Ride like the Devil
A de la Vega Mystery

Written by Nathan Crowder

CONTENTS

ACKNOWLEDGMENTS

The author would like to thank the numerous people who helped make this book possible, many of whom might even appear in disguised form throughout the course of the narrative.

Special thanks go to Lupa and Anthony for their consultation on bikes in general and racing in Portland and San Francisco in particular. A huge thank you goes out to friends, family, and the growing legion of Gato fan-boys and fan-girls for encouraging me to continue the adventures of my favorite broken detective and panda sidekick. And a final thank you to JZ for the inspiration to keep Gato alive.

Also, credit where it is due, the Tesla twins are the creation of Alex "Tamika" Dolphin and Phillip "Xander" Crowder, and Katherine Wilde is the creation of Kathleen Crowder. All are used here with their permission.

The fantastic cover is courtesy of the enormously talented Jacob Giordano.

CHAPTER ONE – BUYING IN

Snowflake pulled his truck to the curb, trusting the intentional cosmetic flaws in the old Ford pickup to distract from the powerful purr of the finely tuned HEMI engine beneath the hood. Dust and mud acquired in the long drive from Buena Rosa coated it and the relatively new but anonymous white cargo trailer hitched behind the truck. The bench seat was a little cramped between his not inconsiderable girth and the two passengers, but at least Manuel and Anita were svelte compared to him. He was thankful the latter rode most of the way from Buena Rosa to Tijuana on her bike, allowing Manuel and the evolved panda driver / mechanic some much needed buddy time.

But now they were here. Despite it being his first trip to TJ, Snowflake suspected tourists got drugged and had their kidneys and livers removed as a matter of course right around the corner. Thankfully, his carefully calibrated holographic disguise made him appear to be an average American middle-aged male instead of the distinctive panda man that he was. He figured panda liver and kidneys went for a whole pile of pesos in this part of town. It had been blocks since he'd seen a streetlight. The only illumination on the pitted street came from the nearly full moon overhead and the bare bulb in a blue, tin-hat style fixture above the door of the tin sided building across the street. "You know it isn't too late for you to change your mind," he said hopefully.

Manuel de la Vega popped open the passenger door and swung his legs out. "By which you mean to say that you are having second thoughts." The lanky detective fished his forearm crutches from behind the seat and stumped a few feet away to give Anita room to

1

exit the truck. He looked across the street to their destination and bit back any of his own trepidation before it derailed him.

No actual sign on or near the building indicated that Manuel had found the right place. The phone number Anita picked up in a recent race resulted in a recorded message asking them to leave a number where they could be reached in the next hour. A calm voice called back fifty minutes later with specific directions, including landmarks, in unaccented Spanish. It repeated the message again in English. The double row of motorcycles parked in the dusty vacant lot next to the rambling tin-sided building served as the only indication that this was the registration point for the Devil's Run International. "This doesn't look like a bar," Snowflake muttered under his breath as the trio approached the two monolithic, sunglass sporting bouncers illuminated by the halo of the lone bulb. "And how do we know this is the place and not just a biker hang-out?"

"Those aren't cruising bikes," Manuel said. "They're built for speed, not comfort—all lightweight café racer profiles. Most bike gangs prefer the bulk and comfort of a touring bike, like Harley or even a Goldwing if they aren't picky about Japanese rides."

"And it isn't a bar," Anita said quickly before Manuel had a chance to finish. "Last time I was here, it was a garage. Look, over on the left side you can see the roll-up doors."

Manuel managed to keep pace with the others despite having to swing along on forearm crutches, but he almost missed a step with Anita's revelation. She caught the break of tempo and smiled prettily over her shoulder at him, one eyebrow raised in a challenge. "And when were you here last?" he asked, his face as neutral as he could make it.

"February. I was in town and needed work done on my suspension and someone recommended a guy who worked out of here."

Snowflake and Manuel shared a look of confirmation that they were both thinking the same thing. "You've raced the TJ before." Snowflake's tone like that of a younger sibling ready to tattle to the adult.

Anita shrugged, the shoulders of her rough, brown leather jacket exaggerating the motion. "So? That's no big deal. I'm not the only one here who has raced in Tijuana, right?" She looked over

2

her shoulder again at Manuel, but he could only shake his head. "Really? You've never raced here?"

Manuel considered the long answer. When he was still street racing, he had a regular day job as a homicide detective with the police in Mexico City. He never saw fit to ride that far north for a street race when there were more lucrative races closer by. And when he did make it up to the border, it had almost exclusively been in the pursuit of criminals. In the end, he settled on the short answer again. "Never raced in Tijuana. But how hard can it be?"

With a snort of derision, Anita crossed the last few strides toward the bouncers—a mismatched set of ogres in wife-beaters, chains, and expensive slacks and shoes. Either of them could have been eyeless beneath the heavy, wrap-around sunglasses, but their heads tracked the trio as they approached, so it was clear that they were awake and could see. The gringo with the wavy blonde surfer hair pulled back into a pretentious pony-tail uncrossed his arms from in front of his chest. "Private party tonight."

"I know," Anita challenged. "And we're coming. I'm here to run with the devil."

The other bouncer, a thick-shouldered Polynesian who looked like he could lift a hot-dog cart over his head without breaking a sweat, stepped to one side, but held out his hand to block Manuel and Snowflake. "You're limited to one guest."

Manuel hobbled over to him. He had to crane his neck back to look up at the bouncer, a full head taller and easily 200 pounds heavier. "I'm here to run with the devil, too."

Both of the bouncers looked him over and assessed what they saw with the fine-tuned gaze of a predator. Six foot and two inches tall when upright, the forearm crutches made certain Manuel was rarely fully upright anymore. That put him more in the five and a half foot range. Lightly curled dark hair in need of a trim framed his dark, flashing eyes. A prototypical Latin playboy plus walking sticks, his clothes hung well on his rail thin frame. There was a subtle charming quality about Manuel, disarmingly rough around the edges, but not a threat by anyone's standards. The bouncers shrugged, and one who had challenged Manuel stepped aside. "Same entry fee as the other racers, no exceptions."

"I wouldn't have it any other way." Manuel smiled and hobbled along after Anita with Snowflake taking up the rear. Once through the door, the lights were only a bit brighter.

Inside they found a garage crudely converted into a makeshift bar. Blue Oyster Cult wailed at them from a large portable CD player at one end of the room. Another pair of bouncers waited inside, demarking the border between what appeared to be a general house party-type atmosphere and the racer's registration table at the front door. A sturdy metal table, probably from a workshop in the back, provided the workspace for a diminutive black man in his late middle years wearing a green banker's visor. A bill counting machine of the type favored by bankers and large scale drug-dealers sat at his side.

Anita handed over the manila envelope from inside her jacket, and the bill counter riffled through her entry fee in a matter of seconds. Once the official confirmed all $10,000 in U.S. dollars, he motioned for Anita's right hand. Without a word, she allowed him to take her hand, palm down. With his free hand, the official plucked a small pneumatic injector from the case next to his seat and pressed it against the back of her wrist with a hiss.

To her credit, Anita didn't make a sound at the injection.

They had been warned by the person who gave Anita the contact number. This race wasn't officially sanctioned by anyone. That was the intrinsic nature of underground races. But the Devil's Run, with a hard cap of thirty racers and a significant buy in, necessitated making it as easy to officiate as possible. With a total prize pool of $150,000 at stake, reducing the number of ways someone could cheat was essential. The race had introduced RFID tags two years ago—tiny chips that broadcast a unique radio signal implanted just under the skin of the racers. This enabled the officials to clock total times from checkpoint to checkpoint down to the second with the right equipment. It also insured that no one deviate from the approved course through the city.

Six races made up the circuit. The first in Tijuana, the last in Vancouver, Canada. In between they also raced in Los Angeles, San Francisco, Portland, and Seattle. Each race offered its own small cash prize for first through third place, but the big ticket was the best time over-all. The person with the best combined time in all six races rode away with bragging rights, $80,000, and however much they won for each individual race. Second place earned half as much. And third place got nothing but the satisfaction of having competed. For an underground street race, it was a pretty rich

4

purse, and anybody who was anybody in the scene tried to scrape together the entrance fee.

Manuel had never raced it before. He had given up illegal street races, refocusing his efforts on being a part time vigilante around the time the Devil's Run Invitational showed up on his radar. But life had a way of changing. For years, he defined himself as a detective with the Mexico City Police, and then in the same position in Cobalt City while at night, he donned the leather body suit and sculpted cat helmet of Gato Loco. The persona and the enhanced tech embedded in the costume proved to have applications well beyond their original purpose—to let him race in anonymity. Circumstances and his own desire for social justice drove him toward the life of a crime-fighter.

For a while, he was happy living that double life. Then someone blew his bike the fuck up with him and that damned costume astride it. The injury that crippled him should have killed him. Instead, it made him reexamine what it meant to be Manuel de la Vega. In the final analysis, racing was in his blood. His sense of self had been birthed there. It was where he would likely end. While he had largely put the crime-fighting thing behind him, recent events had shown him the value of looking at the accident as a new start.

The official taking the entrance fees blinked up at Manuel through smoke-hazy eyes, as if doubting the existence of Manuel's forearm crutches. "You're racing?"

Ten thousand in hundred dollar bills still in their mustard-colored paper bank strap appeared from the inside of Manuel's denim jacket. He set it neatly in front of the mole-eyed banker. "I'm racing."

"It's your funeral, amigo." With sure hands, the banker broke the strap and dropped the entry fee into the bill counter to confirm the amount. Satisfied, he motioned for Manuel's hand and then injected him with the radio tag as well. "Race starts here 24 hours from 2 am. Set your watch by the clock behind the bar, because that's the one we're using. If you're late, you are disqualified and forfeit the entrance fee. If you bring heat down on us, you are disqualified and you forfeit the entrance fee. If you leave the course and re-enter at another point, you are disqualified and forfeit the entrance fee. Any questions?"

Anita raised her chin, signaling toward the back of the room. "I have one. Cash or open bar?"

"Open for racers," the banker said, his gaze flickering toward Snowflake briefly but meaningfully, "but cash for support staff and guests."

Manuel managed to stop Snowflake before the belligerent man-panda launched into a stream of obscenities that would make a marine blush. "I have cash, man. I'll cover your tab tonight."

The ubiquitous panda sidekick cut loose with an easy smile. "Well then, what are we waiting for? Daddy needs a Paloma!"

Manuel forked over a crisp twenty from his jeans pocket. "Make this last all night. Daddy's driving. And bring me back a beer from the bar while you're at it."

If the panda was crestfallen at the twenty-dollar tab limit, he didn't show it. Likely, he reasoned that a Jackson went a long way in TJ in a bar that wasn't being run for profit. "You got it, boss. One Corona coming up."

"If Corona is all they have, don't bother." Manuel secured a seat along the wall on a low shelf with a locked mesh front. "Carta Blanca or Bohemia, or even a Negro Modelo if you have to, but no Corona."

His constant companion for the past several days disappeared into the crowd near the bar with a dismissive wave. Manuel smiled. If anyone there paid enough attention to Snowflake, traveling under the name as Harry Snow, they might notice his hands were somehow wrong as they brushed passed. They might look like the pale, calloused hands of some middle-American gym coach, but were thick and covered with heavy fur to the touch. He had to be careful the batteries on the holographic disguise didn't run down in public, or that he didn't initiate any physical contact to make someone to question what they saw. Still, it was miles better than walking around the world as an upright panda in street clothes with a gravely, but still very human voice.

The panda man had been a short-sighted experiment—an effort by scientists to save pandas from extinction by rocketing them up the evolutionary ladder. By everyone's estimation, it had failed after producing Snowflake. The experiment shut down, the researchers re-tasked to other projects. Snowflake found himself an outcast, bouncing around the world of freaks and misfits until he found a home on the fringes of the super-hero community. Manuel considered himself fortunate to know the gifted mechanic and driver, despite the trouble he sometimes attracted. He was, quite literally, one of a kind.

Manuel noticed belatedly that Anita had already vanished in among the racers, though the underground race community mostly knew her as the Coyote. They were an insular group with whom she was still quite active—unlike Manuel. She knew people in that crowd, friends or even lovers. Though she had shared his bed frequently since Buena Rosa, there was no exclusivity implied in that arrangement.

Back in that corrupt *maquiladora*, Manuel had found justice for Anita's murdered sister. Despite a barely remembered liaison years earlier, he feared gratitude played at least some small part in propelling her into his bed. Every morning for the past week he woke up, surprised to find her still there. The danger, he realized, was when he woke up one morning expecting to see Anita only to find her gone forever. His somewhat turbulent romantic relationships had ingrained in Manuel the inevitability of that scenario. Life was constantly moving, constantly changing. And even the good things were bound to slip from his grasp eventually, no matter how tightly he held on.

He let his gaze play across the assembled racers and support crews. Most of the faces were new. There were some exceptions, of course, but not many. Manuel suspected that those few old war horses he recognized were like him—dreamers trying to hold onto some faded glory. A win in a race of this magnitude would be a feather in anyone's cap, but for someone looking to retire, it provided a fabulous last hurrah. Manuel wondered if anyone there would recognize him. Pride and hubris wrestled within him and even Manuel couldn't tell which would win eventually. Part of him wanted to be recognized, to be feared and respected. Yet the conscious part of him knew that the fewer people who knew who he was, the better off he would be.

After all, the last time he had mixed in these circles, he had been a vigilante with a growing reputation, a sleek black shadow in a brightly-colored world of super heroics. But that was years ago, when he could walk without the aid of the forearm crutches. Back when he was on his way up, not here treading water, wondering how long he could keep his head above the surface before sinking beneath waves forever.

Two weeks ago, before his cousin Esther asked for his help in Buena Rosa, Manuel had resigned himself to a life as a Cobalt City homicide detective and nothing more. Circumstances had changed that. Putting on the black leathers of Gato Loco for the first time in a year, he realized that the mysterious vigilante was too much a part of who he was. And crippled or not, he would be living a pale reflection of a life without him.

That realization had prompted a long vacation of self-discovery, and it started here in Tijuana with the Devil's Run International. Snowflake reappeared with a tall cooler layered with shades of oranges, yellows, and reds, in one hand and a bottle of Bohemia in the other. The holographicaly disguised panda-man handed the beer over before leaning next to his friend. "It's a good crowd." Snowflake motioned around the room with his now free left hand. "Bartender says the roster is just about full. Several of the racers registered and left already, including last year's winner, some guy named Cross."

Manuel raised one eyebrow, suddenly more interested in the race than before. "Cross? What was the first name?"

Snowflake didn't register Manuel's interest initially, his gaze lazily drifting among the crowd for signs of trouble or easy marks, Manuel could never be sure which. "Cross? Oh, I don't know. I don't think he said. He said the name like it meant something so I just smiled and nodded, took the drinks and left." Snowflake blinked and looked at Manuel out of the corner of his eye, suddenly alert. "Why? Does it mean something?"

"Maybe. Did you hear anything else about him, like what he was wearing?"

"No," Snowflake raised one hand, correcting himself quickly, "I mean yes. Not from the bartender, but one of the other racers at the bar reacted to the name. He said this Cross guy wore a red leather body suit with a black cross-hairs over the heart. He gave one of the other racers the heebie-jeebies."

Manuel took a long drag on his beer. *It just couldn't be easy, could it*, he thought to himself. "Marco Cross is a professional killer. I've run into him time and again. Great rider. Better shot. Let's just hope he's here for sport and not work."

Emerging from the crowd like a smiling phantom, Anita approached the pair with a dance in her step. "Have you kissed the trophy yet?"

Manuel finished his beer in three quick gulps before sliding his crutches back on. He had been warned about this on the ride into town just this afternoon. The Devil's Run International had a trophy made of a chromed bike fork with a steel devil's skull mounted on the top, and tradition for the past few years had been for all the racers to give it a kiss for luck prior to the start of the race. Manuel allowed himself to be led through the throng of racers to the trophy, proudly displayed beneath lights in a side room. Several of the racers, young, cocky men who Manuel had never met before, clustered around it, willing themselves to win the race, to claim that trophy for themselves. Manuel could see the fear in their eyes, and knew there wasn't a one of them who would cross any of the six finish lines first.

They laughed and prodded each other in the ribs when Manuel shouldered past to approach the trophy. "Hey, amigo, this room is for racers," a whip-thin red headed racer said. He didn't even try to hide the disdain in his voice.

Manuel made a point of remembering the kid's face and stance. "Well then, you better wait in there, sonny," he said with a nod of his head back toward the bar, "because I'll be crossing the finish line ahead of all three of you."

One of the other racers, a round faced bald man with a pierced ear smiled with just a hint of nervousness. "Oh yeah? And who are you?"

With a smile, Manuel turned his back on them and leaned in to kiss the trophy. "I'm the one with a cat icon on the back of his jacket as he crosses the finish line in front of you. That's who."

He thought he heard two of them whisper his other name— Gato Loco—but he couldn't be sure. For when his lips touched the cold chrome of the trophy's bike fork, a powerful, electric vision washed over him.

Realty snapped away from him, casting him somewhere else. It was night, and the glaring red numbers on the clock near him said it was 3:13 am. He was in an apartment living room, anonymous in its features. The curtain blowing in the breeze from the sliding door to the porch indicated a means of entry. His hands felt sticky, wet, and when he looked down he saw they were gloved in leather and covered in blood. He clenched an exotic looking dagger in his right hand. He staggered and his foot brushed against something solid on the floor. His gaze was pulled down, dreading what he would see.

Framed in light from the street and haloed in blood, was the dead, agonized face of his friend Xander Tesla, the brilliant young inventor who designed his revised Gato Loco leathers.

Reality shifted back around him, and Manuel realized that he had fallen slack. Only Snowflake's quick action had prevented the detective from pitching straight into the trophy and knocking it over. The three other racers were laughing, convinced that if this spastic cripple before them was the fabled Gato Loco, they had nothing to fear. One of them called, "See you at the finish line," before vanishing back into the larger swing of the party.

Snowflake helped Manuel over to a seat while Anita looked on, concerned. Of course she's concerned, Manuel told himself. You haven't told her about your uncontrolled psycho-telemetry, the curse which grants visions of the past or present when coming in contact with some objects. He had possessed the dubious gift for most of his life and had never learned to control it. He hadn't even confessed this ability to his trusted ally, Snowflake, until the Buena Rosa affair was over. The worried panda crouched, looking into Manuel's eyes, knowing only that a vision had downed him, but nothing more.

"You okay, boss?"

"I need to make a call to make sure Xander is okay."

Snowflake had worked closely with the Tesla twins in the past. Their mechanical and engineering passions overlapped to a large degree, and the twins, who were unconventional in many ways, enjoyed the company of the sometimes trigger happy panda mechanic. "Someone hurt the kid?"

Manuel fished the cell phone out of his jacket pocket, hoping that the signal was good enough to reach the twins in Seattle. "If he's not already dead, then he will be soon. And whoever the killer is, he's touched this trophy."

CHAPTER TWO – THE TWINS

Anita helped Manuel de la Vega and Snowflake find a quieter part of the garage from which to make a phone call. She bit her lip, part trying to hide the surprising amount of concern she felt, and part dying for someone to explain to her what was going on. She waited until Manuel was safely seated on a stack of tires in the corner, talking to this Xander he had mentioned, before she turned to Snowflake for answers. "I don't understand what just happened."

Snowflake looked furtive, trying to find a way to explain as much as he could without delving into his friend's secrets too much. "He and I have some mutual friends, including these twins who live in Seattle now. They're super geniuses and did some design work in and around the super-hero community for a while. They did some work on his Gato Loco hardware recently, and used to roll with him back in Cobalt City a few years ago. They're good kids."

"But why does he think one of them is in trouble?" She transfixed the panda with her hard, dark eyes. He squirmed a bit, but she began to suspect that he wouldn't give in out of loyalty to Manuel. She didn't want to put money on which side Snowflake would come down on if she were to push it. She suspected, and not without cause, that the mechanic didn't particularly like her. Anita blinked and smiled, blunting her earlier intensity.

Snowflake's attention was more on Manuel than on her at any length as he strained to make out one-sided bits of the phone conversation. But distracted as he was, the mechanic still worked a casual surliness into his tone. "There's a lot about my buddy's life that I shouldn't be the one to explain to anyone, least of all the woman he's sleeping with. This is one of them. Trust me, there will be more."

She was tempted to raise her voice in anger, and though the muscles in her arm clenched as if preparing to strike at him, Anita instead took a pair of deep breaths. He was right. He was rude, which she had come to learn was par for the course, but that didn't make him less right. If the secretive Manuel de la Vega wanted to share this particular mystery with her, it was his decision to make and no one else's. "I suppose I deserve that." Snowflake merely grunted in distracted agreement.

Gears started to turn in her head as she listened in to what was by now a casual phone conversation full of, "How long have you been back," and, "I haven't heard that name for a while." Something clicked and she suddenly registered that she had heard the names before. Eyes wide, Anita tapped Snowflake on the arm, earning a look that was both laconic and pissed off at the same time. "Do you need the restroom, princess? I think I saw it to the left of the bar."

This time she did slap him, but only on the arm. There was a moment of disconnect as she saw her hand hit a nylon windbreaker but felt the unmistakable fluff of panda fur beneath her palm. "No. Do you mean Xander and Tamika Tesla?"

"Yeah, that would be them. And no touchie." The grouchy mechanic pointed a thick finger at her.

Anita whispered low to herself in surprise. "I thought they were wanted for conspiracy or treason or something a year or two ago."

Snowflake smiled, and comfortable that the kids were okay and that Manuel would fill them in later, he led Anita by the elbow to the doorway of the small side room. "Yeah, that would be them. But things change. It was all bogus anyway. They used to be in a mad scientist club in college, until it turned out that the two founders were only using it as a talent pool so that they could steal and patent ideas. These two assholes took a few of the better ideas, synthetic muscles and kinetic winders and what not, then sold them to the government as their own work. The only way they could get away with that was if the twins were gone, so they painted Xander and Tamika out to be enemies of the state, figuring out that they would be put away in a deep dark hole forever. Or at least long enough to profit from the stolen tech and disappear rich men."

"It was all over the news, even Mexico—something about them supplying terrorists with high tech weaponry." She was surprised. It had been a big story, and then all of a sudden it just went away. She never questioned it, never wondered if the two "terrorists" had been caught or killed or if they were still at large. The news just kept coming, piling in on top of one story with the next until it was impossible to keep track of what was going on.

"Yeah." Snowflake nodded, looking at his friend briefly out of the corner of his eye. "Manuel had worked with them for a while, back before I knew him. Then, shortly before everything went all crazy, he recognized their design styles on some hardware sported by a group of government sponsored spandex. The collusion with terrorists thing was just so against character that he figured out something was going on pretty quick."

"So what happened?"

Snowflake shrugged and offered her an enigmatic smile. "That's where it gets kind of messy. He said he would look into it. The kids turned themselves in, knowing that they hadn't done anything, and then we got a call from Manuel. He said the twins were going to be held indefinitely without trial, and that they were being transferred to a Black Site, which is even less fun than it sounds. He told some mutual friends when and where the transfer was taking place, and the kids got busted out of their military convoy. They figured the crap's really going to hit the fan now, right? But then—" Snowflake held up his hand, palm flat before his face and blew across it. "—poof. Nothing happened. The charges disappeared as if they had never been filed. The government spooks went back into their holes, and the twin's lab space and materials were returned to them."

Anita considered Manuel in a different light, her gaze playing across his thin frame as he leaned casually against the wall on his seat of old tires. Before he had become the shadowy vigilante Gato Loco, she had known him in a different context. He had, as recently as ten days ago, proven the urban legends about him were true when he helped avenge Anita's sister's death. But even after that, she sometimes woke up wondering if any of it had actually happened and that she had witnessed some small part. Having spent most of the past week in the company of Manuel and his unusual and acerbic panda associate, she still had a hard time coming to terms with the fact that the slim and scarred man who needed crutches just to walk was a masked vigilante. "So he never said what happened?"

"I don't even think the twins know for sure. I've never asked, and I don't intend to. Government heat is heat I don't want, being a Chinese national and everything."

"You're Chinese? You sound American."

"My voice coach was from Denver, but you ever hear of a Colorado Panda? I mean, really?"

Manuel folded his phone closed and tucked it carefully back into his jacket pocket before sliding into the forearm crutches. "The kids are fine. Tam has some gigs with her band around the northwest right now. We might cross paths in Portland if we're lucky, and Xander is back in Cobalt City following a lead on a case he's working. Very hush-hush and he wouldn't give me details, but he's wrapping things up and should be flying back to Seattle tomorrow or the day after."

The relief in Manuel's voice was palpable, but there was still something there, an uncertainty behind the eyes that Anita couldn't quantify. Snowflake took a sip of his drink and seemed to relax a little as well, though he made no move to leave the doorway. His cheer and his smile seemed forced. "Great. So he'll be there when we hit Seattle? I was hoping the twins would have the time to meet up, maybe show me this vegan Chinese restraint Tamika was telling me about. Perfect."

"Yeah. Perfect."

The three of them stood there in a fragile bubble of silence in an otherwise noisy party. No, the tension was gone, but there was something else there now, Anita knew. Guy talk. Business talk. She didn't need to be told that she didn't belong in this conversation. Manuel's down-turned eyes were more than clear. "Well. I hear tell there's a low speed drive-along tour of tomorrow's course at three in the afternoon. That should give everyone the chance to become familiar with the route and plan some strategy. I'll hit up some of the other racers for details and let you guys catch up on old friends." She waited until she saw their nod of acknowledgment and put on a smile that was more confident than she felt.

Seconds later, Manuel and Snowflake were alone in the side room, and they were able to stop pretending.

"So what are you not saying, chief?"

Manuel hobbled a bit closer so he wouldn't have to raise his voice too much and leaned against the wall, taking the pressure off his arms. "Clear as day, I saw Xander as a corpse on the floor of an apartment somewhere. It was 3:13 in the morning, and the window or sliding door was open. I looked down and saw a knife in my hand and blood everywhere."

"That doesn't make sense. You kill Xander?"

A hesitant shake of the head dismissed that suggestion. "I don't think so. The vision was through the eyes of the killer, so it felt like me, but it felt off at the same time. And the visions are sparked by touching something, by making some kind of connection to another person through an object medium—" Manuel took in Snowflake's blank stare, and realized he had lost him. "In short, as I understand the visions, they can't show a vision of me. They aren't reflective. So it's someone else—someone who touched the trophy."

Snowflake looked no more cheered than he had been before. "But Xander dies. You saw that?"

"I saw that."

The two of them were silent for a long moment, Snowflake working up the nerve to ask what he felt to be a dangerous question. Manuel, for his part, hoped that the question never came up. In this particular instance, Snowflake won out. "Can you save him?"

Manuel took a deep breath and looked for some escape, but there was none. "I've been having these visions for a very long time. I can't control them. I've told you that. But until recently, they were only looking backward. I got pretty good at reading those. This whole looking forward thing started after the accident, so it's pretty new."

There was a hard tone in the panda's tone that Manuel hadn't ever heard before. He wasn't sure because of the holographic disguise on his loyal companion, but he thought there were tears in Snowflake's voice. "Answer the question. Can. You. Save. Him?"

"I don't know." Manuel wanted to say more, but anything else would be a lie. He put a hand on Snowflake's shoulder, giving the furry bulk beneath his palm a gentle squeeze. "But I'm going to try, okay, buddy?"

Snowflake sniffed and nodded, blinking quickly a few times. He stepped away from Manuel's hand. "I guess that's going to have to do. Well, count me in. He's a punk, but he deserves better than that."

Manuel could hear the affection in the panda's voice but didn't call the bluster for what it was. "Good. Now, let's get back to the party. Tomorrow is a busy day."

"You don't know the half of it." Snowflake chuckled suddenly. "Anita's going to want an explanation, I'll bet."

With a sigh, the lanky detective stumped out into the main floor of the party again where he saw Anita along the side of the room chatting with a pair of young racers. She had a good ten years on them, but they didn't care, each trying to out-do the other with tales of bravado. They probably had no idea who she really was. Among illegal street racers in Mexico, the Coyote was among the elite ranks. *They'll find out tomorrow night*, Manuel thought. *If they're close enough to the finish to see her.* The thought made him smile.

"We should have left her in Buena Rosa." Snowflake grumbled.

"Jealous?"

"What kind of buddy road trip is this, anyway? I mean, you barely know her, and she's already asking questions I have no business answering." He turned on Manuel, a hard and artificial smile on his round face. "You know me, man. She'll roll up on me asking about old girlfriends or your visions or something and I'll fold and spill everything. We're better off just cutting her loose and being done with it."

The idea had merit, Manuel realized. But circumstances were a bit different out here on the road than any time in his recent life. He wasn't trying to hold down a day job and live the secret identity any more. He wasn't sure what that made him—Manuel de la Vega or Gato Loco—and he wondered if there was even a difference anymore. Still, she was nice to have around, as long as neither of them got too comfortable. "It's never going to happen, amigo." He waved to Anita, and she smiled warmly and waved back.

Snowflake snorted and wandered off. "It's your funeral."

CHAPTER THREE – TIJUANA

The blare of The Magnificent Seven theme song on his cell phone jolted Manuel from a pleasant dream where he had been sipping cocoa on his parent's patio terrace while white cranes ambled slowly past. It was a good dream—certainly better than waking to the insistent ring tone in the muggy hotel room. He rolled over, tangled in sheets, only dimly realizing that Anita must have already woken up and left. Left hand flailing in the dim confines of the room, he fumbled his cell off of the bedside table. "What time is it?"

Snowflake's voice sounded concerned on the other end of the line, and it woke Manuel up quickly. "Buddy? Thank all that's holy that you're there. I think I'm going to die."

Manuel swung his legs off the edge of the bed, adrenaline dumping into his heart. *Pants*, he thought. *Pants, pants, pants. Where the hell did I toss them last night?* The underwear could wait, but he couldn't leave the room without pants of some kind. While his heart raced and eyes searched the gloom, he willed his voice to remain as calm as possible. "Ok, walk me through this slowly. Where are you?"

"Across the hall in my room. The bathroom, specifically." The panda was clearly in distress.

Good, Manuel thought. *Just across the hall.* He located his pants draped over the headboard and grabbed them, trying to put them on without losing the phone wedged between his head and shoulder. "What's your situation? Can you describe who is trying to kill you?"

"What? No one's trying to kill me. Well maybe the guy at that taco cart, curse his black heart."

Manuel's heart beat slowed its panicked tempo. He finished pulling the pants up over his long, heavily scarred legs, listening more calmly to his friends predicament. "I don't understand. You said you were going to die."

"I woke up early, still feeling the buzz from last night, and wandered down the street for a little breakfast. The only place that was open was this rolling cart selling tacos. The price was right so I got a few. I don't know what was in them, Manuel. Something crazy. Something wrong. That's all I know. It feels like my insides are on fire."

Ah the wonders of panda digestion. "And how do you want me to help?"

"I want to know what was in those damned tacos so I never get them again, for one thing," the mechanic wailed. "And then I need some kind of medicine. I don't care if it's legal as long as it works. If you can't do that, I'm begging you, buddy. Put a bullet between my eyes, because no one should have to live through this."

Manuel chuckled. He picked up his shoes and shook them out in case they had acquired pests in the middle of the night. "I'll get something from downstairs. But I'm not putting a bullet in your brain, and I'm not telling you what was in the tacos."

"Fine." Snowflake grunted in anguish, and Manuel tried not to think about whatever face his friend was making to accompany the sound. "You guard your Mexican black magic, traitor. I'll remember this when we get Chinese food in Seattle."

"Trust me when I tell you that no matter what I tell you about the tacos, it won't make you feel any better."

"I want the truth!" Snowflake shouted playfully, a hint of his old self shining through the digestive torment he was experiencing.

Manuel shouted back. "You can't handle the truth!"

Snowflake shouted back, "Show me the money!" to which Manuel laughed.

"Well, you're obviously delirious, but you sound like you're going to live. I'll be over with some medicine in a few minutes." He looked at his watch, noticing that it was shortly after one in the afternoon. It was more than enough time to pop down for some Pepto or similar indigestion panacea. Manuel had meant to get up around then anyway, so he couldn't exactly begrudge the wake-up call. But he did wonder where Anita had gotten off to. "You'll be fine by race time. Mexican black magic guarantee."

By the time Manuel had finished dressing himself in black jeans and faded black Calexico tour shirt, Anita returned with a Styrofoam container that was bursting with spicy steam. She appeared happily surprised to see him awake and dressed. "I thought you'd be hungry so I brought you back something for lunch."

"As long as it isn't from the taco cart down the street." Manuel suppressed a shudder at the thought of getting whatever was shaking Snowflake to his spiritual center right at that moment. He suspected that he would be more used to the food here than his friend, but bad, cheap food here was the same as bad, cheap food anywhere—eat at your own risk.

Anita laughed, setting the container down on the small table near the window. She reached for the cord and pulled the drapes open, throwing brilliant light into the small room. "Actually, I went to one of the hotel restaurants and had a burger. I figure we're going to be in America in the next day or so, might as well go native. I got you hot wings."

Despite the incongruity of eating Buffalo wings in Tijuana, just hearing the words made his mouth water a little bit. Then he remembered his promise of digestive relief. "That sounds great, thanks. I just need to pop down and pick up some Pepto for Snowflake and I'll dig in."

"Wait." She went to her own bag, and after a moment of digging, produced an unopened bottle of magical pink elixir. "I always travel with a bottle just in case. You never know from town to town what you'll run into. Just remind him to replace it when he gets the chance."

"Will do. Be right back." Manuel pocketed the medicine and hobbled out and across the hall to Snowflake's door. He fished the spare room key out of his pants pocket and opened the door a few inches. "Are you still alive in there?"

Snowflake's voice came from around the door to the left, from the direction of the bathroom. "Not of my own free will, no. This thing won't let me die. It needs me alive to feed on my pain."

Manuel stuck the bottle through the door. "Get ready to catch."

For the second time in twenty-four hours, Manuel thought he heard tears in Snowflake's voice, though the reason was quite different this time. "If you make me jump for it, so help me God, I will break both your legs and then set you on fire."

"Fair enough." He tossed the plastic bottle lightly into the restroom, reassured when he didn't hear it hit the floor, wall, or any fixtures. "Drink up, and if I don't see you by 2:30, we're leaving to check out the course without you."

"Manuel?"

"Yeah, buddy?"

"It wasn't dog, was it? If I ate dog, you'd tell me, right?"

"It wasn't dog."

"Thank you. Now close the door and leave me to my demons."

Manuel and Anita checked in on Snowflake an hour later and were pleased to see him sleeping peacefully in the darkened room. They both decided that it was going to be a late night anyway and declined to wake him. They went out into the blazing summer sun, soaking up the mid-afternoon quiet. Anita eyed the white trailer where Manuel's ride was secured before turning to him with a sly smile on her face.

"Do you want to let the Gato out or do you want to ride bitch with me and save the surprise for the race tonight?"

He shared her smile. "Why let the cat out of the bag now?"

The underground garage where Anita had parked her bike was much more secure than the open parking lot, but height restrictions in the garage made pulling the trailer down there impossible. With the security on the trailer itself, neither Manuel nor Snowflake had any concerns about theft. They walked around the corner and down the ramp into the noticeably cooler garage. Anita had taken her chopped and customized vintage Triumph somewhere for a tune earlier in the day while Manuel had slept, and her engine glistened like new. "Tune and new oil?"

Anita smiled over her shoulder at him. "I race to win." She mounted her bike, and Manuel climbed on behind her as best as he was able. He found that while his legs couldn't bear his weight well enough to walk, they were more than strong enough to keep from dangling to the ground as he rode behind Anita. *One concern handled*, he thought. But the question of what to do with the forearm crutches suddenly occurred to him as he settled in. "We can drop them into the cab of the truck, at which point you'll be stuck on the back until we get back or you can hold onto them." Anita suggested.

The prospect of having to dismount for one reason or another was not entirely unlikely. If that happened, he wanted to minimize his disadvantages. "I'll hold them." He moved both of the black aluminum crutches to his left hand and held them tightly at the mid-section. It didn't feel as awkward as he would have thought, and he nestled comfortably into Anita's back. He put his right hand on her hip and kissed her briefly on the nape of her neck as she kick-started her bike to life. "You really should wear a helmet, you know."

"You sound like my mother. This is a milk run. I only wear mine to race, and I don't see you wearing one either."

"If I wear my helmet," he said, referring to the sculpted fiberglass helmet made in the shape of yowling cat's head, "then I might as well wear my leathers as well. It's a shame to break up the set. And if I'm wearing the leathers, then why don't I just ride Shadow?"

"You know, just because you're riding on the bitch seat doesn't give you permission to be all bitchy."

He couldn't see her face to see if she was smiling, but Manuel pictured her smiling when she said it. It made her tone easier to swallow.

Despite not being in control of the bike, Manuel found it easy to predict the turns and lean into them. As long as they kept a reasonable pace, he didn't foresee any difficulty in keeping his feet up from the asphalt. With Anita's blatant disregard for traffic laws and her apparent knowledge of the city's layout, it only took them a little more than ten minutes to reach the garage/bar where they had met the previous night.

It was an impressive feat, in Manuel's book. While a lot of the world thought of Tijuana as a lawless border town if they thought of it at all, it was known in Mexico as one of the largest cities in the country, far more than the strip of clubs, pharmacies, and sordid dives that made the city popular among the 18 to 20-year-old crowd from southern California. The two border crossings let through 300,000 people a day on average, making it one of the busiest borders in the world. The sex worker district employed well over a thousand girls, rivaling Bangkok and Amsterdam. And the industrial district along the Zona Rio was filled with industrial parks housing over 200 *maquiladoras*, like factory embassies, little city-states run by everyone from Nabisco to Sony. It was the county seat, and a center of culture, science, and learning for Mexico, having been written up in high-brow publications and journals around the world.

But when the average person thought of Tijuana, their knowledge generally went no further than shady pharmacies, rumors of seedy donkey shows, and some self-destructive blonde girl on a TV show over-dosing in the street while partying with friends. Manuel found it depressing, but only briefly. He had to admit that the unsavory rumors of some of Tijuana's darker corners had made him less than interested in visiting while he lived in Mexico. And once he had moved to the states, to the New England mini-metropolis of Cobalt City, the idea of returning to any part of Mexico was no longer appealing.

The majority of the other racers had shown up by the time Anita coasted her bike to the stop in the dirt lot adjacent to the converted garage. A picnic table had been dragged into the center of the lot, and a map of Tijuana had been taped to the roll-up garage door. Several of the riders were inspecting the map, their gloved fingers tracing the route in anticipation. Several wore leather or neoprene body suits, but for the most part, they had shown up wearing street clothes. Like Anita and Manuel knew, this wasn't the time to be posing or posturing. Blend in, take in the course, and maybe learn a little about how the other riders handled their bikes, and maybe, just maybe, you could find the edge you would need to win.

But though the racers could dress down in jeans and jackets, there was no disguising their bikes. A few were chopped down street racers, built from the ground up around café-racer frames or the occasional touring bike chopped down for a sleeker profile. Most were well maintained and tricked out factory floor models. And then there were the custom jobs, like Manuel's own bike, Shadow. These bikes were made by people with resources and skills. One, a low slung crotch rocket with pearlescent paint and burnished chrome sported a sculpted demon head over the crossbars, with horns that curled halfway up the handlebars. Another was light and flame red, a bike that Manuel instantly recognized as belonging to the hired killer Marco Cross. So it was true. Cross was riding in the Devils Run.

Manuel tapped Anita on the shoulder and indicated the red bike with a surreptitious nod of his head. "Do you recognize that bike?"

"That's Cross. He won last year. You've heard of him?"

"In different circles." Manuel smiled ruefully. "Have you raced against him?"

"Twice, in smaller races, and he beat me both times. That's not going to happen here. This is my year." There was hardness in her voice that reminded Manuel of her intensity when she had been seeking her sister's killer. It was just a touch chilling, and he decided it was best if he didn't bring up that he intended to win the race himself.

"So he can handle a bike, then."

She rolled her bike past the sleek red machine, which looked like it would be more at home in a Japanese cartoon. "Well, his ride is a total custom job. I don't think he has any factory parts on it. On top of that, he has a sharp eye and great reaction time. That's a hard combination to beat."

Manuel remembered well, having pursued Marco Cross through the Cannonade neighborhood of his adopted city two years ago. To evade capture, Cross had shot out the tire of a fuel truck from half a block away while traveling over 130 mph down a busy street. As Gato Loco, Manuel had no choice but to try and contain the damage, pulling injured people out of the resulting wreckage until emergency vehicles arrived. By that time, Cross was long gone. Manuel had to accept the small victory that the ruthless gunman had not returned to Cobalt City since that encounter.

"If I can have everyone's attention, please!" All eyes were drawn toward the speaker, the small man who had collected the entry fees the night before who was now standing atop the picnic table. He was dressed comfortably in an olive drab jumpsuit under a brown leather bomber jacket. "Those of you who've run with the devil before know my name. Some of you new faces do not. I'm Major Tom, and this is my race. That means my words in matters pertaining to this race are like unto you words from God almighty. Am I completely understood?"

Everyone nodded, and Manuel had to admit that he kind of liked the curmudgeonly old biker. It took a lot of *huevos* to command this kind of respect or at least agreement from a large group of outlaw bikers. "In a few minutes, we're going to take to the road and I'm going to show you the course, same as I'll do in the five other races," he continued. "If you want to look at the map on the wall behind me, that's fine, but do it quick. I'm not waiting for anyone. About two-thirds of this race will be on fairly major roads through Tijuana. That means, for all you mathematicians, that one-third will be on minor roads or, in a few instances, not on roads at all. There are two choke points where you will only be able to get one bike at time through. You'll know them when you see them. After this ride through, your time is your own, but be back here by 1:30 in the morning for a 2 am start time. No exceptions. I've already told you what will disqualify you when you paid your entrance fee, so I don't want any damn sob stories if you wash out early."

Manuel couldn't help but feel that Major Tom was looking in his direction for the last part of his speech. He was looking forward to showing up in his Gato Loco leathers more than ever. That should raise a few eyebrows, he was certain.

Everyone moved toward their bikes as Major Tom climbed spryly down from the table and mounted his forest green Ninja. The thing had to be over a decade old, but it looked very well maintained, and when it started, Manuel could hear the smooth purr of a well tooled Japanese engine. He probably wouldn't win a race on a bike like that, but he could certainly keep pace with one.

Within minutes everyone was astride their bikes, and the air in the dirt lot vibrated with the sound of thirty engines revving. Manuel wondered how long it would be before someone called the police, and then reasoned that with a garage here, it was likely no one would much care or even notice. With a wave of a red bandana over his head, Tom signaled the start and pulled smoothly out onto the street. The tour was underway.

They were far enough away from the border at the start point that traffic was no problem, and while the streets were narrow, they were at least streets, decently paved and wide enough to allow traffic flow in both directions at once. And after less than a mile, they turned onto a major street, which was still relatively quiet due to the convenient 2-4 siesta time. The streets, Manuel had noticed earlier, were aligned in a pretty straight-forward grid pattern.

It wasn't until they turned toward Paseo de los Héroes that the route grew a little more random, wending around the walled and fenced corporate estates of the many *maquiladoras*. They cut between two of the large properties suddenly, and encountered the first choke point—a canyon only five feet across formed by two white walls from neighboring corporate plantations. The canyon ran for close to a quarter mile, and the engines of thirty bikes in those narrow confines roared like thunder. At a timid 30 mph, this choke point was nothing. At three times that speed, it was going to separate the wheat from the chaff in a hurry. Manuel planned to get close to the lead early to avoid having to deal with the inevitable problems of someone tipping their bike at the entrance while going too fast to correct.

They shot out onto a quiet service road that dumped onto a larger road and then onto the broad, elevated Highway One. This they followed for about five miles before making an exit toward a huge events and cultural center that Manuel wished he could remember the name of. Here they encountered the other choke point as Major Tom swerved off road between two hip-height concrete guard walls and down a dirt hill. Anita was about middle of the pack, and by the time they took the cut off, Manuel could see that Tom had crossed beneath the highway and cut onto an onramp in the same way he had left the previous one.

It wasn't much of a short-cut, Manuel realized, as the same change of direction could be accomplished by merely following the off ramp to the road below, but it did add a tighter choke point followed by a change in road surface. That could be telling, as any bike with the smooth racing tires would have a hard time making the tight turn on dirt. Looking over his shoulder, he watched as one rider tipped his bike, sliding into the concrete divider below. They hadn't been going fast enough to cause a serious injury, but tonight ...

Heading south now on Highway One, they passed the point they had entered from the *maquiladoras*, and then took a major exit, looping back toward the start point. From there on, it was a pretty straight-forward series of 90 degree turns followed by straight sprints. By then, most of the weaker riders would have been culled from the race. Based on what he had seen, Manuel expected an attrition rate of a few riders each race. If all the courses had as many devious sections, it would either bring out the best in everyone, or narrow the field to about ten or fifteen riders by the time they hit Vancouver.

But before Vancouver was Seattle. And there were bigger things to deal with than merely win the race. One of the people here, one of these thirty scattered riders, was a killer. And he had a week, maybe less, before he had to make the call on which one it was.

And if he couldn't do that, Xander Tesla was going to die.

Snowflake had arrived at the finish line with his truck and the trailer. He was sitting on the hood with a beer when Anita and Manuel finished. The stalwart panda looked a little sallow, but at least he was alive. Manuel looked at his watch. The tour had taken almost half an hour. The actual race would be over in ten minutes, by his estimation. It was a good length, and a good, if potentially dangerous, course. He looked up at Snowflake as he put on his arm crutches to dismount. "We're going to want to go with all-terrain tires, but street suspension should be fine. The course looks pretty smooth, but it's not all paved."

"I can have those tires changed out in, oh, half an hour. I'll tighten up the shocks a bit and flush out the engine while I'm at it. Make it an hour's work. How does the course look?"

"I've seen worse," Manuel answered.

Anita chimed in, "A lot worse. Still, I'll bet you we lose at least four riders tonight, either injury or mechanical."

Snowflake raised his eyebrows. "Really? I'll take some of that action. Twenty bucks American says you lose less than four."

"You haven't seen the course, amigo," Manuel shook his head with a smile. "Or the riders, for that matter. She might be right."

Snowflake slid off the hood of his truck. "What can I say? I live on the edge. Anyway, let me tune up Shadow. You kids mingle and then we can get dinner when I'm done. No racing on an empty stomach."

Anita popped out her kickstand and parked her bike alongside the trailer. "You sure you're okay to eat? I hear you had an incident this morning."

"Is nothing sacred, anymore?" Snowflake scolded Manuel with a hurt look. "Anyway, that taco guy was trying to kill me. But I'm much better now, just a little weak on my knees and starving. And there has to be Hard Rock Café or something around here. We can go get some decent American food, and put this whole unfortunate episode behind us."

Manuel smiled, deciding to pass on pointing out what he felt was an intentional pun. "Whatever you say. Come find us when you're done." He turned to Anita. "Now, since you've raced with some of these guys before, I would love to get some introductions." They ambled off together into the mix of racers, Manuel's eyes taking in every detail. One of them, he knew, was a killer. And time was running out.

CHAPTER FOUR – RACING THE TJ

Despite the day's earlier gastronomic misadventures, Snowflake had eaten a baby's weight in chicken sandwiches and fries, proving that he had been as starving as he had claimed. When they arrived back at the start point, it was after midnight, and the racers were starting to gather. Anita pouted prettily when Manuel and Snowflake denied her access to the trailer, but that part of his life was not for her, and she knew it. She kissed Manuel deeply before the door closed, knowing that the next time she saw him, he would be helmeted.

The next time she saw him, she had to be prepared to beat him.

It made both of them a little nervous, and they had avoided discussing it through dinner and the rest of the evening. Both were very competitive people, and yet they had not competed together since the first race in which they had met, years ago. He had won that day, with Anita a close second, and they celebrated that victory with champagne and ten hours of alcohol and sex. Neither of them was certain how they would react to a win tonight. And though they both hoped for the best, the prospect of a seething resentment building from a series of unanswered victories was all too real of a threat.

It had never been that way between him and the dilettante vigilante Katherine Wilde, though she had been equally competitive. Maybe it helped that generally he and Wild Kat had worked toward a common goal most of the time, rather than against each other. But that was the past, and he couldn't continue to use that as a measuring stick for all future relationships.

With a barely contained sigh, Manuel shut the door on Anita, and turned to face the trailer interior, ready to don the leathers for the first time in days. His bike, Shadow, sat locked in the charging dock. Running on powerful electric batteries, it was whisper silent yet capable of speeds that rivaled anything running on something short of rocket fuel. Around the edges and suspended from the roof could be found everything from diagnostic tools to alternate tires and replacement parts. A computer in the back functioned as a full lab computer, should he need it in the course of investigations, and a thumb-print secured locker stored his Gato Loco costume. All in all, it was a perfect, compact rolling base of operations. Katherine Wilde had outdone herself outfitting him with it. Her goodbye gift. The thought brought a momentary stab of regret that he filed away for later examination.

While Snowflake ran a last minute diagnostic on the bike, Manuel unlocked the red equipment locker to reveal his helmet and leathers. With a sigh of resolution, he sat on the low stool and began stripping off his shoes and jeans, leaving only his socks, boxer briefs and t-shirt. Shoes stored in the small mesh-fronted cubby next to him, he folded his pants carefully and placed them in on top. The pantsuit came first, black leather with silver *conchos* on the outside of the legs, and a black neoprene mesh top. He slid these on, feeling the synthetic muscles in the leggings weighing down his own legs. He pulled out the jacket next, also heavy black leather made heavier by the flat batteries arranged down the spine between layers of leather. A yowling cat head icon was painted skillfully on the back. Manuel cinched the back of the jacket to the pants with the concealed heavy clamp, and power from the internal battery along his spine surged into the pants, activating the synthetic muscles.

Manuel flexed his legs, and then stood. Snowflake glanced at him from above the seat of the bike. "Everything checking out?"

"Feels good," Manuel said. "Xander does good work."

It was a somber thought, and Snowflake pinched his mouth tightly closed. He nodded curtly and turned back to his own work.

It was warm inside the trailer, so Manuel left the jacket unzipped for the time being. He pulled on the black boots and then turned to his helmet. He held it in his hands, staring at the mismatched eyes painted above the visor, one comically large and one small. Fiberglass teeth had been sculpted around the opaque black visor, and swept back ears had been carefully sculpted to be not only dramatic, but aerodynamically functional. It was a helmet that inspired fear in criminals, the grim visage of a crime fighter who had been described as "demonic" only weeks earlier. Manuel smiled, knowing that he was on the side of angels. But best that the other racers didn't know that. If any of them were themselves criminal or old enough to remember the legends of him prowling the highways of Mexico, racing with Gato Loco was certain to shake them up.

He pulled the helmet down over his head. Snug. Comfortable. He plugged in the power leads to the helmet and the heads-up displays blazed to life, low across his field of vision. When he spoke, the integrated voice filters masked it, made it deeper, with a hint of menace. "All lights are in the green. Is Shadow ready to go?"

Snowflake stepped back and released the docking clamps. "Fire away."

Gato Loco started Shadow with a whispered voice command, the only sign it was turned on being the blue tail lights and the faint, electric hum in the cramped confines of the trailer. "Let's ride."

Snowflake popped the trailer door and the short ramp slid out to the ground. Gato Loco mounted his ride and rolled it swiftly down to the cooling Tijuana dirt, taking no small delight in the wave of stunned silence that spread out among the assembled racers. At least two of the racers said his name. Three more swore under their breath. Inside the menacing helmet, Manuel smiled. "Showtime," he whispered.

He took his place with the other riders, and the crowd parted to let him through. There was an air of uncertainty. Sure, this was an illegal race, but there were degrees of illegal, and Gato Loco had raced before. Hell, he was a racer long before he was a vigilante, and dozens of eyes watched him carefully, wondering which way this particular scenario was going to play out. Major Tom walked out of the crowd with a stern look and shake of his head. He held a black device with a small screen in his left fist. "Let's see your hand."

Gato Loco held out the hand with the imbedded RFID chip, and the hand-held scanner passed over it. It was clear from the look in Tom's eyes that he could read the chip and identified it as belonging to the man on crutches the previous night. The mischievous smile on his face showed that he wasn't going to spill that particular secret. "He's registered. He's here to race folks."

Sighs of relief mixed with groans of disappointment. But for every person resigned to lose now that Gato Loco was in the race, there were two more determined to show him up on the streets. It was one thing to win an underground street race. It was an entirely different matter to win that same race against Gato Loco.

A familiar red body-suited figure cut from the crowd, offering a hand for a greeting handshake. Cross. *Well, at least he's cordial,* Manuel thought. "I've heard about you. It will be a pleasure to race against the great Gato Loco. I've heard that you are one of the best." Cross said happily. The voice was wrong. The Croatian accent of Marco Cross was distinctive. This racer was younger, and while there was a hint of an accent, it was very minor.

"Where did you hear that?"

Cross raised the visor of his helmet. A young face, early twenties at a guess, but with the same fierce blue eyes of Marco Cross, stared calmly into Gato Loco's own visor. "I am Victor Cross. My father Marco spoke very highly of Gato Loco. He will be most amused to know that I am to race against you."

Manuel was surprised how much of a relief that news was to him. "So will your father be joining you at any of the races?"

Victor smiled wryly. "My father is retired, but still his travel schedule remains secretive, even to me. Perhaps he will join us somewhere along the circuit to see us race. When he hears that I am competing against you, I doubt he will be able to resist a visit."

"Charming." Manuel smiled coldly behind his visor. "Best of luck tonight." He became aware of a shift of focus back toward Major Tom, and turned to face the old race organizer.

The two bouncers from the other night were there beside him, still in sunglasses. Each held an aluminum briefcase, and as Major Tom began to address the racers, they set the cases on nearby oil drums and opened them. Suspicion flared in Gato Loco briefly, expecting guns to be produced. But instead, each case contain three rows of sleek, black forms, each the size of a pack of sugar-free gum.

"Listen up and listen up good," Tom said loudly. The crown turned mumble-silent in seconds. "This is a tough course. They're all going to be tough courses. I don't abide by short cuts, but I sure as hell don't like getting lost, and I know how easy that can be in a strange city. Mason and Jason here will distribute adhesive flashers to help keep you on track."

Racers began flowing past the two bouncers, collecting their flashers. Manuel looked at his. A little thicker than an old bicycle reflector he used to have on the spokes of his first ten-speed, the screen looked to be a powerful LCD light. "Make sure you put them somewhere on your bike that you can see clearly," Tom continued. "And make sure it's clean so they can stick. When the race starts, these babies will go green. If they turn red, it means you missed a turn and you're off course. You need to re-enter the course at the same point where you left it or you forfeit that stage of the race. As for timing, each racer's time starts when they cross the starting line and ends when they cross it again at the end. The chips we put in your hand to keep you on course will allow me to keep your time to fractions of a second. Once again, this is my race, and my word is final. By my watch, we have ten minutes 'til start, so if you have to throw up or take a leak, now is the time to do it. Be on the line in five minutes."

Knowing that Snowflake had just washed and waxed Shadow that afternoon, Gato Loco was confident in sticking the flasher right at the top of the bike's fork, between his hands. Most of the race, he would be looking ahead, and not down, but that was the case for any of the other racers, he figured. It probably wouldn't help anyone stay on course, but if they missed a turn, at least there was a fast way to confirm the fact.

Gato Loco had lost sight of Anita shortly after leaving the trailer, and he suspected it was probably better that way. He joined the pack at the line, not trying to make his way to the front just yet. With individual times, getting out ahead early didn't matter quite so much, but he was cautious enough to keep mid-pack so that he could keep the lead in sight as much as possible. Things would thin out a bit, and the race would shake down into groups. The important thing, as he saw it, was to get to the first choke point in the top ten or so, and then close the gap with the lead toward the second choke point. After that, he could easily take just about anyone on the open road.

Major Tom stood atop an overturned oil drum that had been rolled out to the start line spray painted across the road in fluorescent orange. "Fire them up!"

The air shook with thirty bike engines thundering to eager life, dancing forward by the inches, hungry for a taste of the road and their opponents. Tom raised a red kerchief above his wrinkled, visor-clad head, and with a smile as big as Mexico, he let it drop. The flashers on everyone's bikes switched instantly to green, and the race was on.

Tires screeched angrily as several racers, more interested in show than they were in a smooth start, spun their rear wheels. The smell of smoke and burned rubber filled the air, and the bikes lunged forward as the racers jockeyed for position. Two racers in neoprene racing suits, one blue with orange stripes, and one yellow and black, took an early lead, but from Gato Loco's position in mid-pack, he could see both Cross and Anita were only a few lengths behind them.

The racer with the demon skull mounted on the front of his bike was not far ahead of Gato Loco, the name El Blanco Diablo painted on the back of the white leather jacket. *Yet another devil obsessed biker*, Manuel thought. *It's no wonder people are afraid of us.*

By the time they hit Paseo de los Héroes, the pack had thinned slightly, with at least one minor accident. Some idiot had been going too fast for the corner and had taken the turn too wide. Gato Loco watched the bike flip when the tires hit the sidewalk at a bad angle at over 50 mph.

By the time the first choke point presented itself, Gato Loco had pulled easily up into top ten, with the bulk of the racers spread out over only about a fifty yards stretch.

One of the early leaders, the one in blue and orange, had almost missed the turn, and had screeched sideways, his momentum sapped. Gato Loco thought he saw another rider slide into the unfortunate biker as he passed by, but there was too much going on. And seconds later, he was rocketing down the narrow canyon like a bullet from a gun.

He anticipated the turn out of the canyon and throttled down slightly, narrowly missing the rear tire of a fellow racer in a canary yellow jacket with dreadlocks falling out of the back of his helmet and some vertical embellishment up the back of the jacket. Gato Loco's amped up reflexes kicked in, and he dodged quickly left, exploding out of the canyon between the suddenly slowed racer before him and left hand corner.

Once out onto the street, he saw why the rider in front of him had slowed down so much. The rider in black and yellow who had taken an early lead had come out of the canyon too fast to make the following turn. He and his bike were wrapped around a now broken power pole across the street. Gato Loco only got a two second glance before speeding off.

It was enough of a look to know that the other racer was dead.

He strongly suspected that Snowflake was going to lose that twenty dollar bet.

Two more turns and the race was out onto major roads, where other racers were not the only traffic. Bikes dodged between the infrequent cars and trucks, blasting past on the shoulder when all else failed. The advantage to the route selection, Gato Loco realized, was that while the city of Tijuana was far from asleep, the neighborhoods they were driving through were largely quiet after midnight. If the race had taken them down into the more tourist-oriented neighborhoods, it wouldn't just be cyclists getting injured.

By the time Shadow's tires touched Highway One, Gato Loco was in a firm fifth place. He opened up the throttle, feeling Shadow thrust up toward 180 mph with ease. He kept his eye on the leader's tail lights, mindful that the exit was coming up, and at the speed he was traveling, it would be easy to miss.

It was difficult to gauge, but it appeared to him that Anita was in a commanding second place while Victor Cross was comfortably out in front of her. Gato Loco passed a rider he recognized from around the trophy the previous evening. From the sounds of his engine, this racer had his neon green bike cranked up as fast as it would go, and Gato Loco almost felt bad glancing down at his speedometer to realize he could easily stack on another 30 mph if he really wanted to.

In his upper field of vision, tail lights flashed and dropped out of sight as Anita cut off the road to make the second choke point. Trusting his brakes and tires, Gato Loco kept his speed for longer than the third place rider, thinking he could hit the choke point first. Not anxious to be passed, the rider in front gunned the engine to cut Gato Loco off. At the last second, Manuel had to brake hard and let the other racer take the turn first

Shadow plunged off Highway One a fraction of a second later, passing into a cloud of dust and grit thrown up by the rear tire of the other bike. For a brief moment, his vision was obscured, and he leaned hard into the corner, braking to avoid a collision. The rider in front of him had laid down his bike and slid into the concrete barrier, leaving the path in front of Gato Loco unobstructed. He nudged the bike forward carefully without spinning out and tossing up a rooster-tail of dust. From the sound of cursing mixed with a revving engine behind him, he gathered that the tipped rider was up and trying to get back into the running. Gato Loco nosed out onto the onramp and back to the highway, determined to close the gap between himself and the lead as quickly as possible.

Shadow exploded up toward 190 mph for the long straight away. Gato Loco felt the almost forgotten rush that had attracted him to racing the first place. It was that thrill that turned him toward building his first bike, the initial Shadow. The dangers inherent in high speed racing necessitated the creation of the leathers with bonus protection of a compact stage field generator that projected hundreds of fragile, molecule thin force fields from his body. Alone, they were useless, but stacked, they acted like an invisible air bag, ensuring he could survive most accidents. The helmet masked his identity, protecting the privacy of his family and the integrity, however thin, of the police force for which he had worked. The entirety of the Gato Loco persona had all been created for this, just for this; racing at breakneck speeds through anonymous city streets in search of thrills and glory.

But his conscience and a buried sense of *noblesse oblige* had other plans. During a race through the midnight streets of Mexico City fourteen years ago, sensors designed to help him better read racing conditions detected a young family being taken hostage at gun point. He could have ignored their calls for help. Everyone else did. Crimes like this were common place in Mexico City, after all. But the same inner fire that led him to becoming a police detective despite his family's objections led him off the course of the race and into danger for what would be the first of countless times.

The night vision lenses that let him see turns and potholes in poor lighting let him see the gunmen in the shadows, and the stage fields that protected him from a crash protected him from the gunman's bullets. The hard-wired reflexes built into the suit that let him corner at speeds that would be impossible for most other riders helped him disarm the two thugs without incident. And the sculpted helmet, besides striking fear and setting off cascading legends of a dark vigilante on the streets of Mexico City, just looked cool.

Maybe it was God's will or the fickle hand of fate. To have been given the uncontrollable psychic abilities that had so marked his life and then the tools to make a difference, it was hard to argue that there had not been some kind of greater plan at work. Some days, he thought he could see the edges of this grander vision. For a while, he even embraced it. When he was forced to leave Mexico after helping the state police in a corruption investigation within his own department, he had gone to Cobalt City, on the Atlantic seaboard of the U.S. For those who called themselves heroes, it was a proving ground, a Mecca for the cape and spandex set. He had built a reputation, established a presence and a real home. It was the first time he had truly felt at peace with what he was— what he had become.

And then his bike was turned into a fireball beneath him, and he woke in the icy river, numb from the waist down and dying. His fancy bike—ruined. His leathers, which were meant to protect him, saved his life, but at the cost of his legs. After months of surgery and physical therapy, he was finally able to walk after a fashion. But Manuel resigned himself to the likelihood that he would never be a hero again. He threw himself back into his work with the Cobalt City Police Department homicide division, and officially retired Gato Loco.

But while he had given up on Gato Loco, Snowflake and the Tesla twins never did. Financed by Manuel's former lover and fellow cat-themed vigilante Katherine Wilde, Snowflake had painstakingly rebuilt Shadow while Xander and Tamika Tesla turned their intimidating engineering skills toward rebuilding the shell that was Gato Loco. It had taken months, all done in secret, as Manuel refused to discuss the topic of his retirement with anyone, especially those closest to him. And Katherine and the twins were very close to him indeed. For a while, they had worked together under the auspices of the Mysterious Five. It wasn't a team or group in the truest sense of the super-hero community. It was a family.

His relationship with Katherine was over, with too much left unsaid and too much water under the bridge to enable him to fix it. The twins had moved to Seattle, their contact reduced to all-too infrequent phone calls and visits. He wasn't ready to give up on his relationship with them, too.

There was no way he could let something happen to the twins while he was still drawing breath. Manuel had only recently started having visions that looked forward rather than back. He had never tried to change the future. He didn't know if it could be done. But he knew that he had to try. He had accepted fate once before when circumstance took away his legs, only to have his friends fight to give him another chance. He owed them too much to not do the same for them, no matter what it took.

He felt the city of Tijuana stream by on the highway, and every sense felt electric. They gave that back to him. And that was everything.

Snowflake's voice pierced his thoughts as it crackled through on the headset built into the helmet. "Gato, buddy! You just shot right past your turn!"

A quick glance down at the flashing red light on his cross bars confirmed the panda's warning. He braked hard, popping up onto his front tire as the rear of the bike swung around at high speed, his heightened reflexes working overtime to keep Shadow upright. At 190 mph, he had shot a considerable distance past the turn, and by the time he came back to it, Gato Loco had fallen back into sixth place.

Every scrap of concentration and skill he had at his command was thrown into the race. The course dissolved into abstracts of corners, straight aways, and other riders, a blur to his conscious mind as instinct took over. When he crossed the finish line two minutes and six seconds later, he had fought back into fourth place, barely within sight of Anita, who had finished second. Victor Cross had crossed the finish line with time to spare, and was already off his bike popping the cork from a bottle of champagne when Gato Loco zipped silently over the line.

"Decent finish buddy," Snowflake said through the helmet communicator. "Give them a false sense of security, then zoom in for the kill the rest of the way."

Gato Loco burned off his excess speed and flipped around, heading back to the parking lot. "I got distracted."

"You sure you weren't just throwing the race to keep the girlfriend happy?"

"I race to win," Manuel said sternly, but he wondered if Anita would think the same thing, or if she would simply be happy with the second place finish behind last year's over-all winner. He looked ahead, and saw Anita, sans helmet already, hard eyes above a thin smile. But her hard eyes were not looking his way, Manuel realized. No, that malice was directed in the direction of Victor Cross.

"Well, then she has two things to be happy about then," Snowflake grumbled. "She placed second and she won a Jackson off of me."

"What? The race isn't over yet. We'll get more finishes."

"Keep thinking that. I have six markers on my GPS of riders who stopped and didn't get back up. Most of them are probably mechanical or injuries. But at least two of the racers died, buddy. Two of them at the first choke. We're down to twenty-four racers going into the Los Angeles race."

CHAPTER FIVE – CROSSING BORDERS

"I heard Cross took the checkered flag," the other racer said with a laconic drawl. "How far back did you finish?"

Manuel looked at the other racer. Athletic build with a dark, acne-scarred face and dreadlocks past his shoulders, he was dressed in racing leathers in a shade of deep canary yellow with forest green accents. Manuel remembered narrowly avoiding a collision with him just outside of the first choke point. "Fourth. I blew a turn and had to double back. Where did you finish?"

The other rider nodded appreciatively, recognizing the difficulty of missing a turn in a tight race like this and still finishing in the top five. "Official word from Major Tom pegs me at sixteen. I could have sworn I was farther up. I'd rather be in the top ten than the bottom ten, but right in the middle is still okay. I play it safe, and I might squeak out a few wins once we hit Cali. And if the field keeps narrowing, I might fare well farther up the coast as well as long as I can keep riding."

"So you're not going for the big prize purse?"

This coaxed a hearty snort of laughter from the other rider. "Yeah, right. Against you, Cross, and Coyote, it's not really likely. You ever heard of a racer named 'King' Arthur?"

Manuel cast his mind back and didn't come up with any connections. He wondered if Anita, if questioned, might have heard of him. But now wasn't exactly the time. "Afraid not, no."

The other racer turned to show the back of his jacket, revealing the vertical embellishment Gato Loco had been too busy to notice in the race was a detailed sword painted along the spine. "My point exactly. I'm Rand 'King' Arthur. Very pleased to meet you."

Manuel smiled behind the anonymity of his black tinted face-plate. "Big fan of Medieval literature?"

Rand looked vaguely embarrassed. "No, actually. I traveled around the country enough that I was kind of a king of the road, and with my last name being Arthur, other people started calling me that. It's more than a little embarrassing, but any moniker lends a degree of mystique and mythology. I'd be crazy not to welcome the word of mouth. But I've never been into the Arthurian or Fisher King myths. And I do not now nor have I ever owned a sword. Closest I ever came was when I almost bought an Excalibur cycle two years ago. But the kitsch value was just too much, so I got a Pegasus V2000 instead."

Manuel was familiar with the V2000. A good bike for a factory racer, though it didn't lend itself to customization well. But for the most part, it could be raced right out of the showroom and perform well. It would never be a world class bike, and a serious and professional racer would likely make another choice. But it was still a respectable if expensive machine. Manuel put the pieces together in his head, pinning Rand down into a simple category. Lots of leisure time to ride around the country on an expensive bike that would win some of the junior league races but barely show in the big leagues, and no strong hunger for the over-all prize purse. This "King" Arthur was a dilettante with the financial luxury of being a pure thrill rider.

Manuel suspected there were several thrill riders in the race, happy to pay their entry fee to race against Cross and Gato Loco. It was like an illegal summer camp for rich bikers. He had raced against the type several times before, and generally didn't mind them. At least they were less likely to take crazy risks to win, because deep down, they didn't race to win. They raced to race, and that was enough. He respected that. "So," he asked Rand casually, "did you earn it or inherit it?"

Rand's face went blank, and he looked nervously around the other bikers celebrating the end of the first race. Once he was certain that no one else was listening, he relaxed visibly. "So much for that big secret. Yeah, I happen to be, as they say on the street, loaded. I managed to parlay a bit of an inheritance from my parents' death into a solid stock portfolio. I've been living off dividends for years now, and it's the easiest thing in the world. I have a condo in Marin County where I bed down a few weeks out of the year, and the rest of the time, I just ride around the country. I started actually racing about eighteen months ago, and I'm getting better, but I don't harbor any illusions about winning."

"Except for San Francisco and Los Angeles," Manuel said with a trace of amusement in his voice.

Rand looked as though he weren't trying to appear self-conscious or cocky, but still managed to let a little of each slip through. "With all the practice I've had there, one can hope. But I must say, with your entry into the race, things suddenly became a lot more interesting. I look forward to competing against you."

"Best of luck." Gato Loco nodded and then started wheeling his bike through the crowd. He saw Anita holding court, celebrating her finish, knowing that she wanted first and not second place. "Hey Snowflake," he whispered into the helmet mic, "do you have the final times for the first race?"

The panda mechanic/sidekick's voice rasped over the headset within seconds. "Already crunched the numbers, boss. If I subtract out the time you were off the grid, you would have won by about seventeen seconds."

"Not the numbers I wanted, but that's actually reassuring. How much of a gap was there between Anita and Cross?"

There was a moment of silence as Snowflake pulled up the screen again. "Thirty-five point eleven seconds. That's pretty close."

But it wasn't close, and every one of them knew it, especially Anita. Thirty-five point eleven seconds must have felt like eternity to her. She hadn't even rounded the last corner by the time Victor Cross had crossed the line. Gato Loco got a good look at Anita's face when she turned to laugh at someone's joke. The tightness around her eyes was fear—fear that she could throw down the best run of her life and it might not be enough to beat Cross. And if Gato Loco got his head in the game, she was all but assured finishing no higher than third for the rest of the Devil's Ride.

He decided to leave her to her celebration. He caught her eye as best as possible through the opaque face plate and nodded a congratulations to her. The small smile on her face spoke volumes. They would talk later, and he would give her the congratulations she truly deserved. But now was not the time. He rolled Shadow toward the trailer. "Pop the door, buddy," he spoke into the helmet. "I'm bringing her in for the night, and then I'm going to take a nap in the truck."

The door was open and waiting when Gato Loco rolled up to it. Snowflake hopped out and helped him get Shadow up the ramp and into the charging dock where the experimental high-test batteries started filling back up to Shadow's energy green line. He was halfway changed out into his regular street clothes when the problem of crossing the border occurred to him. When he mentioned it to Snowflake, the inscrutable panda merely smiled and assured him that it was all taken care of.

Manuel had learned not to question his frequent partner in crime-fighting when he got like this, and instead stumped out of the back of the trailer. The party was already breaking down in the twenty minutes he had been in the back changing, and only a dozen of the more die-hard social animals were there, drinking and singing along off tune to the radio. He didn't see Anita at first, but then he rounded the corner and saw that she had rolled her own bike up into the bed of Snowflakes truck and was strapping it in.

He stopped at the back of the truck and watched her working silently for a moment. She tried to ignore him, working the straps over the seat, looping around the frame and securing to the side ties. The final strap ratcheted down, she shot Manuel an exasperated glare. "What?"

"Good race."

She spat, her words barely above a mutter. "Fuck you. I don't need that from you."

He held his ground and his gaze, trying to lock her down with his eyes, but she was shifting her eyes around, looking for an escape. "Don't need what? I said good race because it was."

Anita opened her mouth to say something mean, something cruel and argumentative, but nothing came out and she closed her mouth again. Instead, she settled for throwing her gloves into the bed of the truck. Eventually, she sat on the back of the truck, close enough that Manuel could take one of her hands. "I lost. It wasn't a good race."

"Anita, you beat the other twenty-eight racers, including me. That's a pretty good race. And you got a cash purse for it, so why the drama?"

She squeezed his hand and when she met his gaze, there was stark fear hidden with her dark eyes. "I don't think I can beat him."

Manuel shrugged. "Did you race your absolute best race? No flaws at all? Nothing you would do different?"

"There's always something I would do different—a corner I would take a little faster or tighter if I knew the tires would grip the road so well, or a straight away that didn't look as long as it was so I didn't get the acceleration I really wanted. How about you?"

He laughed. "Well, for one, I wouldn't have blown that turn."

Anita's eyes went wide with surprise and a barely suppressed laugh. "You blew a turn? Where?"

"I shot past the exit on the highway after the second choke point. Just flew on by and didn't even see it." His voice was rueful. He knew he wouldn't make that mistake again, and it would likely help Anita to know that everyone was human, even him, probably even Victor Cross.

Anita's voice was quiet with wonder as she made sense of it. "I wondered what happened to you."

"What happened was I screwed up. That's my point. The best racers in the world all make mistakes. When you're racing at this level, the trick is to make less mistakes than them. But you know that, otherwise you wouldn't be here." He saw the words coax out a hint of a smile. Manuel bent in and kissed it, and when he pulled back, the smile was in full flower. "Now would you care to lie down with me in the truck for a bit of rest? Snowflake has a plan to get this circus across the border and I want to be alert when it happens."

"Snowflake has a plan?" Her eyes were wide. "This I have to see."

It had been a long day, and now that the adrenaline of the race was flushing out of their systems, both Anita and Manuel were exhausted. She joined him in the cab of the truck, and leaning against the door, Manuel let Anita put her head on his shoulder. They tried once or twice to start conversations about the race, what they had seen, how the other riders had fared, little things that came to them in the half-lucid state between sleep and wakefulness. When Snowflake climbed behind the wheel and started the engine, Anita murmured and smacked her lips, semi-conscious of having drooled on Manuel's chest.

But neither of them woke until they were rocked back into consciousness by the stop and go of the border traffic accompanied by the bright lights of one of the world's most active border crossings. There were already a few bikes lined up with them, and when Manuel opened his eyes, he saw Cross a few spaces ahead of them approaching one of the armed checkpoints on the American side. Snowflake smiled across the crowded truck cab at them, his bland gym coach disguise looking eerily calm despite the rolling crime lab, custom bike, and security measures packed into the trailer behind them. "You have your passports ready?"

Anita patted her jacket to find her passport. Manuel pulled out the small document pouch he had put around his neck and tucked into his shirt when he had changed out of his leathers. "You really have a plan to get us through this? You're not just going to wing it?" Manuel was less certain about the lack of problems the closer they got to the checkpoint. As he had dreamt, he had remembered the final failsafe security device Katherine had insisted on putting in the trailer—a brick of thermite that would level the trailer and everything in twenty feet in all directions should someone manage to breach all the other security measures. He wasn't sure what kind of chemical sniffing they did at the crossing into the U.S. these days, but he didn't know how they could miss something like that.

The space opened up to them and Snowflake pulled into an inspection spot while a border agent approached them. "Trust me, amigo. I have this wired."

While one guard approached Snowflake, another began to circle the vehicle with a mirror on a stick, looking beneath the chassis for explosives or other suspicious packages. The guard at the window looked to be in his late forties, thick around the torso with muscle supplemented by a little bit of comfortable eating. He appeared to be completely devoid of any sense of humor, and his mirrored sunglasses, even at this ungodly hour, covered any emotion his eyes might have otherwise betrayed. "Passports and cargo manifest."

Snowflake gathered the travel documents and handed them through the window. The border guard looked at each one carefully, wrinkles appearing at the edges of his eyes, barely visible behind the glasses as he squinted at each passenger in turn, comparing their face to the picture in their passport. After a long second, he handed the passports back through the window and looked at the cargo manifest. He pursed his lips and looked through the window, his gaze passing over each passenger anew. "It says that you're a race team called Mysterious Five Motors

44

Sports, but I only count three of you. Are the other two in the trailer?"

Manuel cleared his throat and offered up his calmest smile. "Actually, there aren't five of us. That's what makes us mysterious."

"It's a reference to the number of fingers on the hand. In fact, only Manuel and me are on the team, unless you count our sponsor back in Cobalt City," Snowflake offered up helpfully. "The girl here is just a Colombian drug mule we picked up south of the border."

Anita and Manuel froze in shock. The guard didn't move for a long second, his gaze fixed on Snowflake, his face expressionless. Then a smile flickered across his face so quickly that Manuel wasn't sure he had actually seen it. When the guard spoke, his voice was low, but it had very clearly changed. If Manuel was not mistaken, it was the voice of Archon, one of Snowflake's former super-hero employers, and resident expert in just about everything—including disguise and infiltration. "Even through the holographic disguise that Kara whipped up for you, I can tell you're lying. You're really bad at it, Snowflake. Stick to the driving and repair, and you'll do fine."

"Thanks. Tell your boyfriend Gallows I said hi," the panda growled.

The guard straightened and waved the truck and trailer through. Before they pulled away, however, he handed the manifest back to Snowflake. Giving one last look through the window at Manuel, the guard who was not a guard offered a warm and very real smile. "Good luck, Gato. We'll be watching."

The truck pulled past the gates and the guards and onto American soil without further incident. Once the lights of the crossing had faced in the side mirrors, Anita punched Snowflake hard in the right arm, cursing at him in Spanish.

The panda rolled his shoulder, flexing out the pain of the punch with an only mildly hurt expression. "Ow! Hey lady, I'm trying to drive here! Didn't anyone tell you not to mess with the driver of the motor vehicle? And you're in America now. If you're going to curse me out, do it in American!"

"Colombian drug mule?" Anita shrieked. To her credit, she refrained from further physical violence while the truck was in motion. "I should cut you for that! Do you realize how much trouble I would have been in? I have a wad of cash from the race in my front pocket and a few strikes on my record in Mexico!"

Snowflake glanced over at Manuel who was chucking low enough in the back of his throat to escape Anita's notice. "Manny, buddy, better rein your filly in."

That earned the panda another hard jab in the arm, despite the high speed of the truck. "You are lucky I didn't get arrested, otherwise I would have made you a filly before anyone could have stopped me."

"Gelding," Manuel corrected with a smile.

Anita turned on him, as if expecting her recent lover to be in on the joke as well. Her eyes blazed with fury. "Gelding?"

Manuel kissed her quickly on the forehead. "If you had cut his *huevos* off, it wouldn't have made him a filly. It would have made him a gelding. But you're right. It was a bad idea of a joke."

Snowflake pouted, eyes fixed on the highway ahead of him. "Not that we were ever in any real danger of getting stopped, searched, or arrested. That guy was an old friend from when I rolled with the Protectorate. I called him yesterday and arranged a safe crossing. You hang around the cape and cowl set for as long as I do, you pick up a few things. What I picked up was one of the best damn rolodexes on the planet and a log of owed favors as long as your leg. Oh, and you're welcome for getting you across the border, princess."

Not ready to fully release hold on her anger, Anita pursed her lips and stared out the front windshield as well. Manuel glanced across the cab of the truck, watching his two companions briefly before turning his attention to the road side markers, ticking by exits and distances on their way to Los Angeles. Neither Anita nor Snowflake was the type to apologize, nor were they the type to forgive and forget easily. This was going to be a long trip.

There might come time not too far down the road, when one of them would have to get the boot. And there wasn't a second thought to which one it would be. But that was a problem for another night. He gave into exhaustion and closed his eyes. The hum of the tires on asphalt sang him to sleep.

CHAPTER SIX – GHOST FISH

In many ways, the course was simplicity itself. Two dozen bikes set out in the pre-dawn light with the highway traffic already starting to back up. Amid the exhaust fumes and swirling garbage, the tour of the second race course began its slow procession. Gato Loco rode toward the back, interested in watching how the other riders maneuvered the turns at street-legal speeds. Cross took his place at the front, riding just behind Major Tom, as was his right for having won the previous leg. Anita, anxious to find a flaw the armor of the other racer, rode him like a shadow, looking for anything she could use to her advantage.

Starting under the Pomona Freeway in East Los Angeles, the impressive motorcade jogged a few blocks west and then south along South Arizona Avenue until it hit East Olympic, where they turned west again through the largely residential neighborhood full of dying lawns behind chain link fences. A few miles later, Olympic took a shallow bend right, but the racers went straight, cutting through side streets until they hit the river.

Passing between two buildings, they encountered a chain link fence with a wide rend in it, providing the racers with their first choke point. From that point, the bikes dropped down the slope of a concrete embankment to the virtually dry manmade concrete channel that comprised the river bed. They followed this, what Manuel considered little more than a giant, glorified gutter, south for a considerable distance. With no chance of actual traffic and a virtually uninterrupted straight-away, Gato Loco knew that would be the point where most of the speed freaks would make their break when the actual race came. The risk of debris in the occasional patch of tall weeds and varying depths of the sluggish river were acceptable, especially when compared to the greater risks of dodging unpredictable L.A. traffic.

As the racers approached the bend of Interstate 710, they popped back up onto surface streets. This was the point Manuel was most concerned about. A chunk of this portion wound through industrial areas, freight yards, and train tracks. A careless rider could easily get lost or hit a rail wrong with his tire, causing a fatal accident. But once through this particular gauntlet, it was major roads north to the finish line.

While his bike cooled down in the dawn light beneath the Pomona Freeway, Gato Loco checked his odometer. The actual miles made for a longer race than in Tijuana, but the big straight-away in the river-bed would shave off a considerable chunk of time. Looking around at the assembled riders for recently befriended "King" Arthur, Manuel wondered if Rand was familiar with this particular stretch of town. The riverbed was almost certain to be familiar to him, but it was familiar to a lot of people. Even Travolta had raced there once, even if it was only in a movie.

The race was set to start at three in the morning, giving everyone the full day and most of the night to rest up and maintain their bikes as needed. Manuel had slept enough the other night, and with the exception of a nap he planned on taking before dinner, that left him a lot of time on his hands. From the playful smile on Anita's face when she woke him up for the pre-race tour, he suspected that she had plans for at least some of that free time.

Manuel's gaze flickered down to the digital clock readout on the bottom corner of his visor. He doubted Snowflake would be up yet, and even if he was, the holographic disguise would still be charging its batteries for another hour. There was no rush to get back to the hotel they had picked down in Anaheim, just across the high perimeter hedge and walls from Disneyland. Anita had smiled with girlish glee when she realized that she could see the top of one of the roller coasters from the window of their room. Having never been to the theme park before, neither of them could say for certain which one it was, just that it looked like a snow capped mountain, poking up magically just over the wall of green. Snowflake had suggested it was the Matterhorn ride, but wasn't sure himself.

Manuel suspected that a trip to the "happiest place on Earth," might be in his near future. A full day stumping around the park on the forearm crutches sounded like a recipe for disaster. He even wondered if it might be a plot on Anita's part to tire him out prior to the evening's race. It sickened him ever so slightly that he could consider such a possibility, but try as he might, he couldn't shake his impression that his recent lover could sink to such depths if that was what it took to win.

Before the thought was entirely out of his mind, Anita cruised casually over to him on her bike. "How do you feel about breakfast?"

He shrugged, indifference heavy in the electronically altered voice from his helmet. "Not really that hungry, but I could grab a coffee and a cinnamon roll or something. Did you have something in mind?"

"The Copper Kettle down near our hotel had a decent breakfast menu, and I'm starving. Do you think the 'Flake will be joining us?"

Another glance at the digital timer in the helmet was all the confirmation Manuel needed. "No. He was out bowling until after two. He won't be up for a few hours yet. The Kettle sounds fine." He briefly considered heading straight to the diner, and then decided to preserve the tenuous illusion of a secret identity. He could stump the two blocks from the hotel to the restaurant easily enough. "I'll meet you there. I want to change first."

Anita smiled thinly at him and then revved her engine. "Don't keep me waiting too long. You don't want me to get bored."

"GPS," he whispered into his helmet microphone, followed by an equally soft, "Mini-map mode." A compact map of Los Angeles sprang into focus along the bottom of his field of vision. "Opacity seventy percent. Plot to save point one—fastest."

The most expedient route, factoring in distance and prevailing traffic reports, showed up as a red line on his map, with a tiny arrow to indicate his place on the map. He gunned the engine to a silent yet furious life and accelerated away from the cluster of bikes beneath the freeway.

Around him, the city was coming to life, many of the first wave service employees were already up, preparing the path ahead for the white collar office drones and manufacturing workers who would be next, followed by late shift service employees, staffing the movie theatres and book stores and other small business that wouldn't open until ten or later.

Another two hours, and these roads will be full, Manuel thought. Whereas now, it was no small matter to race along the highways and side roads as instructed by his electronic navigator, going anywhere later in the day would require either daredevil riding or patience. Traffic could be bad in Cobalt City, but it was nothing compared to what he had experienced in the truck with Snowflake and Anita when they had arrived. Anaheim was not their first choice for lodging, but it was where Snowflake had lost patience and took the next exit available to him. All things considered, they were lucky that there were rooms available and that they hadn't pulled off the highway into a less hospitable area.

The sun coming up over the Sierra Nevada Mountains turned the air a rarified shade of gold, and even weaving around morning commuters on the highway felt somehow magical. It was good to be riding again, not just to compete, he realized, but to embrace the freedom of a bike between his legs and the open road stretching out before him.

He needed this. Almost as much as he needed food and sleep and air, he needed this. It wasn't as though the life he had built for himself back in Cobalt City was bad. Quite the contrary, he had several friends there, more than he had likely had since school. He had liked his job as a homicide detective, and wondered if only briefly if that job would be there for him should he return. He had bought a converted warehouse building with a strip club called the Kit Kat Klub on the two bottom floors, and the top three floors he had turned into a spacious loft apartment with a view with a headquarters below for his Gato Loco duties.

He had even, for well over a year, allowed himself to be tamed. Katherine had been good for him in many ways—possibly the first woman whom he had regarded as an equal in the more important aspects of his life. She had forced Manuel to confront the Latin playboy lifestyle he had been living, and he had found it ultimately hollow and unfulfilling. The things that were important to him— the concept of social justice and civic responsibility, and the insatiable hunger for adrenaline—he wasn't going to find that in a steady succession of shallow one-night stands. But to reveal more about who he was, what he cared about, exposed not only himself to risk, but anyone he wanted to tell about his dual life. Even his partner on the force, Donegal, had been kept out of the loop, no matter how much it had hurt him to do it.

Donegal had figured it out eventually of course. Manuel wouldn't have respected him as a detective so much if he hadn't been able to crack that particular chestnut.

For a while, Manuel had it all. A fulfilling professional life, and an exciting and rewarding life as a vigilante. Gato Loco had become a known name, even if no one knew that much about him. Among the criminal element, he had been a boogie man. Among most of the law abiding citizens of Cobalt City, he was an urban legend who nonetheless made them feel safer about going out at night.

And then tragedy had struck, turning his legs into a ruin of burned flesh from knees to groin. If not for the suit and the timely intervention of fellow heroes who fished his unconscious body out of the river, he would have died.

And as recovered in the hospital, all the good things he enjoyed in Cobalt City began to taste like ashes in his mouth. A hero? Not anymore. The remains of his vigilante identity went into a box in the "Cat House." And there it stayed, while he moved from the hospital to bed rest and physical therapy in his loft apartment just one floor up from a secret headquarters he couldn't bring himself to enter any more.

Kat was still a hero, while he was a "survivor." She treated him differently. She had been pinned to a warehouse wall and left for dead in the same conflict that had almost killed Manuel. But she recovered, and he did not. His inability to pull out of the death spiral of self-pity made things sour slowly but inevitably between them. While she pulled together the resources and people to rebuild his suit and bike without telling him, they both knew things would never be the same. Some things, once broken, just couldn't be fixed.

Even his promising career as a police detective felt less than fulfilling, knowing that there was no secret life waiting when he punched out for the night. He was just a cop—nothing more and nothing less. While that was a noble and sacred calling, knowing that he had once been so much more and would likely never be again sat heavy in his chest, day in and day out.

And then fate put him back on the bike, reminding him once again of that rush when he reached beyond what he thought was possible. Something came alive in his chest—a soft and secret flutter of his heart awakening again.

Sure, he thought. He could go back to Cobalt City. The warehouse was still there, the apartment and Cat House rented out to a fellow cape and cowl type who went by the name of Regret or something. He found the irony appealing. He could probably have his job on the force back if he groveled enough and didn't take too long to get back to it.

But Kat had moved on. The Tesla kids were in Seattle now. The Protectorate had gone all Beatles on the city, scattering to the four winds—some to other cities, some patrolling the skies they defended as a team now as a solo act, while some went into the private sector. He could go back. But the open road rolled out before him, always changing. And it was calling to him.

Gato Loco reached the hotel parking lot and activated the back door for the trailer, riding Shadow straight into the charging dock as the door closed behind him. It took ten minutes to get changed and the suit stored, and another ten to reach the restaurant, and by then, the sun was burning through the ever-present L.A. haze.

The Copper Kettle was steadily filling up with a few locals and hordes of tourists looking to get a solid and inexpensive meal in them before the park opened up. He saw Anita through the windows as he approached, just being led to the table as he came through the door. Manuel smiled at the hostess and pointed toward Anita's retreating leather-clad back. "I'm with her."

Anita heard the clack of his forearm crutches on the brick floor before she saw him. She flipped his coffee cup over for the hostess and then slid a menu over to his side of the small booth. "Did you get held up in traffic?" Manuel asked, squeezing her shoulder as he passed.

"Fifteen minute wait for a table. You're not that much faster than me." Her eyes were fixed on the menu, perusing row after row of traditional breakfast items. Manuel decided not to distract her and point out that he would have beaten her by close to five minutes if he hadn't stopped to change. The last thing he wanted to do was amp her competitive urge up higher than it was already. When the waitress stopped by their table, she ordered a six-egg tomato, bacon, and sour-cream omelet with a side of hashed browns smothered with green chile and cheese and white toast. Manuel stuck with orange juice, coffee, and a butterhorn, figuring he could always poach off her plate or order another side if he were still hungry later. Worst case scenario, he could grab a bite with Snowflake when the slumbering panda finally rolled out of bed.

"You know this used to all be under the ocean," Anita said idly, her gaze playing out across the dining area. Her voice was disinterested, detached, as though she might not even be aware that she was speaking at all. "There used to be fish swimming around right where we're sitting now."

Manuel paused, coffee cup half way to his mouth. "What?"

Anita focused on him, her fingers intertwined before her on the table. She looked strangely contemplative. Gone was the early morning playfulness of her eyes. "The ocean? You've heard of it, right? Well, this all used to be ocean, and now its desert."

What happened to her on the ride down here, he wondered? Or was it earlier, during the race? Something had happened, had shifted dramatically in her demeanor, and it unnerved him without being able to understand why. "Where did you hear that?"

She motioned toward one of the other tables in the dining area. There were too many full tables for Manuel to sort out which one she was indicating with a simple head gesture. "I heard someone telling his kid when I was waiting for a table."

"I don't think that's historically accurate. The La Brea Tar Pits are pretty close by, and those were above ground millions of years ago."

She offered up a dismissive shrug, and then began idly toying with her empty coffee cup. *Not a big coffee drinker, that girl*, Manuel thought. "Take it up with the guy in the Buckeye's sweatshirt over there. I'm just repeating what I heard."

Manuel took a sip of forgettable coffee and poured in a touch more cream. He tried to make eye contact with Anita, but she was being dodgy, her gaze on her hands, on the window, on the waitresses, on the ceiling fans over the dining area—anywhere but at him. "This conversation isn't about the ocean, is it?"

One corner of her mouth flickered up in a tiny, brief smile. "It took you long enough, mister detective. No, this isn't about the ocean. This is what they call a relationship discussion."

Manuel's back tightened instinctively. "You don't say? I'm not really good at relationship discussions."

"Me either." She smiled a little more warmly and a little longer, her gaze locking with his for only a second before she went back to looking at the sugar packets on the table. "It's just that, I don't really do relationships, and I get the feeling that you don't really do them either."

"You're breaking up with me," he said quietly and without emotion, only half serious about the suggestion, "and you're doing it in a public place so I won't cause a scene. How, may I ask, did I become the hysterical woman in this scenario in your head?"

Anita laughed quickly and reached out, taking one of his hands in her own. "No, that's not what I'm talking about. Not really. It's just—we've never really talked about us. We've been together for a little while, and I don't really know what this is."

It was a tricky proposition for Manuel. On one hand, she already knew some of his biggest secrets, having figured them out on her own weeks ago. On the other hand, she and Snowflake had already proven to mix poorly. The more time they spent together, the more they tended to grate on the other's nerves. He had come to suspect that every day he spent with her was one more day of delaying the inevitable. "I don't know what this is either, Anita. I like having you around, but I don't exactly see a white picket fence in the future either."

She nodded, apparently having come to the same conclusions herself. "So I'm just filler? A rebound hoochie until something better comes along?" While her voice was filled with mock indignation, the color around her ears suggested that she believed her own words. It gave Manuel pause, derailing him from a quick and easy denial that might not be true. Sure, she was a good fit for his life now. But his life was changing, maybe like moving from ocean to desert in its own way. Maybe the idea of a real adult relationship was nothing more than those ghost fish—just memories of lifestyle that might not fit anymore, and he was too stupid to realize it yet.

She hadn't struck him as the settling down, committed relationship kind of person either. His instincts could be wrong. When it came to women, it wouldn't come as much of a surprise if his instincts were in fact very far off base. "Do you want to be my girlfriend?" Manuel asked with an overly earnest smile on his face. He squeezed her hand for extra emphasis. "We can go steady and get matching t-shirts like the people over there near the window."

Anita's gaze took in the couple in the matching cartoon t-shirts, and she stifled a laugh with the back of her free hand. But Manuel thought he saw, for just the briefest of seconds, a hint of a tear in the corner of one eye. But she shook it off too quickly for him to be sure. "That wouldn't be so bad. But you never answered the question. Am I a placeholder?"

His voice was firm and sincere, which surprised him just a little bit. "No." If he was being honest with himself, he wasn't looking for anyone else. He hadn't even been looking for someone when he met Anita, so the idea struck him as odd. There was always the chance, he supposed, that someone might come along who was absolutely perfect for him. But he couldn't imagine that being the case. He thought he had found her once, and had been wrong. "I'll be honest, though. There is a little bit of the rebound in me. I was in a big relationship. Biggest I've been in before. I learned a lot from it, but when things fell apart, well, there was no fixing it."

She looked deeply into his eyes, as if trying to determine if he was lying or not. "If you could have her back, would you?"

There wasn't any point in lying to her. He shrugged. "Maybe. But there isn't any chance of us working things out even if I did see her anymore, which I don't." He believed every word, and he could tell by the look on Anita's face that she believed him too. There wasn't any chance of him getting back together with Katherine. The last time they had spoken in person, he had kissed her good-bye, and the vision he had let him know. It was over.

But what if, he found himself thinking ...

If I can change the future of the visions, which needs to happen if I'm to save Xander, then maybe nothing was truly set in stone. The thought gave him pause. Had he accepted the visualized fate without question because he believed in fate or because he had wanted to believe in that fate?

Thankfully, the food arrived, and Anita dug in eagerly, saving him from further questioning.

Manuel secretly hoped that his wistful smile hadn't planted the wrong impression in her mind. That smile, he realized, might not have been about Anita at all.

"Would we sound too much like a couple if I asked if we have a plan for the day?" Manuel said around a mouthful of butterhorn.

The question made Anita smile anew, sending to her a shade of glowing that Manuel felt might be a shade excessive. "I was going to let you spend the day with Snowflake doing guy stuff. I want to spend some of my winnings at Disneyland. I would love if you came with, but I don't want to tire you out right before the race. If we have time, maybe we can go tomorrow before we head up to San Francisco. But today, I just want to hit as many rides as fast as I can."

Trying to hide his surprise, Manuel took a long sip of coffee, finishing off his cup with no waitress in sight for a quick refill. Since their acquaintance had begun, Anita had never once suggested he spend the day without her. On the heels of her sudden ambush of the relationship conversation, it was a curious if not altogether pleasant change of course. And the prospect of seeing a movie in a classic Hollywood theatre and maybe sushi somewhere for lunch with Snowflake was appealing. "Would you like to join us for dinner tonight?"

She rolled her eyes around, thinking it over while she chewed a mouthful of egg and bacon. "Maybe a late dinner, around eight or nine?"

That worked for Manuel's time table, giving them more than enough time for a relaxing meal, and then last minute tune-ups on the bike. "Give us a call late in the day, and we can arrange where to meet you."

Only half an hour later, Manuel found himself back in his room with a handful of brochures from the lobby. Snowflake joined him twenty minutes after that, and they began planning their day. After two movies, a China Town lunch, and a few hours watching the waves at Malibu later with Snowflake complaining about the sun and the heat and the sand, they finally heard from Anita, who had called from a payphone. They agreed to meet at an East Coast style deli called Mr. Rosewater's that Snowflake insisted came highly recommended.

Anita was unexpectedly delayed, and both Snowflake and Manuel had already finished two sodas by the time she finally showed up. They saw her ride in on her bike and park right outside the front window of the non-descript 24-hour white cinderblock deli. "At least she looks contrite," Snowflake muttered. Manuel was impressed that it was the first negative thing his friend had said about Anita all day.

The bell over the door dinged as she came in, alerting the two counter staff to her entrance, and they looked up at her expectantly. She only took a second to decide on a sandwich, and then asked for directions to the restroom. Anita passed them, a sheepish look on her face as she showed the greasy tire smear on left palm. "My tire was low when I filled up, and now who knows what kind of Los Angeles street crud I have on my hand. I'll only be a few minutes, I hope."

Snowflake and Manuel approached the counter and put in their sandwich order. The panda also got three of the huge kosher dills out of the case in a baggie for later enjoyment. He was uncharacteristically quiet, and Manuel was thinking of asking him what was going on when Anita joined their table. The sandwiches followed shortly thereafter, and then racing and travel talk, and then preparation for the race itself.

Before he knew it, Gato Loco was at the starting line, Shadow purring quietly between his knees. It was only then, as the race was about to start, that he remembered the quiet moment in the deli. Whatever it was, he decided, couldn't have been that important. There was always time to ask Snowflake about it later.

CHAPTER SEVEN – RACING ANGELS

The roars of engines woke those unfortunate enough to be asleep as the second leg of the Devil's Run rounded the first corner onto southbound South Arizona Avenue. Two blocks into the race, and Manuel was already in place where he wanted to be, right in the middle of the pack, with a clear view of first. Cross had once again taken the early lead, and Anita was pushing hard after him, keeping the faster racer within one bike length.

Gato Loco didn't envy Cross. It was hard being the leader, with everyone gunning for your position. And you constantly had to divide your attention between the road ahead and the competition behind, because a clever racer could snake up and capitalize on a moment of weakness. No, being lead wasn't for everyone—at least not for the entire race, which is how Cross seemed to like it. It took a special kind of narcissist to covet the lead for the entire race, and only someone with that magic combination of skill, speed, and hubris could hope to hold onto it.

Gato Loco edged up into fourth rank, directly behind El Diablo Blanco, by the time they hit the turn off Arizona to East Olympic. The lead position was only fifty feet away, and Manuel decided to get into the head of the young Cross. Popping Shadow up across the sidewalk as he made the turn, Gato Loco cut the corner tighter than anyone else had dared. This time of night, there was no one on the sidewalk for several blocks. It seemed no one walked in L.A. if they could help it, especially in East L.A. at three in the morning.

Cycling Shadow's engine up toward max output, Gato Loco lunged ahead, accelerating faster than perhaps even Anita would have expected. He nursed the bike back off the sidewalk and into the street even with Cross. For two breathtakingly fast blocks, Gato Loco kept pace, and then he gave Shadow just a bit more juice, and he inched past Cross, moving to half a length ahead. It wasn't a maintainable position, at least not comfortably, and Gato Loco knew it. Cross probably knew it too, but now Cross also knew that he had some real competition. But top speed wasn't everything. On a real race course or the salt flats, a bike could hit in excess of three hundred miles an hour. But on an actual urban street, with uncertain road conditions and turns, no one, not even Gato Loco would push those kinds of limits.

The bikes hit the side street like thunder, heading for the river. Gato Loco held position, trusting Snowflake's skills as a mechanic and engineer. He hit the breach in the fence at a clean 195 mph and sailed out into the air above the concrete river bed fifteen feet below.

It was a stupid, showy stunt, Gato Loco realized as soon as Shadow's tires left the ground. He wasn't familiar enough with this area to have calculated a safe landing zone. And even if he did, the landing forced him to take the turn much wider than necessary, allowing four riders to get back ahead of him.

But for a few seconds, Cross had lost the lead, and that blow was likely to change his performance. It might have even shaken him a bit, and if that was the case, he was likely to make mistakes. With luck, Anita would find an opening and exploit it, knocking Cross even further back in the rankings.

The low-light filters gave him enough light to see the path ahead where he saw a landing space as clear as anyone could hope for under the circumstances. Shadow's tires bit down on the weeds and dirt of the river, the performance shocks absorbing the bulk of the impact. Leaning hard into the turn, Gato Loco swept the back tire over to his left without sacrificing too much of his speed. But the damage was done, and he found himself sixth out of 24 riders now, and on the wrong side of the anemic river as well.

He could only hope that his intimidation of Cross would pay off down the stretch for someone. As he sought an opportunity to safely cross back to the other side of the sluggishly moving river, he watched as both El Diablo Blanco and "King" Arthur swapped the lead back and forth between them before Cross managed to gun past by riding high up on the concrete embankment.

Anita was keeping it competitive, her front tire close enough to Blanco's bike at one point that Manuel was certain a collision was unavoidable. But instead, Blanco cut hard left and dropped off speed to let her pass, circling around behind and far right to pass on the other side of Cross.

The four racers jockeyed back and forth, Cross, Arthur, Blanco, and Anita, while a fifth racer, in a black Gore-Tex jacket with gray sleeves dogged their heels, looking for an opening. Every time the pack leaders parted slightly, the fifth racer would edge up and then back down again, too cautious to make his break. Gato Loco saw a wide shallow spot in the river and gunned Shadow for it, kicking up a plume of filthy water as he shot through at over 150 mph, settling in behind the rest of the pack at a close sixth.

Ahead, the bend of Interstate 710 loomed, and the window to make a decisive move began to narrow. Gato Loco went high on the embankment, confident in his ability to brake and make the tight turn at this sharp approach. The fifth place rider gunned hard around on the right, through the high weeds, slipping past Anita and El Diablo Blanco. But something solid, perhaps an engine block or the ruins of a sofa, lay in wait in the tall weeds. At the high rate of speed the other racer was traveling, he never stood a chance. The tweaked out street bike hit hard and crumpled, throwing the rider high and hard to the grit of the riverbed, which was little more than sand and gravel on concrete. He bounced and skidded like a rag doll fired from a cannon for thirty feet before coming to a stop.

The wreckage of the bike flipped left, and El Diablo Blanco nearly tipped his bike to avoid the collision. The defensive maneuver caused the devil-styled biker to shed a lot of speed, and he ended up getting passed by several bikes following the pack leaders. When they hopped up out of the riverbed into the industrial portion of the race, Cross was back in the lead, with Gato Loco and Arthur jockeying for second, with Anita tight behind the both of them.

With the tighter turns and rougher road surface and unnerved perhaps by the closeness of the race, Cross tried to shave as much of an advantage as he could, cutting corners around parked rigs and trailers as close as he could. "King" Arthur wasn't as willing to take

61

those kinds of risks, and Anita edged up on him as Gato Loco pulled away.

They were all close enough to Cross to see the front wheel of his bike bounce off and away as the lead racer hit some train tracks. To Manuel, it seemed like everything went into a sickening slow motion, as he ducked to avoid the flying wheel. Without support for the front end of the bike, the fork dug into the ground, pitching Cross head-first into the hitch plate of a parked diesel rig. Even over the roar of the bikes, Manuel could swear he heard the crunch of collapsing helmet and skull. The other rider who had spilled down in the river might live through the night. There was no doubt in Manuel's mind that Victor Cross was dead instantly.

And as certain as he was of the young Croatian racer's death, Gato Loco was certain of something else as well. What had happened to Victor Cross's bike was no accident. It was sabotage. He activated the cell phone in his helmet with a sub-audible command and dialed his sidekick and mechanic. "Snowflake, this is Gato. Do you have your ears on?"

"Reading you loud and clear. What's the situation?"

Distracted as he was while calling in the terrifying accident, all the while being laser-focused on the course ahead of him, Gato Loco almost didn't notice Anita inching ahead of him. "Victor Cross just died south of where I am. It looked like his front wheel came off the forks. Any chance you can jet down here and take a look at the wreckage before someone official shows up?"

Over the headset, Manuel could hear the engine of Snowflake's truck roar to life. "You mean can I get to a crash scene in an industrial section of East Los Angeles at three in the morning before L.A.'s finest show up? I don't think you have anything to worry about. Just win the race, and I'll work some panda magic for you."

"Thanks. Over and out."

Gato Loco felt the road surface change beneath his tires, signaling the end of the challenging section. From here on out, it was surface streets to the finish line with a minimum of turns. Anita was good and her bike was fast, but with a faster acceleration and deceleration, Gato Loco was able to pop around the corners cleaner, and she ended up crossing the finish line a few lengths behind, still much closer than she had finished against Cross in the previous race. "King" Arthur placed a solid third and seemed happy for the ranking. When his helmet came off, a shaky smile spread across his face. "Good race," he called out to Anita and Gato Loco, "but when we get to San Fran, I think I'm going to be the one crossing first."

Major Tom was standing nearby, lips pursed as he looked at a small GPS reader in his hand. The two bodyguards were standing near-by, watching on, and he saw one hold up three fingers to the other guard. Three. He didn't understand at the time, but as he started counting racers crossing the line, the enigmatic number made sense. Three racers. They lost three more racers.

The field was down to twenty-one. One-third of the Devil's Run was finished, and they had lost nearly one-third of the racers to mechanical issues, injury, and even death. There would be more. Gato Loco looked around at the assembled riders, to a man elated to have lived through the experience. *Oh yeah*, he thought. *There are definitely going to be more losses.*

CHAPTER EIGHT – LEGWORK

As Manuel understood it, there was supposed to be a party of some kind after the race. He had been counting on the gathering to get a better feel for the racers and hopefully ferret out some clues as to who was on trajectory to kill Xander. But with the news of the death of Victor Cross, the celebratory mood had been extinguished. It left Manuel in the uncomfortable position of having to take his best guess based on what little he already knew.

While Major Tom was giving instructions to the racers on where and when to meet in San Francisco for the next race, Manuel reprocessed the vision as best as he was able. He had a general sense of height based on the surroundings. His best estimate put the killer somewhere between five-nine and six foot. That dropped the list of suspects to sixteen people.

The size of the hands in the gloves ruled out the three women racing, dropping the suspect list to thirteen people.

Manuel considered the knife. He hadn't seen anyone with a knife, but suspected several of the bikers here would have one for utilitarian purposes if nothing else. But the knife in the vision wasn't just some simple jack knife. It was a fixed-blade affair, with a serpent head at the end of the grip. The blade itself was wickedly jagged, and reminded him of the fantasy knives from replica catalogues and cutlery stores. It wasn't a functional knife—not in any real sense. They were meant to appeal to the type of knife owners who liked death metal, Michael Moorcock novels, and Vallejo paintings. Looking around his suspect pool of thirteen people, Manuel realized that he didn't know any of the racers well enough to eliminate them based on that limited of a profile. However, El Diablo Blanco seemed to visibly fit the mold much better than most, with the demon painted on the back of his jacket.

The jacket, he realized. That was another factor he had overlooked. The room was relatively dark, so colors were difficult to make out, but the killer wore a leather jacket. It only shaved three more names off the list of suspects, but the jacket had been light colored, and with the biker fondness for black leather, that information narrowed the suspect list considerably.

Three suspects, Manuel thought. An unnamed racer in pale gray leathers who had finished in the bottom half of both races, El Diablo Blanco, and the recently befriended "King" Arthur.

The voice of Major Tom at his right elbow shook Gato Loco out of his focused stare. "That was some race. I hear tell you caught some impressive air at the river. That must have been something to see."

"It was stupid showboating," Manuel said almost without thinking, reacting to his most recent self-deprecating memory of the incident. Then he thought a second more about it. "But yeah, it was something to see. It put me on the other side of the river, but it was something to see. I think it shook Cross up."

Major Tom shook his head sadly. "Damn tragedy. He was a fine racer. Better than his father, I think."

Manuel was thankful for the anonymity of his helmet's opaque visor, which masked his surprise. "You raced with his father, I take it?"

The elderly race organizer didn't make eye contact, his gaze off into the far distance of memory. "Several times, and quite some time ago, back when we were much younger men. He isn't going to take his son's death well. I expect I'll be seeing him up San Fran way for an earful."

Considering what he knew about Marco Cross, Gato Loco figured they would all get off lucky if the worst they had to deal with was an "earful." He considered his list of suspects again, the gray jacketed racer with a clump of other racers, while Blanco was in a heated argument with Anita of all people. Arthur had his helmet off and was sipping on a can of soda that one of the other racers had offered him, relaxing against his bike. "How well do you know the other racers, Major?"

Major Tom squinted at Gato Loco, considering him carefully. "My understanding was that you were just here to race."

"That is why I'm here. But things change." Gato Loco turned

66

the full effect of his grim visage on the smaller, older racer. The grizzled old Major didn't blink. "I have reason to believe one of your racers is a killer. If you know anything that can stop them from taking their next victim, you need to say something, or you're partially responsible."

The Major pursed his lips stubbornly. Manuel didn't know him well enough to tell for certain which side of the law-and-order fence he would come down on, but he had to play the odds. "I've known a lot of these racers for years. Not well, but I've seen them ride in events, and drank with them. I can't just share everything I know. There's too much water under those particular bridges."

"Then how about three racers. Tell me what you can about three racers of my choice, just a little bit, and it will be something."

Eager to strike the compromise, Major Tom jumped at the chance. "Done. Pick your men."

Gato Loco pointed toward the cluster of riders near the highway support. "The one in the gray jacket."

"His name is Kemp. I think it's his last name. No first name, just an initial. S. He's a good kid, heart of a competitor, but a little out of his depth in this race. He finishes higher each race, and he races smart, knowing just how hard to push without taking too many chances. But to be good here, you almost have to be willing to die for a win. And quite frankly, that isn't him. He has some other kind of job that pays the bills and keeps his bike in shape, and he only races a few weeks out of the year. Who else ya got?"

"How about Rand Arthur?"

Major Tom chuckled. "Oh, so you want to know about the King? He's personable enough. He's a decent racer and he has the money for a bike that matches his abilities. But he's a freedom rider. He loves to race and loves to ride, but he isn't neurotic about winning. I know a few people who used to ride with him, who gave him the nickname. They say he has this natural leadership thing. Lots of charisma. He had a group of friends who followed him around everywhere. But then he took off on a cross-country trip two years ago, and when he came back he was riding solo. Been riding solo ever since. If he's a killer, then I'm the Queen of England."

"Fair enough. Then tell me about El Blanco Diablo."

Major Tom sighed, as if expecting he question. "He's a southern boy, from Texas to judge by the accent, but he spends a lot of time in Mexico. I've even heard tell that he rides farther south, all the way into South America, but I can't prove it. I don't know his real name. He only answers to Diablo. He has money, but I don't know where it comes from. The bike is a custom job, but I've never seen him do anything more complicated than change the oil, so I doubt he built it himself."

Manuel looked at the Blanco's bike again. Yeah, the ornamental stuff was definitely custom, but it wasn't signature enough that he could identify who might have done the work. "Any idea where he might have gotten a bike like that?"

"If you believe him, it was a gift from the Devil himself so that he could do His work on Earth. And I don't believe him. At least not most days. He's a mean customer, and more than able to look after himself in a fight. I wouldn't be surprised if he's killed someone. I heard about a scrap he got into in Humboldt last year where he left a few people with holes in them because they touched his bike. He doesn't race to win. He races hard, but he just doesn't have the fire. And I doubt he races for fun since I've never seen him smile once."

"Go back. You said he left holes in some people for touching his bike. What did he use to do that?"

Major Tom kept his eyes on El Diablo Blanco, as if afraid that the other racer could hear him across the distance and commotion. "Way I hear it, he has one hell of a pig sticker on him. I've never seen it, and if you're lucky, you never will either."

But Manuel was almost certain that he had seen it. Now he had to make sure it was the right pig sticker. "Thanks. I'll try to keep from disrupting the race."

"Much appreciated." The Major handed Manuel a wad of bills, rubber-banded together in a tight roll. "Your winnings from tonight. Again. Good race, and I'll see you in the San Francisco Bay area."

Gato Loco tucked the bankroll into a concealed pocket at his hip, nestled down amid cords of synthetic muscle. It was an awkward fit, but it would have to do for now. He started his bike again and rode smoothly over to Anita and Blanco, the sounds of their argument starting to rise above the celebratory noise of the other racers.

El Diablo Blanco towered over Anita, his every muscle signaling imminent aggression, but she was keeping her cool surprisingly well, a lazy smile spread across her pretty, tanned face. "If you try to crowd me out again like that, I swear to hell that it will be the last thing you ever do!"

"Sorry devil-boy, but if you can't handle the pressure of being in the pack, then you should just stay out of it." Anita's voice was glaringly un-threatened, and Gato Loco could tell it wouldn't go over well even before the words were all out her mouth. He chose that moment to roll right up on top of them, close enough for Diablo to fog up his face plate if he chose to do so.

Gato Loco's electronically altered voice was clear and unaccented, but laced with hidden menace. "Is there a problem here?"

Diablo weighed the prospect of tussling with both Anita and Gato Loco, and seemed to be considering it. Anita didn't put forth the appearance of any real physical threat, and Gato Loco had dealt with smaller and quieter men who thought they stood a chance. "This filly here tried to nudge me into a crash out there."

Manuel let the silent stare of El Diablo Blanco bore into him for a few seconds, not moving an inch. Secretly, however, he wished that Diablo would go for his knife so he could get a look at it. "Where was this? Back in the river bed?"

"You saw it too, then! She cost me time and almost scuffed up my bike!"

He became aware of the eyes of the remaining riders on this little conflict. Out of his peripheral vision, Manuel noticed "King" Arthur had stood up, as if debating if he should intervene as well. *Might as well*, Manuel thought. Arthur had been in that pack too, and might have seen something if he hadn't been too focused on the race and his own safety. But no, Manuel saw Arthur watch, curious how things were going to turn out, but not ready to commit himself to any action. "I saw it," Gato Loco said. "Bike and rider combined, you have a good two-hundred pounds on her. And she would have tapped your fixed rear tire, where most of the weight was, with her front tire. Who was in more danger there, Diablo? It sure as hell wasn't you. Anyway, you had more than one option to deal with her nudging up on you, and you chose the one that cost you time. That's not her fault. That's yours."

El Blanco Diablo flexed his gloved hands, gaze flickering between Gato Loco's face plate, Anita, and the crowd of other riders who had gathered. Manuel saw the fingers on Diablo's right hand graze a bulky pocket on the outside thigh of his leather pants. The pocket, he realized, was easily big enough to conceal the knife he had seen in the vision, and he rethought the placement of the pocket. It was a sheath, he realized. Crafted into the leg of the pants was a sheath with a sturdy leather flap covering the grip that secured with a steel snap. He couldn't be certain if it was the same knife from the vision, but Diablo was looking like a better suspect each second that went by. "Watch your ass next race, *punta*," Diablo growled as he looked at Anita again. Then he shifted his gaze one more time to Gato Loco, looking him over with a sneer. "That goes for both of you."

Satisfied that his honor was more or less intact, Blanco backed off and mounted up on his bike, parked only a few feet away. "I could have handled him," Anita whispered, confident that Manuel could hear her. He didn't reply, but did afford her a sideways glance, noting that she was unshaken and serious. He wondered if she could have handled Diablo. He also wondered if Diablo had been right, and that she had intentionally tried to nudge him into a crash, as insane as that would have been. "Meet you back at the hotel?"

Gato Loco shook his head. El Diablo Blanco rode to the street and then started off to the north. "I may be late," Manuel said quietly. "I have work to do." Without another word, he rolled swiftly and silently out onto the street after his prey. The low-light filter in his visor activated as he shut off the headlight, his eyes all the while on the retreating tail light of Blanco's bike.

He hung back two blocks, carefully staying in his target's blind spot. With Shadow running silent, and without a headlight broadcasting his position, it wasn't long before El Diablo Blanco had settled into a casual ride. A softly flashing light in the top corner of Manuel's field of vision alerted him to an incoming call, Snowflake's number appearing in the caller ID line. He answered with a whispered voice command, and heard, in the background, a distant sound of sirens. "Did you manage to get anything for me?"

"You're lucky there was a good camera in the evidence kit in the trailer, or we might not have much of anything. Someone called in the accident and put enough pressure on the powers that be to get emergency crews down here."

Manuel wondered if it might have been Major Tom who got the crews down there, and then considered it might have even been

Victor's dad, Marco. The idea that the former assassin might have biometric sensors in the suit to alert him of any problems with his boy was not entirely outside the realm of possibilities. Marco Cross was a meticulous planner, and had always worked out every possible angle with the most up to date information. That kind of obsessive attention to detail could easily have overflowed into his private life. "Were there any troubles?"

The siren sounds were fading, and from the background rumble, he realized that Snowflake was driving away from the scene of the accident, leaving the emergency vehicles behind. "I got a close look at the tire and at the fork, and photos of the fork from two angles. I'll have to play with them a bit and see if I can enhance any details, but it looks like sabotage to me. The fork just snapped off, which it shouldn't do. And the cut was clean for most of the way through. Whoever did it was counting on the rough conditions to finish his work."

"Go ahead and make your way back to the hotel. I'm following a lead and will be back before morning."

The panda was silent on the other end for a few seconds, as if considering some other option besides the one offered him. "You think whoever did this is the one who is going after Xander?"

The thought hadn't had time to occur to Manuel yet. Until now, he didn't have the confirmation of his earlier gut instinct. And with that confirmation that Victor's death wasn't an accident, he wasn't sure if there was a connection or not. "We don't have any evidence to support that yet, but I'll take it into consideration. How long until you can get a closer look at the photos?"

"Baring unusual traffic, I should be back at the motel pretty quick. I'll grab a coffee somewhere and dive in. How long before we have to report for the next race?"

Manuel realized that he didn't know for certain, but that Anita would have the information memorized by now. "Don't worry about it. We'll find time for you to sleep when you need to."

Up ahead, Blanco pulled into a parking lot of an after-hours club called Prospero's. A bouncer in a charcoal gray suit and sunglasses stood at the door with his hands crossed in front of him. With dark, mirrored glass windows and steel fixtures, Prospero's looked more upscale than the kind of place Manuel pictured Blanco frequenting. As the biker approached the front, the door opened and a young-looking couple stumbled out toward the sidewalk. The man was wearing black leather pants and matching suit jacket over a fishnet top. Heavily made up with artfully crafted hair, he looked like a rock star of some kind. The woman had long, blonde hair and over-made up eyes, and was wearing a scandalous red satin dress. Manuel was certain he had seen her in the news recently, and instructed the mini-cam in his helmet to record so that he could research them later should he need to.

The bouncer stepped aside to let the couple pass as a black limo with tinted windows pulled up to the curb. He seemed to recognize Diablo, and rather than moving to block his access to the club, he nodded with a smile. *So*, Manuel thought. *This El Diablo Blanco is a regular here. How very interesting.*

The dark windows to the club made it impossible to see what was going on inside or who else might be there. He considered looking for another entrance, but realized that he couldn't afford to let Diablo know that he was being followed, particularly by Gato Loco. So instead, he did the next best thing.

Leaving Shadow parked quietly in the darkness of a nearby alley, Gato Loco crept across rooftops to the parking lot of Prospero's. He scanned the lot carefully and identified two separate stationary security cameras. It was only a matter of a few seconds to determine which one covered Blanco's bike, and only a few minutes more to approach the camera from behind and twist it hard to the side so that it pointed at a blank wall instead of the lot.

Moving quickly, Gato Loco dropped twenty feet from the roof of the neighboring building down into the lot, letting his stage-field generators absorb the kinetic energy of his landing. The battery that stored up excess kinetic energy showed him a little, glowing green dial in his readout labeled "B.P." for Boom Points. He sprinted across the lot to the bike, keeping low to the ground to avoid the one spot the other camera could pick up. Then, he carefully looked over the other bike without touching it. The digital recorder in his helmet recorded the entirety of the bike from all sides. Once back to the trailer, he could dump the images and let Snowflake pore over those.

El Diablo Blanco was far too protective of his bike for Manuel's comfort. First the stabbing in Humboldt, then the confrontation with Anita tonight, no, there was something going on. Maybe Snowflake would be able to figure it out. Before leaving, he hovered one hand above the bike, hoping for some tingle, some sign that a vision was coming.

Nothing.

He couldn't risk the bike being alarmed to be sure.

Gato Loco was up the wall and halfway back to his own bike before anyone came out to look at the re-oriented camera. By the time Blanco was back to the lot, Gato Loco was already on the freeway south to puzzle out the day's mysteries and, if he was lucky, get some much needed sleep.

CHAPTER NINE – A HELL OF A LEAD

It was a polite yet insistent tapping on the door woke Manuel from a fitful sleep in the darkened San Francisco hotel room. The tapping, he realized distantly, had the rhythm of a song that he was certain he had heard before, even if he was unable to recognize it in his current hazy state. Manuel disentangled himself from Anita's limbs, which had flopped over on top of him during the night and fumbled for his crutches. Behind him, he could hear Anita moan, half-awake despite what was likely to be an impressive hangover. The empty bottle of Patrón skittered away across the room when his foot found it accidentally in the dark. A glance through the peephole revealed Snowflake waiting patiently, or perhaps not so patiently, as the musical tapping continued on the frame of the door.

Manuel opened the door as far as the chain would allow and blinked against the perceived brightness of the hallway lighting. "What song is that?"

Snowflake looked disappointed by the question. Manuel caught a whiff of coffee, and he spotted the cardboard carry-tray with two, steaming, paper cups balanced on top of a brown pastry box. "California Über Alles," met with Manuel's blank stare, prompting a further, yet unnecessary explanation from the disgruntled panda. "It's the Dead Kennedys. Classic Americana. I'll play some for you when you ... sweet Jesus, when you put on some freaking pants!"

Despite his shock, Snowflake managed to steady the coffee with his second hand, and not a drop was spilled.

Manuel realized belatedly that he had neglected to cover up, and shifted his torso back around the edge of the door. "Sorry. I'm not awake yet."

"You should be sorry. For the love of God, man, no one needs to see that this early in the morning."

Despite the panda man's grumbling, Manuel found it hard not to smile. "Anita doesn't seem to mind."

Snowflake kept his gaze averted lest he see more of his partner than he should ever want to again. "Whatever. Put some clothes on and meet me in the trailer." Without waiting for an answer, he turned and headed down the tan and burgundy carpeted hallway toward the elevators.

Stumping over to the chair in the corner, Manuel dressed in jeans, cowboy boots, and a concrete colored Calexico t-shirt with a horny toad on it. Anita had stopped grumbling and was curled up around his now vacated pillow. He considered leaving a note, but she knew where to look for him should she wake up before he and Snowflake were done.

Double-checking his jeans pocket for one of the room key cards, he slid on the forearm crutches again, undid the chain, and made his way to the lobby. The truck and trailer were parked around back in a lot reserved for RVs, busses, and other vehicles too large to fit in the underground garage. The hazy gray cloud cover made it look earlier than his watch indicated. And there was a fine mist in the air, which chilled the skin enough that he wished briefly for an over-shirt or jacket.

Snowflake had his holographic disguise turned off, and was halfway through a glazed donut, hunched over the computer in all his panda glory, when Manuel entered. "The database search turned up a few possibilities."

Manuel hobbled through the cramped space quickly and sat on the folding stool Snowflake had set up for him. Once they had blown up the close-up shots of the fork that Snowflake had shot the other day, they had determined that whatever had caused the damage might have been distinctive. Once they hit San Francisco, they hooked up with a forensics database and started an automated comparison. With the size of the database and the uncertainty of getting any good matches, they had no choice but to leave it running overnight. "How many and how close of a match?"

"Four are within the 80% threshold." Snowflake's tone indicated that it wasn't all hugs and puppies. "Two are highly specialized and it's unlikely they were used. One is uncommon, but not too high end. I even have one in the truck's tool box in case I need to slice through something in a hurry. The fourth and final mystery date is a high tensile wire coated with diamond dust that is used like a garrote, sawing back and forth. That, my friend, is pretty much exclusive purview of very shady individuals, and without being able to test the edges of both pieces for residue, I'm afraid we can't rule any of those four out easily."

Manuel puzzled over the list of four tools on the screen. He could recognize none of them by name. Times like this, he was thrilled to have a mechanical tools specialist around. "Can you rank them from most portable and easily concealed to bulkiest?"

"No problem. The diamond wire is number one, followed by the McKindrick tool there, followed by the Herswie saw that I use, with the McKindrick 8000c dead last."

"And speed it would take to make that kind of precision cut? Fastest to slowest."

This one required a little more time out of Snowflake, and he bobbed his head from side to side thinking it over. "In field conditions like they probably had, the 8000c then the smaller McKindrick, followed by the Herswie saw, and probably the diamond wire last."

"Probably?"

"For a first timer, that's the speed. But someone who was used to using the diamond wire could pop that cut faster than the Herswie, maybe faster than the McKindrick, but not as fast as the 8000c. That baby is just like, bam! But it's noisy and requires an external power source. With that in mind, let's just take that one entirely off the list."

Manuel was hesitant to remove anything from the list entirely, but decided to trust his mechanic. "Not that I'm arguing with you, but why exactly? Just too much noise and logistics?"

Snowflake looked proud of himself, getting to explain something to his detective role-model. "The way I see it, to use the 8000c, you either had to already have access to it in Los Angeles on short notice or you would have to cart something the size of a 400 cc engine around on the back of a motorcycle. With this being a touring road show, the chances of someone having easy access to something this specialized is astronomical."

Rand Arthur knows this area pretty well, and he has money to burn, Manuel thought. But Manuel didn't see the motive. Yeah, taking out last year's winner might improve your chances, but Rand didn't seem to need the money, and he didn't seem to care enough winning for winning's sake. It was too early to rule him out, but it did seem highly unlikely. "Ok, point taken. Any word on the investigation from L.A.?"

"Nothing on the news. I was waiting for you to see if you could weasel your way into the LAPD computers." Snowflake rolled away from the computer to give Manuel easier access. "But the word on the street is that there is a wave of street racing moving up the California coast. The local police are working with the California Highway Patrol to clamp down on it. Is there any chance that the Major will pull the plug on the race?"

Manuel shrugged. "I don't know. This is my first time, but the whole thing is illegal. We knew that signing up. And I'm pretty sure this isn't the first time the police got bent out of shape about the Devil's Run. The two deaths in Los Angeles probably crawled up their ass a bit, though."

"There were two? I thought it was only Victor."

Anita had gotten the news from one of the other racers last night. It was part of what had driven her into finishing a bottle of expensive tequila largely by herself. "The one who flipped his bike in the river didn't wake up. Too much internal damage is what I heard. It wasn't as immediate or dramatic as Victor Cross, so it didn't make the news, but I expect there will be a small write up in the back pages of the *L.A. Times* today."

True to his prediction, a quick search online turned up an article with the lead in of, "Night of reckless cycling claims second life." Their reporter drew connections between the deaths and similar incidents in Tijuana just a few days earlier. An officer with the highway patrol rattled off the party line about how motorcycles could go faster than a sports car, but had no protective measures like airbags or crumpling frames. For anyone who knew the first thing about motorcycles, it was nothing new. However, it did seem to confirm the rumors that Snowflake had heard. Local law was going to be prepared this time.

But something else was nagging at the back of Manuel's mind. He sipped on his coffee while he turned the aspects of the case around, looking at it from all angles. "I think we might be looking at this sabotage all wrong."

Snowflake hunched forward on his stool, his tone confident and level. "I'm no detective, boss, but I stake my driver's license on that damage being done intentionally."

Manuel glanced at him out of the corner of his eye and smiled. "I'm not doubting you. Victor's bike was definitely sabotaged. But I don't see any reason to think that it's related to the impending attack on Xander."

"Why not?"

"Primary intent," Manuel fished a cruller out of the pastry box and then looked up to see Snowflake's blank stare compelling him to elaborate. "What's the primary intent of sabotaging Victor's bike?"

"To cause a crash." Snowflake's tone suggested that it was the obvious answer and, as such, could not possibly be the right one.

"More specifically, it was a way to remove him from the race while remaining hidden. Whoever did it could have damaged the bike in any number of ways that would have been spotted and potentially fixed before the race. But this was subtle—done in such a way that he would likely never notice in time. And if they just wanted to cause a crash, they could have forced one out on the streets, but if he lived, then they would have an enemy."

The panda man nodded, not finding any flaws with the reasoning. "And if they made an enemy of Victor, they might make an enemy of his dad, and his dad is a scary individual."

"Taking that further, whoever did this probably knew who his dad is. But what is the primary intent of killing Xander?"

This line of questioning had Snowflake stumped, and he opened his mouth several times to offer an answer, only to close it wordlessly.

"Exactly, we don't have a motive for someone involved in the race to kill Xander."

"But it might sidetrack you enough to give the killer an edge in the race."

Manuel shook his head dismissively. "For the final race in Vancouver, or maybe the Seattle race, if they make their move quickly enough. But that's at most one-third of the races. To think their intent to kill him will impact how I perform in the race presupposes that they know about my visions and could predict I would foresee the attack. Even I can't predict that, so it's doubtful anyone else could. Secondly, they would have to know a lot about both involved parties: Xander and me. They would have to know of my connection to him, and where to find where he lives in Seattle. With the exception of you and Anita, who even knows who he is or what city he's in?"

Snowflake bit his lip, but eventually had to state the obvious horrible suggestion. "Well, there is Anita."

Manuel couldn't ever admit to Anita that the thought had occurred to him as well, but his process of elimination had removed her from the equation already. "I thought about that, but the person in the vision was bigger and dressed differently. And I know she wants to win, but if I thought for a second she could kill a friend of mine in cold blood to gain the advantage in a race, then do you really think I would be spending time with her?"

Snowflake muttered, begrudgingly convinced. "The heart is a mysterious thing. There are some days when I would take Kim Jung Il with breasts and a willing temperament."

Manuel blinked, processing what he had heard. "I'm going to forget what you just said."

The panda looked up at him with wide eyes, somewhat surprised that it came out of his own mouth. "Yeah, I really wish you would. What with you exposing yourself to me and me not engaging my internal censor, I'm thinking maybe we're too comfortable with each other. From now on, I'm wearing a suit and calling you 'Sir'."

"I'm going to hold you to that," Manuel smiled and turned back to the computer, pulling up the images he had downloaded from his helmet's camera the other night. "Ok, so on to Diablo. He seems to frequent this club, Prospero's in L.A. I can't find any public records of it, with the exception of a brief mention of an up-and-coming video director dying of a drug overdose out front of the club three years ago. I was there around three-thirty in the morning, and they still had a bouncer on the door, and people were going in and out, so it's definitely an after-hours place. They value their privacy. The two guests I saw leave had money. It turns out that the guy is Terrence Park, the guitarist for Rhino Hymen. The woman is Sylvia—"

Snowflake jumped in, having recognized her already. "Sylvia St. Paul. Adult film starlet."

"Former adult film starlet," Manuel corrected him. "She's trying to enter mainstream media."

"A cameo on that Jim Belushi sitcom doesn't constitute mainstream media. She'll be back on the black leather couch of love in a year, mark my words." Snowflake snorted.

"Regardless, they have money in the bank and a certain degree of visibility. I find it odd that they travel in the same circles as El Diablo Blanco."

Snowflake scooted forward, his gaze having caught something in the photo on the screen. He squinted, trying to make it out. "Is she wearing a necklace? Zoom in."

Manuel selected an area of the photo with a cursor and magnified the image several times until a clear view of the necklace presented itself. Both Manuel and Snowflake stared at it for several long seconds. It was a crucifix, perhaps two inches long, and ornate in a Roman Catholic style. And it was hanging upside down. Manuel did a screen capture and then zoomed out again, and started selecting frames to see the hands and neck of both Terrence Park and the bouncer as well. Several minutes later, they had screen captures of silver horned devil rings on both men, as well as a tiny inverted cross necklace around the musician's neck.

"You know, I think we found the missing link between our friends, here," Manuel murmured. "And probably why there isn't any info about that place. I think Prospero's might be a members-only Satanic club."

Snowflake pushed himself back. "I don't think we should be too surprised by a guy calling himself El Diablo Blanco, but Sylvia is a bit of a shocker. Do you think killing Xander might be a ritual thing?"

Manuel shrugged. He didn't know much about Satanism, except that in a world where people could fly and shoot lasers out of their eyes, the possibility that someone could really entreat with devils was not so far-fetched. Dr. Shadow, one of the former members of the Protectorate had once described the supernatural world to Manuel over sweet potato fries at an all-night diner. The millennia-old Egyptian sorcerer had explained the world as tightly coiled tube filled with marbles. Each marble was its own reality, and there were higher and lower realities. Some people could step from marble to marble, and others could pass down the core of the spiral and go to any marble. Some of those might resemble heaven. Some, however, were very much like hell.

Was El Diablo Blanco's Satanism a religious observance or was there more too it? In short, how much danger was Xander—and by extension himself—really in here? There was no way to know. And until he could prove the other biker was responsible for some kind of criminal activity, there wasn't a damn thing he could do about it.

"What time is it?" Manuel asked the panda hollowly.

Snowflake looked at his watch. "Still early. Not even nine yet. What time is the preview of the course?"

"This afternoon at two, up on Telegraph Hill. Have you heard anything about the weather forecast for tonight?"

"Overcast most of the day, with high chance of fog, last I heard," Snowflake grumbled. "It makes me happy, but I don't have to ride in it. Decent chance of rain in the afternoon, but things could always change. I have a set of tires that will funnel the water away no matter what speed you're doing. I'll pop them on after the tour, but I got bupkis to help with the fog."

Manuel stood, feeling more tired now than when he had been awoken. "Fate will provide. I'm going to go avail myself of the hotel's hot tub before lunch. Then we can grab some sandwiches before the tour."

The panda mechanic had already turned his attention to Shadow. "Grab me before you go. With the sabotage of Victor's bike, I suddenly feel compelled to go over Shadow with a fine-toothed comb. I don't want anyone messing with my baby."

"Oh, that's sweet, but I'll be fine." Manuel smiled as he stumped toward the door.

"I'm not worried about you. I'm talking about the bike."

The misting outside had become even more aggressive in the short time Manuel had been inside the trailer. He wasn't looking forward to racing in it, but he couldn't control the conditions. And at least it was better than riding in the New England winter ice storms of Cobalt City.

When he got to the room, he was immediately aware of the unmistakable smell of bile. The bed was empty with the sheets bunched up on the floor. The sound of the shower let him know where Anita was, and he stuck his head into the increasingly steamy bathroom. "I'm heading down to the hot tub in a minute. Do you feel like joining me?"

Anita's voice was hushed, and it was hard for Manuel to hear her over the sound of the running water. "As long as we take it slow."

"Are you feeling okay?"

It took a second for her to process the question, but at least her voice was a little stronger when she finally answered. "I sat up too fast and felt sick. I figured I would be better off if I just threw up. I'm much better now."

Manuel nodded and then realized that she probably couldn't even see his head through the fogged up shower door. "Ok. Take your time and I'll wait for you." He closed the door and went to sit in the green easy chair in the corner.

As he settled in to wait, he felt his cell phone ringing with the distinctive theme from Magnificent Seven. He fished it out of his pocket and looked at the caller ID for a long moment until the ringing stopped. A few seconds later the phone beeped to let him know a voice mail had been left. Manuel sat staring at it for several seconds, and then opened the phone, acknowledging the voice mail without listening to it. He was about to put the phone away when an impulse struck him and he opened it again and dialed.

Xander answered on the third ring. "Hey! Long time no talk! How is the race going?"

"Number three is tonight. I'm only second overall, but I'm sleeping with the racer in first place."

The young inventor laughed on the other end of the phone. "Well, that's almost as good. I just hope he's gentle, because you're a fragile little flower."

Manuel joined in the laugh. "His name is Steve, and I can't wait for you to meet him. So, have you made it back home yet, or are you still being a globe-trotting smart ass?"

"I'm at the airport to fly back now. Kara Sparx and I got delayed on an out of town job, and she's going to fly back with me to catch a few meetings with tour promoters. She's saying 'Hi' to you around a mouth stuffed with Cinnabon now. Such a lady! How long before you guys make it up to Seattle?"

Manuel calculated by the pace the Devil's Run had been marching up the coast so far, visualizing by counting out an estimate on his fingers. "Best guess? Four days. Maybe as few as three, but don't count on it."

"Great. I'll tell Tam and she'll bake a cake or something."

The shower shut off in the other room and Manuel realized he had to tie this up quickly lest Anita hear more than he was comfortable divulging. She might not be high on his suspect list, but there was still no reason to involve her in the investigation. "So, reason for the call—have you been dealing with any occult threats lately?"

Manuel could hear the surprise in his young friend's voice. "Occult?"

"Satanic, specifically."

It didn't take long for Xander Tesla to ground himself in the conversation. It took a lot more than a sudden change of topic to knock the kid off balance. "Not really my bag. I've been focusing on commandments six and eight lately."

Raised a Catholic, Manuel remembered his commandments quickly. "False witness and adultery? What kind of cases are you working on these days?"

"What? Six and eight are murder and theft."

Manuel was positive that he remembered his bible better than that, but resolved himself to look it up later in the copy conveniently left in the bedside table by a Gideon. "So, no Satanism?"

"After the juju that Stardust had to deal with during the whole Darla Spider thing, you really think I want to mess with occult forces? Trust me. Theft and murder—good old six and eight—that's all I've been doing. That and Kara is teaching me to ballroom dance."

Anita came wandering slowly out of the bathroom wrapped in a towel to dry off. "Keep your nose clean, kid, and I'll be there in a few days. Call me if anything changes." Manuel said. Once Xander acknowledged the goodbye, Manuel folded the phone closed and tucked it back into his pocket. He looked up at Anita with his most comforting smile. "You feel better after the shower?"

He watched her struggle with the decision of which would hurt more—a nod or speaking, and speaking won out eventually. "Some. Thanks for waiting, but I think I'm going to try and sleep a little more instead. Do you hate me?"

Manuel stood and hobbled over to give her a kiss on the cheek before digging around for his swim trunks. "No. I was going to go solo and let you sleep anyway, but I figured I might as well ask since you were up. Sleep, and I'll make sure you're up for lunch and the tour of the course."

The mention of food made Anita turn slightly green, but she managed to control her gag reflex. "I'm not hungry."

Manuel sat on the edge of the bed and began changing into his swimwear. "Well, no, not now you aren't. We'll see how you feel in a few hours, okay?"

She lay back on the bed, still wrapped in the towel. She nodded slightly with a cute frown as the motion caused her brain to slosh around in her skull. *Probably floating on a sea of expensive tequila right about now*, Manuel thought. "You're good to me."

Changed into pool-wear, he leaned across the bed to kiss her again, thankful that she had gargled in the shower and brushed her teeth. "And no more tequila for you."

"Never again." She agreed, a weak smile showing that she would promise anything now, but did not anticipate honoring that promise at an inconvenient future time.

CHAPTER TEN – STREETS OF SAN FRANCISCO

The sun was trying to fight through the persistent gray haze of clouds, and while the soft rain had let up, the streets were still wet, and the sun was only a softly glowing suggestion overhead. Twenty-one bikes had assembled in the parking lot at the top of Telegraph Hill to the north of Coit Tower. Anita was still feeling a little blurry, and had elected to ride behind Gato Loco on Shadow. As Major Tom walked to the middle of the group, asking for their attention, she leaned out slightly to look around Gato Loco's shoulder.

"Due to some unfortunate attention, were going to do this next leg of the race a little differently than the first two," the Major looked and sounded tired, as though the extra scrutiny had worn him out. A murmur went up from the assembled racers at the mention of a change. Manuel wondered if some of them might not have even known that there was extra attention being paid to their illegal road rally.

"First off, this will not be a closed loop circuit. Your individual timer starts as you cross the start line at the edge of the parking lot here. It stops when you cross the finishing line where northbound Transverse Drive crosses John F. Kennedy Drive. At that point, keep riding. Find your way across the Golden Gate Bridge and to the address I'm going to give you all in a second. I'll distribute the prize purse there, post the cumulative score board, and buy the first two rounds of drinks."

At the mention of drinks, Anita squeezed Gato Loco's upper arm with her left hand. He hoped that she wasn't feeling sick again.

Especially riding behind him like she was and with a belly full of grilled ham and cheese and tomato soup in her.

"Secondly," the Major continued, "twenty-one riders is going to attract a lot of attention, so I'm breaking the racers up into three flights of seven, leaving in five minute intervals. We'll be less likely to attract unwelcome attention this way, but there is the possibility that the third flight might encounter a bit of police presence. For that reason, I'm asking for volunteers to bat cleanup."

Gato Loco raised his hand, as did "King" Arthur and two other racers whom hadn't placed particularly well in the first two legs of the race. Major Tom noted the four racers and marked them in a small notebook in his hand. "Anyone else? Ok. I'll select three more at random prior to race start. The final change is an earlier start time. First flight takes off at ten sharp tonight, the next at five after, and etcetera. That will mean for more traffic, but the course will be more straight forward than before, and with smaller groups, the traffic won't be as much of a problem. Now mount up and follow me in an orderly manner."

Those who were not already on bikes hoped on and fired up the ignitions. Manuel took the honor position immediately behind Major Tom as they began to file out of the parking lot and down the hill. At the bottom, they turned west onto Lombard. Several blocks ahead, Manuel could see what had been known as "the most crooked street in the world" where eight switchbacks negotiated the 27 degree climb for a block. He was almost disappointed when the turned off Lombard onto Grant after only one block, removing the challenging obstacle from sight. Another block later, they turned left on Chestnut, continuing their migration west through Nob Hill and Russian Hill.

A short uphill climb to Hyde Street and they turned left and then right onto Lombard, the tantalizing switchbacks now behind them. A quick glance back indicated that it was one-way, and not in a direction conducive to their starting point, otherwise he suspected Major Tom would have had them navigate the turns. Then again, perhaps it had been part of the original course and it had been revised to reduce the likelihood of another high-profile accident or death.

The course was relatively simple after that, as Lombard turned into the wider Highway 101 shortly thereafter. They stayed on 101 as it changed name to Richardson, passing the Palace of Fine Arts and its adjacent lagoon, and then turning into Doyle Avenue. The course continued along the northern edge of the Presidio, jutting into the water of San Francisco Bay, a former military base that was now a large park area. To the north, the Golden Gate loomed large in their vision. Shortly past a large cemetery, the route went south along Highway 1. A pretty much straight-forward run south, through the Douglas MacArthur Tunnel, down a wide and scenic boulevard, and then into Golden Gate Park followed. They crossed John F. Kennedy on an overpass headed south, and then doglegged back around to the right, heading back toward Kennedy from the south.

With the wide east-west drive in sight before them, Major Tom pulled off the road to the left down a dirt road toward a park maintenance area. He stopped his bike and got off. Several of the other riders followed his example, although Gato Loco didn't dismount, nor did Anita. Once everyone was gathered, the race organizer took off his helmet and fished business cards out of his pocket. "The finish line is JFK Drive. We would have crossed it if we had kept going another few hundred feet, but then I wouldn't have had a good place to stop and hand these out." He split the handful of cards and started circulating one stack left and one right. "This here is the meet-up place after the race. Present the card at the door and they'll let you in. You can either take the Golden Gate across the bay and loop around to the east, or double back and cross the Bay Bridge on Interstate 80. However you want to get to Oakland is your choice."

A murmur that made the previous sound of discontent pale in comparison rolled through the assembly. Manuel found it strange that people who would risk life and limb racing at breakneck speeds through crowded city streets would get nervous going into a rough neighborhood. When the cards got around to him, he took one for himself and one for Anita. He would explore a few routes to the site, but suspected that it would involve heading back along Lombard so that he could chance the switchbacks. Manuel suspected that he was not alone in that desire.

As the racers peeled away from the pack, Gato Loco noticed Major Tom motioning for him to wait. As the last of the cyclists left to make their way back to make race preparations, the Major nervously cleared his throat. "I realize you are under no obligations to do anyone any favors—"

The fact that Major Tom was nervous made Manuel nervous as well. "What can I do for you?"

"Marco Cross has asked to meet with you."

In a way, Manuel was glad that the suspense was over. He knew it was only a matter of time until Victor's father put in an appearance, and he was glad that the former assassin treated the matter with a degree of civility. "When and where?"

Major Tom cleared his throat again, "Now. Due south. And you should probably go alone. I can take Coyote back to your hotel, if you like."

Anita hopped off the back of the bike, her complexion a little pale, either from the ride or the concern for Manuel's safety, he couldn't be sure which. "I'll wait here, if it's all the same to you."

Scanning the terrain to the south, Gato Loco had no doubt that if Marco Cross had intended to shoot him, he could have done it a dozen times by now without anyone knowing where the shots came from. "I'll leave Shadow here with you and walk it. He's not far, is he?"

Major Tom shrugged, apparently relieved that the suggestion had been received with diplomacy. "I don't know, but he said he would be close enough to be persuasive if you were reluctant."

Charming, Manuel thought. "I'll see you tonight at the tower," he said to the Major. *You probably don't want to be here right now anyway*, he added mentally. *Then again, do any of us?*

He struck off toward the trees beyond the dirt lot of the park maintenance area, aware that he probably had cross-hairs on his heart the entire time. Gato Loco didn't give Marco the satisfaction of looking down to check. Shortly after passing a high mound of fill dirt on the south edge of the lot, he heard the familiar Croatian-accented voice of Marco Cross. "That is far enough."

Gato Loco turned to see his one-time nemesis leaning comfortably against the fill dirt, dressed in his full red leather body suit. Marco was not wearing his helmet, nor the Lycra black stocking mask he used in his professional career, and both hands were surprisingly empty. "No gun? Should I be insulted?"

The dark haired contract killer smiled, the puckered scar tissue on the left side of his face creating a ghastly rictus. "On the contrary. Why waste a bullet on you and your force-fields when I can put a rifle in a secondary location and keep it aimed at your friend with a smart-trigger. I doubt she will be so well protected as you."

The distance between them was reasonable enough that Gato Loco knew he could close and strike if he should need to. However, if Marco was telling the truth about having another gun trained on Anita, it would be linked to a precision robotic armature trained to fire on a voice command. *Just like the job in Cobalt City the last time we met*, he thought. "Ok. You have my attention. I understand you wanted to talk to me?"

Marco's cold smile slipped beneath the surface of his face like a child beneath the ice atop a frozen river. His icy blue eyes were cold and deadly. A predator's eyes. A shark's eyes. "My son was murdered. I trust that you might believe this yourself, yes?"

Manuel fought the urge to nod or to make any move whatsoever, lest it be interpreted as hostile. "I checked it out, and I have every reason to believe it was sabotage."

"You are looking for the monster who killed my son, then?"

Oh, delicate ground, Manuel thought. While he was interested in whoever sabotaged Victor's bike, it wasn't the primary focus of his energies. With Xander's life on the line, it just couldn't be. But he wasn't sure that Marco would see it the same way. "It is an ongoing investigation. It looked like it might overlap with another matter I was already working on, but that seems unlikely now."

Marco's eyes narrowed, burning through Gato Loco's faceplate, and Manuel felt beyond all reason that the killer could somehow see through the opaque shatterproof plastic and see his real face and the concern etched across his brow. "Perhaps I made mistake. I did not mean that to be a question. You will find the person who did this, or I will start looking into the matter myself. You do not want me to do that. I think we can both agree on this point."

"Your son said that you were retired."

At the mention of his son, Marco's expression softened and for the briefest of moments Manuel saw real, raw emotion on the hired gunman's face. But it was gone as quickly as it had appeared, and he was dealing with the shark again. "Yes. For now I am retired. You do not do this for me, and I will come out of retirement. I give you this chance, Gato, because of all the men who tried to stop me over the years, you were the only one I ever respected. We are very alike, you and I. Men in a world of gods, and yet we strive to grasp the fire from Prometheus. You will do this, not because of any love you had for my son, nor of sense of duty to the law. You will do this because it is who you are. And when you find this person, you will give him to me."

Inside his helmet, Manuel felt his jaw clench. "And let you kill him? Why would I do that?"

The icy cold smile slid to the surface again. "Because if you don't—"

A loud BANG, from a gun positioned somewhere in the trees behind him, made Gato Loco spin instinctively, looking for the fired weapon. Too late, he realized that it had been a ruse, the smart-linked rifle Marco had set up to keep him in line. Spinning back around, he was not surprised to see Marco, the famed Black Cross, long gone. Gato Loco raced around the mound of fill dirt to check on Anita.

Crouched behind Shadow, Anita Cruz looked terrified but unharmed. Gato Loco closed the distance as quickly as he could on foot, bounding across the packed dirt in fifteen-foot leaps. Anita looked up at him, her eyes as wide as saucers. "Are you okay?"

She nodded, the words stumbling on the way out of her mouth. Anita reflexively and frantically began probing the right side of her head, inspecting for a wound of some kind. "He ... the bullet ... there was a shot and I felt my hair move. He tried to kill me!" To everyone's relief, she had not been touched.

"It was a warning. If he had wanted to kill you, neither of us would have known he was there until it was too late. You should have gone with the Major." Gato Loco swung his leg over Shadow and started the bike up. Anita climbed on behind him, her arms tight around his stomach more for reassurance than any need for support.

There was a nervous tremor in her voice that was completely understandable considering how close she had just come to death. "What did he want?"

"Vengeance."

Neither of them had much to say after that, and rode all the way back to the hotel in silence. With the moved up timetable, Manuel decided to give Snowflake a call en route to give the mechanic a heads up. They found the panda man waiting for them when they rolled into the lot. Anita squeezed Manuel's arm for a good-bye and then slid off the bike to go see to her own pre-race prep. She called out, "I'll see you at the race tonight," before Manuel and Snowflake disappeared into the trailer.

Once Shadow was locked into the charging dock, Snowflake clicked the hydraulic lift, raising the bike just high enough to swap out the tires easily. The panda motioned in the direction Anita had wander off in with an emphatic waggle of his wrench. "What's gotten into her? Too good to eat dinner with us?"

Manuel sat and began changing into his street clothes while Snowflake got busy. "Marco Cross showed up wanting to talk. He fired a warning shot at her to make his point."

Snowflake didn't bother looking up from his work. "Well, it was nice knowing her." He didn't sound sincere, but Manuel had concerns other than the camaraderie between his current traveling companions. Once he was back in jeans with a heavy chamois over-shirt, he hunkered down at the computer to work while Snowflake got Shadow competition ready.

With the list of four possible sabotage tools at hand, Manuel dug up images and item specifications for each so he would know what to look for. Knowing that two of them were highly specialized, he played a hunch that distribution lists would be easy to find, and while he could narrow down which stores in the greater Los Angeles area carried the two tools, it presupposed that someone had bought one shortly before using it, and that was highly unlikely. The more he looked at it, the more his suspicions turned to the diamond wire or the Herswie saw—one being almost impossible to track point of origin, and the other so ubiquitous that any well stocked tool chest might reasonably have one.

Narrowing the possible list of suspects by motive was no easier. Victor Cross had won the year before and was likely to do so again. Anyone who wanted to move up in the ranks could be responsible, whether they intended Cross to die or not. And with Victor's notorious father being who he was, another layer of potential motive sprang up. How better to strike at a shadowy killer than through his highly visible and accessible son? Without knowing the other racers better, there was little chance of him eliminating suspects from the list.

He knew he had been stand-offish. Gato Loco wasn't like the other racers, and it wasn't a matter of ego that made him think that. At the end of the race, the other racers could take off the helmet and sit down for a beer and a chat. Manuel didn't have that luxury.

While the connection between the mysterious black-clad vigilante rider and the tall, crippled Mexican detective was a cloudy one to the casual viewer, that separation did not bear close scrutiny. And if anyone should take issue with Gato Loco, they only had to wait until the leathers were off, when Manuel de la Vega was vulnerable. Not helpless, he reminded himself, but certainly at a much greater risk.

The perils of a secret life, he knew. But he could still retain a level of mystique. A cross-country road rally was a much different circumstance than living in a city where he had to maintain an established dual presence. True, the other racers might see the face behind the mask. But who knew the name of Manuel de la Vega? He might as well be anonymous out here on the road. And the show of trust might open some doors for him, letting him better determine who might be capable of the life-ending act of sabotage that had claimed Victor Cross. It was a risk, but if it stopped the Black Cross from unleashing the hounds of war on the race, it was a risk well worth taking. And it wasn't like they hadn't seen his face at the sign-up party and first race tour.

"Snowflake, since Anita won't be joining us, let's have an earlier dinner. I want to get to the start point early and chat up some of the other racers."

Not too many hours later, Gato Loco pulled into the lot at the top of Telegraph Hill alongside a handful of other bikes as a light rain fell. He recognized "King" Arthur's bike almost immediately, as well as Major Tom's vintage ride. Snowflake was finishing packing the truck, and would be set up in Oakland near the bar by the time the race started. The clock in his helmet gave him the better part of an hour before the race started, and he parked Shadow and went off in look for other racers to make the most of his time.

He found Major Tom and Rand in the park under the cover of some trees. Standing around at the edge of the lot, they were sipping on cans of Jones Green Apple sodas from a twelve-pack at their feet and sharing stories with three other riders. The stories trailed off as Gato Loco approached. *Moment of truth*, he thought. He popped the strap on his helmet and pulled it off. He motioned toward the cans of soda with a nod of his head. "Any more where those came from?"

Two riders bumped heads trying to dive into the cardboard carton to retrieve a soda. Major Tom noticed and laughed, not bothering to comment on their school-girl nervousness. "These gentlemen are going to be joining us in the third group," Rand said with his ever present lazy smile. "Meet Terry, James, and Kemp."

The rider identified as Kemp took the freshly retrieved soda from Terry's hand and tossed it to Gato Loco. Manuel belatedly recognized him as the gray-jacketed racer who he had asked the Major about the other night. His head had been shaved, leaving only a back-knot, monk style, and Manuel estimated his age in the early thirties. "Greetings, boyo. Hope you don't mind warm soda."

Rand pointed playfully at Major Tom with his free hand. "We were just complaining about the simplicity of today's race to our esteemed race chairman. No choke points, no terrain challenges—"

"I don't know," Gato Loco interjected, seeing the look on the Major's face. He knew the race organizer had a reason for plotting the course he did, and suspected it had pained him to do it that way. Manuel figured "King" Arthur knew it as well, but was comfortable enough with the old man to tease him on it. "The hills in traffic will be a different element, especially if the rain gets worse. Just riding over here, I got a feel for what the traffic will be like, and it will be its own kind of challenge."

Rand's head bobbled on his shoulders, conceding the point for the most part but unwilling to let go entirely. "It just seems like a shame to ride so far on Lombard but not use the switchbacks between Hyde and Leavenworth."

"The King here is from the area and is looking for some kind of home field advantage," Kemp explained to Manuel.

But Rand's words had struck a chord with Manuel's competitive nature, and he couldn't let it go unanswered. "It is a shame we aren't racing the switchbacks. Maybe we should make a side bet?"

Eager to avoid any complicity in a potential accident on what was arguably San Francisco's most famous street, Major Tom threw up his hands. "Whoa there, boys. That street is one-way going the wrong way, and if you deviate from the course—"

Rand's eyes sparkled at the idea of a separate challenge, and without looking at the race organizer, he lifted a finger in a "tsk-tsk" gesture. "The rules state we have to re-enter the course from the same place we left it. If, for instance, we turn left on Lombard rather than right, we just have to circle the block to get back on course."

The other racers looked at each other nervously, and at Major Tom for any cues. The organizer's jaw was clenched, but it was clear that he had painted himself in the corner with the rules. They had been clearly stated at the beginning, and to make an exception would be seen as singling someone out, thus calling the impartiality of the big money race into question. "You'll lose a lot of time with a stunt like that—enough to move either of you out of clear over-all time contention."

It was clear from the look in "King" Arthur's eyes that he didn't care about over-all time. But he wasn't in strong contention for that title anyway, whereas Gato Loco was. "I have another solution," Manuel offered. "You can stop and start the timer whenever you want, right? How about a side bet? From the finish line to the address in Oakland, best time wins, any course you want to plot, as long as it goes down Lombard from Hyde to Leavenworth."

Rand "King" Arthur smiled so big it looked like the top of his head would flip open like a PEZ dispenser. "How confident are you feeling?"

Manuel considered the prize purse he had won in Los Angeles, all two-and-a-half thousand of it, and felt confident about winning tonight's race as well, although he couldn't say the same for the side bet. "Is a thousand too rich for your blood?"

"It will be a pleasure taking your money."

Major Tom shook his head gravely, but Manuel could see a hint of a smile on the old man's face. "I can't be a part of this. Officiating a side bet contributes to your criminal negligence. I'm trying to run an honest, illegal road race here."

"We're both in the same group, which is conveniently running ten minutes behind the lead pack," Rand said confidently. "We should be in sight of each other at the end of the official race. And some of the other racers will likely already be at the bar when we get there."

"And if we need a tie breaker, there are other ways to confirm times with the RFID tags we're using," Manuel added. Rand and the Major both raised their eyebrows.

"Man of mystery, indeed!" Rand said with a laugh. "See you at the starting line."

Manuel took a long drag on his warm green apple soda under

the only vaguely disapproving stare of Major Tom. He couldn't help but notice the older man had not mentioned the visit paid to him by Marco Cross. Manuel suspected that conversation might never happen. Kemp and the other racers began making odds on the Gato Loco and "King" Arthur side race, and before race time, just about everyone had a little money placed on one or the other.

Two minutes before ten, the heavens opened up and it began to rain. Manuel barely noticed, still buzzing about the side challenge. It was good to be alive.

CHAPTER ELEVEN – A PARTIAL LIST OF OTHER THINGS LEFT IN SAN FRANCISCO

The first two waves of racers got off the line without a hitch, and "King" Arthur and Gato Loco rolled up to the line with the other five racers. Kemp gave Gato Loco the thumbs up and a hearty, "Cheers, boyo," before dropping his faceplate in place.

Major Tom, eyes on his watch, stepped out to the front of the line and raised his red kerchief above his head. Everyone held their breaths in anticipation as the engines revved. The five minute mark hit and with a flourish, the elderly race organizer snapped the starting flag down. Seven bikes lunged off the line and down Telegraph Hill Road. Gato Loco's faceplate was treated with a chemical that caused the mounting rain to bead and pool off his faceplate quickly, but he still had a decreased visibility. And it wasn't just his visibility that was going to be an issue in this race— it was the visibility of all the other drivers he would be dealing with throughout San Francisco. Every cyclist knew the deadliest thing on the road was other drivers.

At ten after ten on a weeknight, the traffic was light when they turned onto Grant and then again onto Chestnut, but it wasn't non-existent. There was plenty of room at this point to weave around the scattered cars, even zipping between two parallel cars when space permitted, or dodging across the center line on the rare occasion when oncoming traffic thinned.

With the race broken into three groups, setting his pace by the six he happened to be racing with was a fool's gambit. The King might be a solid racer on Californian streets, but he was no Coyote, and she was going to push for her best time. The only chance he had of beating her was by taking chances. He pushed the tempo, taking an early lead, determined to run the fastest time he could. Rand and the others endeavored to keep up as best as they were able.

At the six-way intersection of Chestnut and Taylor Streets and the wide diagonal of Columbus Avenue, there had been a multiple vehicle accident that blocked most of the intersection. It looked recent, as sirens were still approaching but no emergency vehicles had arrived yet. As Gato Loco slowed to an even 30 mph to hop the sidewalk around the smoking vehicles, he was relieved to see no motorcycles among the wreckage. But there were several drivers and passengers standing next to three wrecked cars and a hotel shuttle bus that pointed at the speeding bikes with accusing glares. It left little doubt in his mind that a previous wave of racers had caused the commotion. There would probably be more of the same along the route.

As long as Gato Loco didn't have to dodge police vehicles, he would end the night happily. With the restrictions about leaving the course, he was limited in how he could shake a pursuit. And as any cop knew, the longer a high-speed pursuit went on, the greater the chances were for innocent bystanders to get injured.

Gato Loco cut the left hand corner onto Hyde Street tighter than was sane, and had to immediately deke hard right to avoid running headlong into a beaten sedan with one broken headlight. He heard a screech of tires from the sedan, and a loud crunching sound of impact and wondered which of the racers had followed his lead but not reacted as quickly to the hazard as he had.

"King" Arthur took the same corner just a bit wider and faster, and since he had not been forced to make an emergency correction, he was able to pull a full length ahead of Gato Loco. Hopping the curb to the right around the next corner extended his lead another two lengths, and Gato Loco suddenly found himself in a race. He was thankful that they were on Lombard now. From this point, there were no real turns until they switched highways, exchanging the 101 for Highway 1 on the north edge of the Presidio Park.

By the time the 101 curved north, turning from Lombard to Richardson Avenue, Gato Loco and the King were exchanging first place about every block. Gato Loco had driven at high speeds through traffic all the time in his duties as a vigilante in Cobalt City, but it had been a long time since he had ridden in the same circumstances with someone who could match him block for block. To be fair, Manuel admitted, Rand had warned him that San Francisco was practically his back yard. If Gato Loco was going to fall to him anywhere, it stood to reason that this would be the place.

But Gato Loco wasn't willing to give in—not for anybody. If the King wanted this crown, he was going to have to take it. He knew there had to be some way to squeeze out enough of a lead on Rand that the win would be sealed, but he was hard pressed to come up with it.

Richardson turned to Doyle Avenue, and still the constant back and forth ensured that no racer had the lead for more than a few seconds at a time. Gato Loco spared a look down at the speedometer, and saw the needle tacking up into 80 as his bike wove through the traffic at death-defying speed. The exit to Highway 1 ahead of them, the Golden Gate Bridge dominating the view to his right, Gato Loco felt the lead begin to slip away from him.

He took the exit ramp fast and low to the ground, his knee skimming above the asphalt and concrete and managed to close to two lengths. The road signs to his right mentioned the approaching Douglas MacArthur Tunnel, and Manuel felt a moment of inspiration sneak in. It was a gamble, but this race was all about chances anyway.

As the curved, rainbow arch of the tunnel mouth loomed ahead ready to swallow the lanes of light traffic, Gato Loco popped Shadow to the right. The emergency walkway was a tight fit, but not an impossible one. A cruiser would never have made it, but with a café racer style bike—a street bike like Shadow—all it took was *huevos* the size of cantaloupes and a steady hand. Whispering a silent prayer to Saint Augustine, the patron saint of madness, Gato Loco gave the throttle all the juice he could spare. The speedometer shot up and Shadow rocketed down the emergency walkway like the bullet from a gun.

"King" Arthur rode the center line as much as he could and tried to follow, but there was too much oncoming traffic hogging the center of the tunnel, and he had to cut back into the main lanes or get sheared in half by a truck or SUV. Gato Loco widened the gap by over a hundred feet by the time the tunnel was behind them both, and there was nothing Rand could do to completely close the gap.

Shortly, Gato Loco crossed the finish line, and confident that they were not being pursued by police, he nosed over to the side and came to a complete stop. "King" Arthur pulled over after him several long seconds later. Rand's helmet was off before his bike was at a complete stop. "Are you kidding me with the walkway?" Manuel couldn't tell if the other racer was angry or thrilled.

"I had to do something to get a little distance on you. You're too good on these streets."

Rand started laughing. "Oh, man, I am so not worthy of that, but thanks."

"You still on for the side bet?"

The King in his yellow jacket put his helmet back on. "If you think I'm going to change my mind now, you're even crazier than your name suggests."

On the road next to them, they saw a gray-jacketed rider who could only be Kemp shoot past with two other riders tight on his tail. The last rider in the trio peeled off from the pack and circled back around to Rand and Manuel. The colors on his jacket belonged to James, he was pretty sure. The other rider flipped up the visor on his helmet, revealing a thin Chinese face behind round glasses. His eyes were wide with surprise. "Did you see what happened to Kemp?" The other riders shook their heads, not feeling the need to mention that the other three riders had been behind them the entire time. James took the hint and continued. "He bounced off the front end of a sedan up on Hyde. The knee guard on that side was shattered and it looks like his leg is broken, but he just kept going."

The collision, Gato Loco thought. He had heard the collision. Kemp must have been right behind him when he took the corner on Hoyt too tightly. "It looks like his leg is broken?"

James nodded. "It looks bad. He might be in shock. I think Terry is following to try and stop him and get him to a hospital."

Rand nodded. "If bouncing off the front of a sedan and breaking your leg doesn't stop someone, then I don't think Terry will be able to do it either."

Manuel had to agree. Most likely, Kemp was running on pure adrenaline, and when that ran out, he would realize how badly his leg was damaged. If Terry was still with him at that point, they could get him to a hospital. He wished them both luck. And as an afterthought, he whispered another prayer to St. Augustine, just to be safe. James took off in pursuit of the other racers, and after a quick nod of acknowledgement, Gato Loco and the King gunned off the line in their second race of the night.

They lost sight of each other within half a dozen blocks, the California native knowing his own tricks and secret routes. When Gato Loco reached the hairpins of Lombard Avenue without having seen his opponent, he became a bit concerned with the uncertainty of his position. He gave the voice command to speed dial Snowflake. "Are you monitoring the race?"

"Your time looked good. I don't have all the racer's RFID tags marked, so I don't have everyone's time, but I know for sure that you beat Anita."

"Can you find where King Arthur is now?"

There was silence on the other end of the line while Snowflake thought it through. "Oh, you mean the other racer? The one in the yellow jacket? I don't have his tag flagged, so I don't know which one he is."

It hadn't occurred to Manuel that Snowflake hadn't labeled the other tags, but realized it made sense. As far as the panda was concerned, the dots on his screen were just markers. The only ones he needed to know the identity of were himself and maybe Anita. "He finished second in my group tonight. Does that help?"

"Sorry, buddy. I was watching live results, not recording. What's the problem?"

A solution to his El Diablo Blanco problem suddenly occurred to him, sidelining the importance of finding how he was faring against Rand in the race. "Nothing, just a side bet. Do you have something hand-held that can scan an RFID tag? If we can read Blanco's tag and flag it, we can track him a little easier from here on out."

Snowflake sounded more than a little indignant on the other end of the line. "Ok, first off, side bet? That's an irresponsible thing to be doing with your money. Second, um, no. But I can cobble something together pretty quick. I'm not sure this isn't an unethical invasion of privacy, but if El Diablo Blanco is going to stick a shiv into one of my friends, it becomes a much more gray area. I'll try to have it ready by the time you hit Oakland."

Manuel knew better than to underestimate the shifty King again, and pushed Shadow as hard as he could, crossing the bridge into Oakland in what he felt was an impressive time. His earlier efforts of trip planning had not gone unrewarded, and he went straight to the bar—a little dive with brick exterior called the Cat and the Fiddle, without any hesitation over directions.

Several bikes were already parked out front, making it clear that this was a biker friendly bar, but most of the rides were of the wide-body touring variety. And tucked neatly in amid the Harley Davidson's and vintage Indians, he saw "King" Arthur's distinctive ride. "Well I'll be dipped."

"How much did you lose?" Snowflake said from across the street. He was holding something that looked like a cell phone, and on closer inspection, was in fact a cell phone. He handed it across to Manuel. "Get within about five or so feet to reduce risk of getting someone else's info, point it at where he has the tag—back of his hand or whatever—then hit the dial button. It will capture his tag signature and I'll download it later. Now, again, how much did you lose?"

"A grand."

Snowflake whistled low in appreciation. "A little confident in our abilities, are we? I just hope this doesn't impact my compensation."

Manuel tucked the phone-like device into his hip pocket. "I don't pay you."

"Yeah, I've been meaning to talk to you about that. Maybe later, when you're not out fighting crime or something." Snowflake smiled and headed back toward the trailer parked down the street. "I'll have my eyes and ears on. Let me know if you need anything else."

Beneath the grim visage of the Gato Loco helmet, Manuel smiled. Despite the rough edges, he could do a lot worse as far as friends were concerned.

Gato Loco fished out the business card for the Cat and Fiddle, and presented it at the door when he entered. There were two bouncers stationed just inside the door—monoliths of meat and muscle. Gato Loco considered that they might even be meta-humans merely based on their size. Not everyone who developed super powers of some kind got them to the same degree. There were plenty of people who changed just enough to set them apart, but not enough to put on the cape and cowl and join the spandex set. The bouncers seemed to recognize him, and they looked down at the card he had offered twice, weighing whether they should allow entrance or not. Begrudgingly, their dedication to the job won out and they parted to let Gato Loco through.

The interior of the bar was not as squalid as Manuel had expected. The space behind the bar was decently lit, as was the back section where three pool tables occupied an area separated from the main bar room by a half-height wall. Several of the other racers were there already, and they had set themselves apart distinctly from the "regulars," a pack of bikers wearing identifiable gang markers. It was interesting, Manuel thought, that the racers would be so competitive with each other, but in an "us" vs. "them" situation, they seemed ready to bond protectively with each other.

Major Tom was seated at the bar as close to the door as possible, chatting with the lanky, mustached man pouring beer. The bartender saw Gato Loco enter first, and even though the jukebox was playing the Rick James song "Superfreak" too loud for Manuel to make out the words, he was relatively sure that the mouth beneath the mustache formed the words "Holy shit!" Whatever he had said, it got the Major's attention, and his old, dark face swiveled around on his shoulders to see Gato Loco standing just inside the bar. He pushed away from the bar and approached the helmeted vigilante, and reached out to shake his hand.

Gato Loco took the offered hand, and felt the roll of bills palmed within. He curled his hand around it, careful not to broadcast the exchange to the bike gang, a hardened bunch with "Gabriel's Devils" painted or embroidered across the back of several of their jackets. "One and a half thou," the Major said, just loud enough for Manuel to hear.

With the time he had finished in, Manuel was surprised for the thinned bankroll of a second place finish. "Who finished first?"

Major Tom raised one eyebrow, a wry smile on the corner of his mouth. "Well, you did, of course. But I settled your bet out of the winnings. You finished first, but with that side bet, the King ended up taking home the first place purse."

"And third?"

"That would be Coyote, Miss Anita Cruz. She had an excellent time. More than enough to keep her in second place overall."

Second place overall, Manuel thought. Most racers here would be thrilled with that placement in a race of this caliber, but he suspected that it wasn't sitting well with her. "How far behind me is she in overall time?"

"Eight seconds and change. Don't get too comfortable with being in first place." The old man's smile was growing. "She was breathing fire when she saw your time. I wouldn't want to be you right now."

Gato Loco nodded. He didn't see Anita anywhere in the bar, but he dimly remembered seeing her bike out front. Before he could ask, he saw her come out of the restroom with a look of disgust on her face that probably had little to do with her placement in the race. She noticed his entrance and stared daggers into him from across the room. Manuel swallowed involuntarily. Yeah, there was going to be trouble in paradise for the next day or so, until she had a chance to even the scales in the next race. He should have learned his lesson by now when it came to dating competitive women, he realized. "Did Rand tell you about Kemp?"

The Major shook his head, the smile fading. "What happened?"

"He got clipped. James said it looked like his leg had been broken."

"After the race?" Major Tom fished his GPS device out of his jacket and tapped through several screens. "He finished the race, and with a decent time actually. His first time in the top half this run."

Gato Loco shook his head. There was sudden competition for his attention as, simultaneously, El Diablo Blanco entered the bar and a table of the Devils began harassing Anita and a pair of Asian racers who were seated close by. "No, he got clipped turning onto Hyde Street. He finished the race with an injured leg."

Major Tom only seemed to be half listening as the building commotion behind him demanded his attention as well. "That crazy bastard. I'll make sure he gets his leg fixed when he comes in. He's halfway across the Bay Bridge now, and it looks like James and Terry are right with him, so he's with good company." His voice trailed off.

Manuel knew what he was thinking. At least Kemp was with good company. The same couldn't be said for his fellow racers at the Cat and Fiddle. The two Asian racers were strong competitors on the streets, but they weren't nearly as aggressive off their bikes. However Anita was full of piss and vinegar, and El Diablo Blanco approached both sets of tables as if uncertain which side of the argument he was going to come down on.

"Maybe this was a bad choice of venue," the Major muttered.

Manuel hardly felt it was worth a sarcastic, "You think so?" so he kept it to himself. Instead, he closed on the tables, making sure he was in Diablo's peripherals enough to not startle him into action. "—this little sumbitch might ride a rice burner—in fact, most of us ride rice burners—but he happened to beat my pace in TJ by twelve seconds," Diablo growled, pointing to the racer with spiked hair and thin, rectangular sunglasses. He had stylized Chinese monkeys painted on the front panels of his black leather jacket, and a look of calm determination on his face, as though he was prepared to accept the ass beating that was surely coming his way. Manuel was strangely proud to see El Diablo Blanco standing up for his fellow racers. It was a shame he was the prime suspect when it came to stabbing Xander to death. "Lo Ping here has earned my respect the hard way, and he doesn't have to take shit from a bunch of faggot posers in devil drag."

If there was any doubt in anyone's mind that them there was fightin' words, the abrupt melee that exploded from the biker gang's table put those doubts to rest. Manuel did the quick math. There were eight racers there, and of those, most of them didn't appear to be fighters. The Gabriel's Devils Motorcycle Club outnumbered them a solid two-to-one, and there wasn't a man among them who didn't have murder in his eyes.

The Devil closest to Blanco lunged with a small knife that Manuel hadn't even seen, but the white-jacketed Satanist was ready. He caught the weapon hand tightly at the wrist with his left hand and pivoted, tapping his assailant hard in the side of the head with his right fist as he went past. The suffering bastard was unconscious before he even hit the floor. *Great*, Gato Loco thought. *He can fight.* That would come in handy now, of course, but when it came time to apprehend him, it would make for a more exciting experience.

Gato Loco saw leveling the playing field as the best immediate option and dove into the thick of the Devil's two tables. Punches, knives, and bottles lashed out at him, driving the B.P. meter in his in-helmet display up incrementally. The stage-field generator in his suit, designed to protect him in the case of a wreck, was more than capable of absorbing the blows of his attackers. He waited, timing until most of the blows were pulled back, ready for another assault, and then triggered a sub-audio command. Hundreds of tiny force-fields generated by his suit rippled out invisibly in a pulsing cascade for several feet in all directions. The minute waves of force washed over eight of the nearby Devils and did the hokey-pokey with their inner-ear. A targeted pulse on full charge had once taken down a pro defensive lineman high on PCP. A full 360 degree burst, while not having the same range or strength, was more than enough to plunge the eight bikers into an unexpectedly sudden unconsciousness.

Looking behind him at the racers in his group, he discovered to his delight that there were more scrappers among the Devil's Run competitors than he had anticipated. It was no surprise to see that Anita had hopped the half-wall to confront the Gabriel's Devils members, but the fact that Rand had joined her was a pleasant surprise. Anita had one of the members on the ground and was kneeling on his chest while she punched him repeatedly in the face. The King stood between her and the four other gang members, all of whom had pool cues in their hands. It was impossible for Gato Loco to hear what the yellow-jacketed rider was saying, but it was clear from the nervous expressions on the faces of his opponents, that they were unlikely to join the fray anytime soon.

The furious El Diablo Blanco was delightedly pummeling the remaining two gang members with his bare hands, yelling something about how scum like them gave the devil a bad name. Gato Loco noticed that both of Blanco's combatants had stopped fighting, and he grabbed the powerful fist as it pulled back for another punch. Blanco's head swiveled, his eyes blazing. "I think they get the idea," Gato Loco said with authority.

El Diablo looked back at the two bikers who at this point were holding onto the table to avoid falling over. He shook off Manuel's grip and then straightened his jacket. He glared into the billiard area at the cowed gang members holding position inside. He puffed out his chest. "Better grab your friends and get them the hell out of here before I remember that I'm a gentleman."

The four men looked to "King" Arthur for as if for confirmation, and then tossed their pool cues quickly onto the closest table. Rand had to put his hand on Anita's shoulder to coax her off of the biker she was still pounding on. Two of the bikers hoisted her punching bag up with an arm around each of their shoulders. His face was an unrecognizable ruin of blood and meat.

Anita turned to face Gato Loco, her eyes wide and feral, her nostrils flared. She hopped the divider and stepped up to him with authority. "You," she growled, "Now!" She turned on her heel and headed out the back door to the alley.

Manuel had hoped this discussion would wait until later, but with her blood still boiling from the unexpected fight, he couldn't really hold it against her if she wanted to rip him apart for knocking her out of lead position. Someone made the sound of a whip crack as he followed her out the door. Manuel was pretty sure it was El Diablo Blanco, but no one was stupid enough to laugh at it.

She was pacing in a tight loop amid the discarded boxes and dumpsters. Anita wheeled on Gato Loco as soon as he was outside and the door was shut behind him. He was glad that she had made this a private discussion rather than tear into him publicly. If the extent of their relationship became common knowledge, she ran the risk of more episodes like Marco Cross firing a warning shot at her to make a point with Gato Loco. "Take the helmet off," she commanded.

As soon as Manuel slipped the yowling cat head helmet off, she was on him, her lips pressed fiercely against his. She forced him back against the alley wall as she ground up against him. He was suddenly reminded of the first time he had beaten her in a race, long ago on the Baja Peninsula before he was using the Gato Loco identity to fight crime. She had damn near killed him, and her intensity then paled in comparison to what he was experiencing now. Her hands, sticky with blood from the face of the defeated biker gripped his head tightly, and he had to fight to pull back enough to speak. "So, you're not mad?"

"Jesus, Manuel, you're an idiot sometimes," she kissed him hard again. "I'm furious."

When they re-entered the Cat and Fiddle fifteen minutes later, the rabble had been cleared out, and most of the other racers had arrived. Major Tom was happily buying the first two rounds of drinks for everyone, relieved that despite two injury accidents, there had been no deaths or arrests. And despite the mangled leg, even Kemp had joined the party to celebrate the good news.

CHAPTER TWELVE – THE DEVIL, YOU SAY?

"So when can we take you to the hospital?" Manuel asked, trying not to look too long at Kemp's leg. Terry and James had supported him on their shoulders, and lay him down on one of the pool tables. At the bartender's insistence, they put a clean garbage bag under his leg to keep the green felt surface clean. Rand had cut the pants leg away from the injury and had cleaned the abrasions with a bar rag soaked in watered down vodka. If not for the disturbing angle with which the lower half of the leg was hanging, the injury would have looked no worse than a bad bruise and scrape.

Kemp's face was pale and sweaty, with a distracted smile broken by an occasional wince of blinding pain. "No hospital. I'll be fine. I just need to cowboy up and walk it off. And maybe a quad hazelnut mocha."

Manuel, Rand, Major Tom, and Anita shared the same concerned look.

"Hate to tell you this, Tex," Rand said calmly, "but you're not walking anywhere on this. The tibia and fibula are broken, and they weren't clean breaks, which you would expect from a crushing blow like you took. I can't just reset it, even if I was a doctor. The patella—your kneecap—it was torn loose and is free floating right now, so that will need surgery too. Honestly, I don't know why you're still conscious."

"Someone's bedside manner sucks," Anita mumbled, but only Manuel was close enough to hear her.

Kemp was adamant. "No hospital. End of discussion."

Manuel leaned in and put his hand on the injured racer's shoulder. "You had a good race, but you need to see a real doctor now."

Intense, fevered eyes locked on Manuel's. "I said no—"

The hammered iron voice of El Diablo Blanco interrupted Kemp. "I know a guy." All eyes turned to look at the broad-shouldered racer who had been quietly sipping a beer since the fight had ended half an hour ago. "He's off the books, and he isn't cheap, but he owes me a favor. He's in Berkley. I can have him here in twenty minutes."

Major Tom's eyes flickered down to Kemp, considering it. "Is he legit?"

El Diablo laugh sounded more like a deep bark. "The guy running the illegal race wants to know if my doctor is above-board? He ain't no Marcus Welby, but he brings certain things to the table that a valid medical license won't."

"Such as?" Anita piped up.

"Discretion." Blanco said. "And a willingness to make a house-call to Oakland after eleven on a week-night."

"I'm not sure—" Manuel began, but Major Tom's hand on his arm stopped him.

"Call him."

It wasn't his call to make, Manuel knew, but with his suspicions of El Diablo Blanco, he wasn't comfortable with the situation. The idea of sending the injured rider off in the care of a doctor attached to a suspected killer with a history of violence and occult affiliations tied Manuel's stomach in knots. *The phone*, he thought suddenly. He fished the jury-rigged phone out of his pocket, pointed it toward Diablo as subtly as could be managed, and pressed the Dial button. As far as Manuel could tell, the improvised device worked, recording the RFID tag signature, and only Anita and possibly Rand had been aware that he had done anything at all.

Major Tom stayed with Kemp while Gato Loco shared a quiet table off to the side with Anita and Rand. Dealing with the injured racer had quenched much of Anita's fire. She leaned her chair back against the wall, eyes closed, while Neko Case sang "Look For Me (I'll Be Around)" from the vintage Wurlitzer in the corner. Gato Loco and Rand, the cat and the King, watched Major Tom tend to Kemp. "He needs a nickname," Rand muttered around the lip of his glass.

"Who? Kemp?" Gato Loco knew who he was thinking of, and he considered the same thing earlier but had said nothing, because his first thought for a name was too grim. Calling the kid the "Gray Ghost" based on the color of his jacket and brush with death seemed to be tempting fate.

"Yeah. A ride like that, that's the kind of thing that earns you a moniker. I told you how I got mine." Rand didn't take his gaze off the kid on the table. Manuel told himself not to think that. He wasn't a kid. A kid wouldn't have made a ride like that. But Rand was right. "Where did yours come from?" the King continued. "Was it careful market research and a super-hero think tank?"

Manuel half smiled, shaking his head at the memory. "My uncle Chuy called me that when I was a kid. I was always trying these crazy stunts on my bike, and I kept landing on my feet against all reasonable odds. A kid I knew at school drew the cat thing I have on my jacket when he heard the nickname. He was a good friend at the time, but I can't even remember his name now. He got killed by a drug gang when we were thirteen. Just wrong place, wrong time, you know? I came across it in my notebook when I was looking for something to decorate my leathers. Ricky. Ricky Lorenzo. I knew I'd remember his name eventually."

"You never told me that before," Anita said, her eyes still closed, lost in the song.

"You," he said, pointing at her with the mouth of his bottle even though she didn't see it, "never bothered to ask. Where did the name Coyote come from?"

"I gave it to myself," she said, a vaguely embarrassed smile spreading across her face. "Coyote was like my totem—all tricky and a survivor. It's how I saw myself—this lone coyote, out on the asphalt, outwitting the world."

"Your totem, eh?" Rand nodded. "You know, sometimes the name we choose for ourselves is more defining than the ones we're given. I wasn't real keen on this whole King thing. Then I decided to own it. I may not be into the whole Arthur myth, but there are a lot of kings out there."

"Like Elvis," Anita said, saluting with her own drink, a diet cola to make up for her tequila excess the other night.

Rand laughed. "Yeah, like Elvis. So Kemp needs a nickname. Maybe he'll embrace it, maybe he won't. But the fact remains that he's earned it."

"We don't know anything about him," Anita pointed out.

"He's one tough hombre," Manuel said.

"We could call him Hombre," Anita suggested with a smile. "Or Hondo. Wasn't that a Charles Bronson character in a western?"

"We're not naming him after a Charles Bronson character," Manuel said.

"He's a librarian. Maybe we could do something classical?" Rand suggested.

Anita lifted her head from against the wall and fixed Rand with a skeptical eye. "How do you know he's a librarian?"

"People like me," he smiled. "They tell me things. Unlike your boyfriend here, who just scares the piss out of most people."

Manuel flashed back to less than an hour ago when the King stared down four hardened bikers without doing anything. *Yeah, and I'm the one who scares people*, he thought. But Rand did have a point about the name. "Ok, so characters who are damn hard to keep down. What do we have?"

"Achilles," Anita said without hesitation. Both Manuel and Rand looked at her with open surprise that she was the first one to come up with the name. "What," she responded indignantly, "now a girl can't watch a Brad Pitt movie a few dozen times without people giving her grief?"

Rand and Manuel looked at each other for the other's approval. Satisfied, they toasted the newest nicknamed rider in the Devil's Run history. "To Achilles!"

The other tables looked over in their direction, and Rand pointed at Kemp, resting fitfully on the pool table. He raised his glass and waved one hand, encouraging the other riders to join him in the toast. "To Achilles!" Most of the riders joined the toast, even though several didn't seem to understand why. The question of, "What's an Achilles?" floated in hushed whispers around more than one table. It didn't matter. To the racers who got it, the name would stick. And Kemp could take ownership of it or not. All things considered, it was a damn good name. Dipped in the River Styx as a child, the hero's one weakness was his ankle where his mother held onto him, the only part that hadn't been treated in the river of the dead, granting him invulnerability.

The conversations returned to normal around the other tables. Anita took a few big sips of her soda and then put her head against the wall again as Blue Oyster Cult came on the jukebox. "So what's your interest in Otis?" Rand asked Manuel quietly.

"Who's Otis?"

Rand's gaze flickered over to El Diablo Blanco, still sitting alone along the far wall with what was his third beer. "Otis Lee Merriwhite. From Texas."

"Sounds like a serial killer," Manuel whispered, regretting the words almost immediately.

"It's the three name thing," Rand said. "You know, that and the fact that he's probably killed and skinned more than his share of hitch-hikers."

Manuel fixed the King with a probing eye to determine if his new friend was joking or not. It was hard to tell, and he decided to take it as a joke and see where it went. "We get a share of hitch-hikers to kill and skin?"

"Four." Rand said without missing a beat. "I can't believe no one told you!" Then he winked at Manuel and took a long sip on his drink. "No, I think there are a lot of rumors about him, but I can't say for sure which are true and which aren't."

"I heard he stabbed a few people in Humboldt a year or two ago."

Rand scooted forward and put his elbows on the table. "Yeah, that much is true. Saw it for myself, but wasn't about to intervene. He said they were messing with his bike, which is probably also true. And to be honest, seeing him stick up for Lo Ping this evening was probably the biggest surprise I'll have all week. You know, other than having you race down the emergency walkway."

"I'm still not apologizing for that." Manuel smiled.

"Not asking you to. So is that why you're interested in Otis? Those people in Humboldt?"

"This isn't about your friend being in trouble, is it?" Anita asked.

What a wonderful time this would have been for her not to be paying attention to the conversation, Manuel thought. "Yeah, it's about my friend."

Rand heard the terseness in Manuel's voice even if Anita did not. "You have a friend in trouble?"

Well, cats and bags and whatnot, Manuel thought. "I have strong reason to believe someone is going to kill him when we hit Seattle."

"And you think it's Otis?" Rand said quietly, guardedly lowering his voice as if afraid that El Diablo Blanco might hear them.

"All I know is that whoever is going to do it is in the race, and he fits the profile."

Nervous confusion knotted Rand's dark features as he thought about it. "So it's a foregone conclusion that your friend will be killed? You just said that they're going to do it. Not try to, but actually do it. How do you know that?"

Manuel kicked himself for saying anything, but as much as he hated to admit it, all signs pointed to Otis right now, and the more eyes he had on his suspect, perhaps the better. "I know things."

"He's Gato Loco, bitch," Anita said with mock seriousness. "He knows things!"

Rand looked down into his glass for a long second, and then from Anita to Manuel to Otis and finally back to Manuel. "Is there anything I can do to help?"

Manuel looked long into Rand "King" Arthur's face. It was a sincere face, and while it betrayed a hint of fear, he felt he could trust it. "I'll let you know." He tapped Anita on the knee, and she opened one eye to glare at him. "And you, darling, should finish your soda. We have the gear packed and are heading up to Portland tonight."

Anita smiled at Rand, conspiratorially. "He calls me darling," she said. She redoubled her efforts to finish her soda.

"That's a nine or ten hour drive," Rand pointed out. "Why such the hurry to get to Portland? The grand tour won't be until after midnight tomorrow anyway."

Eager to get away from Marco Cross, for one, Manuel thought, but there was no point bringing that up. Not with Anita around, certainly. "I have business to take care of, and my support staff is ready to go, so there isn't any point in waiting."

"I won't ask," Rand said with a cryptic smile. "Not information for the likes of me. I understand. But if you have time for dinner before the race, I know a good Chinese place—August Moon on 23rd in uptown. I'll probably be settling into a booth for a late dinner around ten or so if you care to join me."

Anita drained off the last of her soda and set the glass on the table. She and Manuel both stood, tugging their jackets down snug. "That sounds good," Manuel said, almost surprised that he meant it. Something about this pretend king put him at ease, and he was finding it nice to know people who weren't a part of the whole vigilante aspect of his life. "I don't know how my schedule will work out, but I'll try to make it."

"And I'll be there no matter what," Anita said, eliciting a warm nod from Rand. She fought the impulse to wave goodbye to the room as she followed Gato Loco out into the fresh rain. "That was nice." She grabbed a hold of Gato Loco's arm and gave it a squeeze before collecting her bike and rolling it toward the truck and trailer. "It seems like we never go out and do anything anymore."

"I'll schedule a dinner party for next week," Manuel laughed. He felt strangely giddy. The stress of the day and the extremes of adrenaline flow must have just wiped him out. But there was still room to be cautious. There had been a lot of people with access to his drink in the bar, and even though he hadn't been drinking anything hard, it was always possible that his cheerful mood was not a natural occurrence. He helped Anita roll her bike up the ramp and into the bed of the truck first, and while she set about strapping it down, he rolled Shadow up into the trailer.

Snowflake was dozing in front of the computer, the screen now blank, and when the door opened, he blinked away surprise. "Just resting my eyes."

"Are you going to be okay for the drive?" Manuel was a bit concerned. A ten hour drive while tired was risky under any circumstances, but pulling a heavy trailer behind was just asking for trouble.

"I had two naps, counting this one. I'll be fine," Snowflake assured him, and true to his word, Manuel saw his friend starting to perk up quickly.

Manuel locked Shadow into place and then sat to strip down to street clothes. "This may sound like an odd question, but do we have anything to take a blood sample in the ol' crime kit?"

Snowflake looked at Manuel sideways as he ran a mental inventory across the inside of his eyes. When he responded, it was slow, and uncertain. "We should. But we don't have the stuff to analyze it here. We can take a sample and keep if fresh until we need it though."

"Do you know anyone in Portland who can run a toxicology screen?"

Concern replaced confusion in the panda's eyes. "Do you think you've been poisoned?"

Manuel shook his head. "No, but maybe drugged, and better safe than sorry. I'm just feeling, what's the word, bubbly."

Snowflake pulled out a sterile hypo and rolled up Manuel's sleeve. "I ask you, what is this world coming to when grim, black-clad vigilantes start feeling happy? It's madness, I tell you. Madness!"

"Just take the sample, smart ass." He winced slightly as the needle missed the vein, pulled out, and then struck true on the second try. "When can we get this analyzed?"

"If it's not poison, then it's not an emergency, so no need to call in any big favors. Is Seattle good enough for you? Xander can do a complete bio-chem work up on it."

Manuel nodded, rolling the sleeve of his over-shirt back down and buttoning it snuggly at the wrist against the impending cold. It would have to do. But the real chill that he felt came from the realization that Seattle, and a date with a potential murder, was not very far away at all. And he still had no idea if it was a fate he could prevent or not.

CHAPTER THIRTEEN – FRIENDS, LOVERS, AND KILLERS

AC/DC powered them through the long, hard hours before dawn. The combination of Snowflake blaring "Shoot to Thrill" off *Back in Black* for half an hour, the resulting argument over whether it was the best rock song ever recorded, and then another half hour of even louder playing of the song, kept tempers high and eyes open. And then the sun started cracking through the pines on the passenger side of the truck, glaring off the windshield just enough that it made Snowflake squint. Once his eyes were that close to completely closed, he found himself dangerously close to falling asleep at the wheel.

Just over the state line into Oregon, they took the next available exit to something like civilization and found a diner for some breakfast and high-octane coffee for the panda. There were only a handful of vehicles in the muddy parking lot of the Log Cabin Pancake House, but it was still early, and Manuel and Snowflake decided not to take it as an indictment against the place. At least the two cars and three trucks in the lot all appeared to be local, which was usually a good sign.

Packed with rustic, homey charm, the Log Cabin featured a long breakfast counter, and four and six seat tables all the way through the softly lit depths of the dining area. The waitress was pleasantly smiling woman in her thirties who wore a heavy yellow uniform dress with a nametag that said Moonflower. She brushed a stray lock of honey-colored hair behind her ear with the back of her pen while the tired trio looked at the menu.

Snowflake kept looking up from his menu as if entranced by Moonflower, though Manuel couldn't really see why. In the vast rotation of diner waitresses that he had been exposed to in their travels, he saw nothing in particular about her that made her stand out. But his friend was clearly distracted, and he hoped it wasn't anything more than sleep deprivation and a little home sickness. "What's good here," the panda asked, with what he no doubt thought was his smooth voice, "besides you, that is?"

Moonflower didn't miss a beat. Manuel figured that either she was an old pro, used to breezing past the clumsy advances of her customers, townies and travelers alike, or she just didn't see the effect she was having on his companion. "Oh, it's all good, but we're known for our pancakes."

"You have good ... pancakes?" Snowflake raised his eyebrow, half a smile spreading across his face.

She smiled proudly. "Sure do! That's why we're a pancake house and not an omelet house. My favorite are the Country Apple Griddlecakes."

Snowflake sighed, resigning himself to failure. "I'll have those. And keep the coffee coming."

The waitress turned to Anita, who appeared to be lost, staring at the large laminated page full of pancake-related meal options. A look of relief passed over her face as she reached the meat and eggs portion of the menu. "A number three, eggs over-easy, white toast, and an extra side of bacon."

"And a short stack of the buckwheat, side patty sausage, and a large grapefruit juice," Manuel said when she looked up from her pad.

"You got it, sugar," Moonflower said with a wink. "I'll be right back with more coffee."

When Manuel looked across the table, Snowflake was staring daggers at him. "Sugar? Why did you have to do that, huh? Why did you have to flirt with my waitress? You know I liked her. I was using the Tao of Barry White on her and everything."

"I wasn't flirting with her. I just ordered breakfast."

Snowflake turned to Anita for confirmation. "Was he flirting with her?"

Anita smiled mischievously, turning to look at Manuel over the top of her sunglasses. "A little bit, yeah. I'm going to have to keep him on a shorter leash."

Manuel shrugged. "I wasn't flirting with her, but maybe she saw the crutches and it brought out some caretaker thing. I don't know. But I didn't encourage her."

"You're like a poor, injured kitten. Who wouldn't want to take care of you?" Anita cooed.

Snowflake snorted indignantly, and looked like he was about ready to jump up and storm out when Moonflower came back with the coffee. She filled Anita and Snowflake's upturned cups, and left a small, cream dispenser. She didn't say anything, and Manuel was careful to avoid eye contact, but by the way Snowflake's hands were clenching at the edge of the table, he must have seen something. Once she left, Snowflake seethed in his chair. "Oh, that just tears it. I'm breaking my leg the first chance I get."

Manuel paid for the breakfast with winnings from the Los Angeles race while Snowflake got his Thermos filled with even more of the decently strong but otherwise unimpressive coffee for the road. They all hit the washrooms before heading back out on the road, refreshed and ready for the last five or so hours into Portland.

Being the only one who hadn't had more than a sip of coffee, Manuel sat on the far passenger side and dozed. He fell asleep to Anita and Snowflake playing "Name that obscure one hit wonder" on an eighties music station on the satellite radio, and woke up hearing the panda telling her about Xander and Tamika Tesla. He cracked open his eyes, and glanced out the window for some kind of road marker. No sign of Portland yet, and no highway markers of any significance gave him an indication of where they were. "You know, I'm not sure how much the Tesla twins are going to like you spilling their secrets to someone they've never met." He said after stifling a yawn.

"I'm not giving up any secrets," Snowflake snorted.

"Xander does some sub-contracting work for the government as part of a settlement they reached over a wrongful prosecution last year or the year before. He's a savant in bio-mechanical engineering and chemistry," Anita recited, each word taking another notch off of Snowflake's smile. "He built a costume with synthetic muscles and other enhancements, and used to go by the name Lily-pad Man, but changed it to Dart Frog, which is a much better name. His sister created an armored suit to mock him, essentially, and worked alongside you as Steel Pan, but only briefly.

She has a degree in acoustical and electrical engineering, but quit the science world to focus on her band. Did I leave anything out?"

Anita looked damn proud of herself, which more than balanced the sheepish look on Snowflake's face. "All things considered, it could have been worse," Manuel said. "It's not like Tam is still active in the cape and cowl set anymore, and Xander would be bragging about pretty much everything you just told me within ten minutes of meeting you."

"Because I'm a girl?" Anita smiled coyly. "I would wonder about a person who feels compelled to put 'Man' in their super-hero name. It's like they're compensating for something." She batted her eyes at Snowflake, but the panda refused to acknowledge it.

"First off, the name thing came about because he was, what, fifteen when he decided to risk his life to be a hero. But that's not why he'd spill the beans. It's because you're with him," the panda said, nodding toward Manuel. "He's always looked up to Gato Loco, and if he impresses you, then it's like impressing Gato Loco by proxy."

Manuel sat up straighter and looked down the length of the cab at his friend and sidekick. "That's insightful. I didn't really think about it that way."

"Well, you know me," Snowflake interrupted the thought with a loud burp. "I'm like a fucking philosopher."

Despite the promises made when the reservation was booked, their hotel wouldn't allow them to check in for an hour. Manuel talked the desk clerk into letting them park the truck and trailer there only to find his companions had been lured into a sleepy, near-hypnotic trance by the flyer rack near the front door. Once Anita was convinced that Manuel didn't know why Portland was called the City of Roses and Snowflake was encouraged to leave the brewery tour flyers promoting "Beertopia" and "Beervana", they crossed the street for a leisurely lunch of Vietnamese noodle soup at a place called Pho-Shizzle.

Through it all, Manuel felt disconnected, and he wondered if he had really woken up from the nap in the car. The sun had broken through the clouds, but it wasn't warming anything, and the hard won and languid camaraderie between Anita and Snowflake was dreamlike. He found himself drifting in and out of conversations. And for long minute he found himself staring deeply into his humongous bowl of soup, completely lost. As tired as they all were, he considered that all three of them having bowls of soup big enough to drown in was a recipe for disaster. Despite his concerns, no one fell asleep in their pho.

The room was ready for them when they returned to the hotel, and Manuel decided to bring his duffel bag up later, heading straight up to the room while Snowflake and Anita collected at least a little of their travel gear. He sat on the wide bed to take off his boots, barely managing to get both off before stretching out on the top of the bedcover and falling into a deep slumber.

At some point, Anita had come to the room and covered him up. He woke from a troubled sleep finding that four hours had passed since he had taken off his boots. Anita had fallen into bed beside Manuel and had curled up so tight behind his back that he was in danger of being forced off the edge of the bed. He heard the muffled strains of the Magnificent Seven theme from his jacket on the floor and realized it might have been the ringing of his cell phone that had woken him up.

The ringing had stopped by the time he sorted it out, and then beeped to let him know he had a fresh voice mail. Manuel closed his eyes again and go back to sleep, but his thoughts were too chaotic and jumbled, as if his brain rebuffed every attempt to go to let go of consciousness. Finally, he gave up and sat on the edge of the bed, careful not to wake Anita. He slid on his boots and collected his forearm crutches from where he had let them fall haphazardly to the floor.

Manuel fished out his cell phone, opening it to see who left a message. He recognized the Cobalt City phone number, and decided not to bother listening to the voice mail yet. He folded the phone closed and tossed it back onto his jacket, far too awake to think about sleeping, but exhausted enough to know he needed the rest.

He needn't have worried about waking Anita, as she barely registered his disappearance from the bed. Manuel double checked the presence of the key card in his over-shirt, and found that he had fallen asleep with it. He stumped across the hall and raised his fist to knock on Snowflake's door, but the sound of his friend's hearty snoring reached his ears almost immediately. Manuel paused, curled fist above the aged wood, and then turned and headed down the hallway for the lobby. There had been a hotel bar, he remembered—the Sandpiper or something nautical. He decided that a drink and little while to collect his thoughts on the two separate cases haunting him might make falling asleep easier.

As he navigated the two steps up into the drift-wood paneled bar, the last person he expected to see was Marco Cross. The grizzled assassin raised a drink in his direction as a friendly salute and motioned to one of the spacious captain's chairs at his table. "I'm expected," Manuel said under his breath, "How completely discomforting." The hired gun pulled out a chair and waited for Manuel to join him.

"I would like to begin," Marco said with a trace of mirth shining through his thick Croatian accent, "by telling you how easy you are to find."

"I didn't know I was supposed to be hiding," Manuel flagged down the cocktail waitress, "Ask your bartender if he knows how to make a Fire Ant Torture, please."

"He probably doesn't," the waitress said conspiratorially. "But tell me what's in it and he can whip one up."

"One shot tequila with five jigs of lime and five jigs of Tabasco. And set me up with two." She went to put in the order and Manuel looked over the corner of the table at Marco Cross. "You have until I finish my shots, and then I'm going back to my room. So you better make it quick."

Marco cut right past the small talk. Manuel figured it was a hired killer thing—no time to waste with pleasantries. *Then again*, Manuel thought, *he started the ticker.* "Have you found my son's killer yet?"

"I'm working on it."

"You're not working hard enough on it," Marco said, his jaw tight.

It was a mistake to come down here and chance into this conversation when he was tired, Manuel realized. "What's the matter? Is Victor getting any deader?" Marco's ice blue eyes flashed dangerously, and Manuel moved on, realizing that he couldn't see one of the killer's hands. "And what I mean by that is, of course, that whoever sabotaged his bike did it to win this race. They're in it for the long haul, and aren't going anywhere. I start coming out of the woodwork on very little information, making accusations, hinting that a professional killer is looking to settle a score because of what happened, they're going to rabbit, and you'll never catch them."

Marco accepted the answer and relaxed as much as possible in his chair. The waitress brought the drinks, setting one in front of Manuel and hovering with the second, not sure if they were both for the crippled detective or not. She avoided looking at Marco, visibly frightened by his facial scar and his predatory grace. Manuel tapped the table next to the first drink and handed her a twenty. "Gracias." The only thing that vanished faster than her was the money, and the two mystery men were left alone again to talk.

"The Devil's Run is half over," Marco stated. "You do not have unlimited time, and I have not seen you making any progress."

"We narrowed the tool used to damage the bike down to two likely suspects, and we're eliminating people who would have stood to benefit from Victor's crash." Manuel said. The fact that one of the tools was pretty damn ubiquitous didn't need to be brought up, he figured. He slammed back one of the shots, feeling the sting of tequila, lime juice, and Tabasco hit the back of his throat and then march angrily down into his stomach. He tapped the glass back on the table, empty, and pointed at Marco Cross. "And that's one. Now it's your time that's running out."

The icy blue eyes narrowed as Marco scrutinized the rail-thin detective. "When you were trying to stop me from earning a living, you were a different man. More focused. Driven. What happened to that man?"

"He got blown up." Manuel picked up the other glass, "Tick, tock."

"When the sun rises on the morning after the Vancouver race, you will have lost your chance to do right by my son," Marco said. "I raised him right. I kept him away from the violence, taught him respect, the importance of hard work. And yet this happens to him. There is no God, Mr. de la Vega. There is only a father's vengeance. And I will see it done on the person who did this to Victor."

"So you know my name now? Is this going to be a thing for us—a General Foods International Coffee moment or something?" Manuel tried to keep the tremor out of his voice, all the while his brain was screaming, *he knows my name now!*

"As I said, you were easy to find. You are not hiding, because things are different for you now," Marco's tone was calm, casual, with no hint of hidden menace. And that alone was strangely menacing to Manuel. "You do not have a home or friends who do not know your true identity. You are free, unencumbered by the illusion that you are any different than you are. You are a hunter. Like me, but not like me. And I respect that. It is an honest life."

"I'm not like you. I won't turn the person who sabotaged Victor's bike over to be killed."

Marco's jaw clenched slightly, but he didn't look particularly surprised. "I said nothing about killing him."

"You didn't not say anything about it either," Manuel said. "Am I supposed to believe that you'll slap him on the wrist and let him walk?"

"Then give him a choice," Marco conceded tenuously. "Let this monster turn himself in to the authorities. He does that, he will suffer in jail for what he did to Victor. Jail is worse than death anyway. He chooses jail, and I will not touch him."

They both acknowledged the unspoken truth between them. Marco knew people inside. The Croatian death merchant might not touch the person who gave himself up, but he could damn well make sure that there would be people waiting to make that person's life a hellish experience. Maybe death was preferable, as much as Manuel hated to admit it. The lanky detective looked hard into the frozen eyes until he felt them chill his soul. He slammed his second shot to warm up. His veins danced with liquid fire, and he knew falling back asleep would be easy when he hit the comfort of the bed, but that sleep was likely to be filled with nightmares. Marco Cross was a lot of things, most of them very, very bad. But in the final analysis, he had always been a man of his word. "Ok. Let's say I give them the choice, and they pass. What then?"

"Then they are mine." A wolf's smile appeared on the scarred face.

Manuel pushed his chair back from the table and got his weight atop the forearm crutches. He hated to ask the obvious question, but it had to be done. He licked tequila, lime and a hint of Tabasco from his lips. "How will I know where to find you?"

Marco smiled. "Stand in the sun, and then turn around to look at your shadow. You'll see me there."

"As always, it's been charming," Manuel made his way back to the elevator. Before long, he was back in the hallway between his room and Snowflake's room.

Manuel fished the key out of his pocket, and held it above the card slot for several seconds. Marco's words rattled around in his brain. *More focused. Driven. What happened to that man?* "I got blown up," he repeated to himself. And yes, that was true. But it wasn't too long ago that the old Manuel, the old Gato Loco began to heal and became strong. And then ... then something happened. Marco was right. He wasn't himself.

He was a good detective. He had used those skills for years. The visions, while never necessary and never on command, had always been there somewhere, tucked in the back of his consciousness. When had his last vision been? Kissing the trophy in Tijuana? That didn't seem right. It was like they had abandoned him, and it began to seem that their persistent absence was having some other kind of numbing impact. Even stranger than their absence in his life was the startling fact that he almost missed them.

After sliding the key back into his pocket, Manuel turned and crossed the hall, knocking softly on Snowflake's door until the panda answered, his holographic disguise turned off. Snowflake blinked away sleep in his eyes, wearing khaki's and a poorly buttoned Hawaiian shirt, his black and white fur spilling out from the cuffs and collar. "What's the problem, buddy?"

"I don't know." But he did know. He realized that he had known for a while. "I think I'm lost."

Snowflake smiled. "Your room is just across the hall. Jeez, you sound as tired as you look." He took a sniff of the air. "And you reek of tequila. Has that harpy been plying you with alcohol again?"

"No. I needed it to sleep. And I know where my room is, but I don't think I belong there right now. You mind if I crash in your easy chair?"

"Dude, they gave me a double by accident. You can have the other bed if you want it." He opened the door wide and ushered Manuel in. "But just so we're clear, this isn't a Brokeback moment, is it?"

"No. God, no." Manuel shuffled past to sit on the untouched second bed. He kicked his boots off with ease and dropped the crutches next to them at the foot of the bed.

"Jesus, no need to be mean about it." Snowflake said with a smile of mock dismay.

The pillow was welcoming, and the bed, for some reason, was softer than the one he had in his room. Manuel pulled the

127

bedcover up over himself. "Thanks, Snowflake. You're a good friend."

Snowflake closed and chained the door before coming in and climbing back into his bed. "Damn right I am. Get some sleep. We'll discuss direction when you're rested."

"And, Snowflake?"

"Yes, Johnboy?"

Manuel smiled into his pillow. "I don't know how to quit you."

Snowflake sighed and shut off the side light. "Get some sleep, wiseass. We have some 'splainin to do to the missus when she comes looking for you. And she will come looking for you, mark my words."

But Manuel didn't hear his friend's dire warning. He had already drifted back to sleep.

☐

CHAPTER FOURTEEN – GATO WRESTLES THE DEVIL

———

The smell of garlic and sausage woke Manuel from a deep sleep, and he realized that it was dark outside, the sun long since gone down. Light from the parking lot illuminated the ceiling, and Snowflake was nowhere to be seen. The sound of the door opening compelled him into motion, and he swiveled his legs off the side of the bed and fumbled for his crutches, not finding them anywhere. The sound of ice rattling in a plastic bucket preceded the panda's arrival as he entered the room with the hotel ice bucket under one arm and a pair of sodas in his hand. He smiled when he saw Manuel sitting up, and pointed to the foot of the bed with the soda-filled hand. "Good to see you awake. Boots and walkin' sticks are there at the front where you left them."

The fog was starting to lift in Manuel's head. In the back of his throat, he could taste a reminder of the Fire Ant Tortures he had drunk a few hours ago. He distantly wondered what time it was, but trusted Snowflake not to let him miss the tour of the course. But he felt like he was forgetting something and was entirely unable to put his finger on it. "Do I smell pizza?"

Snowflake set the cans of soda down and started filling plastic cups with ice. "Two kinds of sausage and onion on a garlic crust from some local place that the guy at the front desk swore by. I used your cash to cover it, which I hope is okay, and then wandered off to get race fuel down the hall. I would say that I hope I didn't wake you, but it was about time to get up anyway."

"What time—"

"Half past ten. Enough time for you to eat and get changed and get to the tour." Snowflake handed Manuel a cup of cola.

Dinner with Anita and Rand, he remembered. He had made some kind of vague promise to have dinner with them at this Chinese place, but he couldn't even recall the name of the restaurant now. "Has Anita been looking for me?"

Snowflake sat down at the table and opened up the pizza box, releasing a puff of fragrant steam. Manuel's stomach notified him eagerly that it had been some time since his last real meal. He reached out and, grabbing the back of the other chair for support, pulled himself to his feet briefly, swiveling into the chair. "She came poking around the trailer when I was detailing Shadow earlier this evening," Snowflake mumbled around a mouth of pizza.

"And what did you tell her, because if she came up here looking for me, she must not have knocked very loud."

"I said you hadn't been down around the trailer since we checked in as near as I could tell," Snowflake smiled. "Then she muttered something in Spanish that was probably impugning my character or heritage or something."

Manuel fished out a piece of the pizza for himself. He felt vaguely guilty about not leaving a note for her, but the feeling soon passed. She was an adult, and he was his own person. He didn't need to clear everything with her first. "You didn't need to lie to her."

"Nope, but I wanted to. I don't like her. I don't think I've tried to keep that secret from you. Anyway, I didn't lie. It was selective truth-telling."

Manuel shook his head. He took a bite of the pizza and found it every bit as tasty as it smelled. He chewed for a while, thinking it over. "Yeah, you know, I don't think she's going to see it that way."

"Pffff," the panda snorted dismissively. "Manny, in our brief association, I've been chased down a darkened elevator shaft by a man-eating tiger-woman and held captive by a corrupt sheriff's department with a predilection for torture. What, my friend, makes you think that I would be frightened of your crazy Latina girlfriend?"

Manuel smiled. "That she's a crazy Latina. That's enough for most people. And you didn't see what she did to that biker back in

Oakland. And crazy is such a loaded word. Let's just say potentially dangerous."

Snowflake mulled it over while he sipped his soda. He had many fine qualities, chief among those being a strong sense of his own mortality. "Yeah, you might have a point. So did you skip out on couples night or something?"

"Dinner with Rand."

Snowflake looked confused. "Rand ... Oh, wait, the King guy? I don't like him either. Let them have their filthy dinner! We're better off without them. You, me, this pizza that, I swear, that angels must eat in heaven."

Manuel smiled. "It is good. Ok. Let them enjoy their dinner. I didn't know you weren't a fan of King Arthur, though. When did this happen?"

The panda shrugged. "Never did like him, I think. There's just something off about him. A scent I pick up that doesn't sit right with me. I don't know."

"Well, he's the last of my concerns. I need to figure out what to do about El Diablo Blanco." Manuel pushed his seat back from the table to give his food a chance to settle before he went in for another piece of pizza.

"He's going to murder, or at least try to murder Xander." Snowflake pointed out.

"But he hasn't done it yet, so I can't arrest him for it. I don't have anything to pin on him that will stick."

"I could do a search on his name, see if anything turns up," the mechanic offered. "A name like El Diablo Blanco should get some entertaining results if nothing else."

"Merriwhite," Manuel recalled. "Rand said his name was Otis Lee Merriwhite. See if there are any outstanding warrants on that name. If he has a clean record, I'll have to consider something else."

Snowflake finished writing the name down on the back of a flyer advertising Beervana. "Three names, just like a serial killer."

"So it's been said." Manuel took a deep breath and then picked up another slice of pizza. "One, maybe two more slices and we need to get me suited up."

Two slices and the rest of his soda later, Manuel followed Snowflake down to the trailer and changed into his riding leathers. He stopped by his room first to check for Anita, but there was still no sign of her. A softly flashing light in the dark hotel room led him to his cell-phone lying on the un-made bed. Manuel knew that he had left his phone on his jacket, and theorized that Anita had left it there. After picking up the phone, he realized that the slow, red flash was a message alert. There were also two new missed calls, both from a Portland area code, but only one of them had left a voice mail. He figured the first might have been from the room. He pictured Anita waking up alone and sitting on the edge of the bed, calling to find out where he had gone, only to have his cell phone start ringing in the jacket not ten feet away from her.

Either that or someone else had called and woken her up. Manuel checked the time on the missed call again. He wasn't sure, but it looked to be about the time he had woken up and went down to the bar. On a hunch, he dialed the number shown on the phone. Two rings later someone answered, "Pelican Lounge."

"Are you located at the Riverside Hotel?" Manuel was pretty sure he knew the answer, but there was nothing wrong on covering all his bases.

"Yes, sir."

"Gracias," he said, pressing the call-end button. So, Marco Cross knew his cell phone number. He had clearly underestimated the Croatian hired gun. Worrying about how Marco found the number wouldn't do much good now, but it did make him wonder how many of his secrets had been uncovered.

The second call was from nine forty-five and was from a different local number. He tried calling it, but received a message saying that the number he had dialed did not accept incoming calls. He was aware that in some places payphones refused incoming calls to avoid having drug dealers use them as office space. Shut down, he dialed in for his voice mail message instead, skipping ahead to hear the most recent. He wasn't surprised to hear it was from the 9:45 call, and that it was Anita on the other end. In a terse voice, she gave the time of her call and the name and address of the Chinese restaurant where Rand had invited them to dinner.

Great, he thought, suppressing a tightening in his stomach over the impending argument. Just a few weeks in, and already they were on the path of missed dinner engagements. What was next, he wondered? Arguments over the way he dressed or the company he was keeping? He sat on the bed, trying to quell a sudden onset of frustration.

He held the phone in the darkness of the room, staring at the LCD screen until it went dark as he debated listening to the other voice mails.

Snowflake knocking on the open door snapped him back into focus. "Buddy, come on. Time to get your mojo working."

Manuel looked around the hotel room and took stock. She wasn't even here, and she was impacting his performance, his focus. He snapped the phone closed.

There were only so many hours in the day. If he tried to divide them up between finding the person who caused Victor's death, stopping the person who was going to cause Xander's death, winning the Devil's Run, and relationship issues, he was going to tear himself apart. He knew that now. And for the first time, he began to strongly question if Anita knew that as well, had, perhaps, known that all along. He pulled on his jacket, tucking the phone back into the breast pocket where it belonged. "I'm coming." Manuel hoisted himself up onto his forearm crutches. "And when you get the chance, could you gather up my stuff and move it into your room? I'd recommend you do it before Anita gets back."

Snowflake's smile threatened to split his head in half. "I thought you'd never ask. If you ask me, she was no Katherine Wilde."

Manuel flinched slightly at the thought, but kept moving. "If by that you mean she never handcuffed me to a shower curtain rod, tortured me, and tried to kill and eat you, then no," Manuel smiled ruefully. "But she had her charms."

Snowflake closed the door after Manuel. "You know, one of these days, you have to start dating normal women."

Manuel laughed, pushing the elevator call button. "I hate to break it to you, but I've met a lot of normal women, and they bore the hell out of me."

"Or you could go back to Cobalt City, maybe work things out with Wild Kat—"

"We're not having this discussion." Manuel's voice was suddenly weary. He wasn't sure, but he suspected that Snowflake took the hint.

"Fair enough. But from here on out, I got dibs on panda women."

"I thought you were the only one of your kind?"

The mechanic shrugged. The elevator arrived and they both stepped on. "I probably am. My project was shut down after they produced me. But if there are panda women, whatever freak-woman magnet you have going on is bound to bring them out of the woodwork eventually."

The thought that the rest of his life would be a succession of, well, not freaks, but at least challenging women should have concerned Manuel more than he found it to. He filed that away for later self-analysis. "You have a deal. I meet any panda women, and I'll send them your way."

They had to hurry to get Manuel suited up, and Snowflake helped by handing gloves and helmet over. And once Gato Loco and Shadow were out on the quiet near-midnight streets of Portland, the panda sidekick guided Manuel to the meeting point using the GPS in the trailer. He was pushing his luck speeding on his way to the preparatory tour, but it couldn't be helped. Thankfully, Gato Loco kept the speed just above the limit yet just below where the local police seemed to care about him, and he rolled into the start point just as the bikes were starting up.

Anita was pulled up to the line near Rand, and while King Arthur's face plate was down, rendering his expression unreadable, there was no hiding the venom in Anita's eyes. The discussion after the ride promised to be an exciting one.

Major Tom dismounted and walked over to Gato Loco, an expression of almost fatherly relief on his deeply lined face. "I just finished telling these yahoos that the official race begins at 3 am sharp tonight. Show up to the start line no earlier than five minutes before the race. It's a quiet neighborhood, and I don't want any extra attention. Got it?"

Gato Loco nodded.

The Major patted Gato Loco firmly on the shoulder and leaned in, keeping his voice just above the level of the nearby bikes. "Oh, and Achilles will be fine. Doc says he'll be able to rebuild the bone around the knee, and the boy will be up and riding again in no time."

It was the best news Manuel had heard all day. He smiled behind the opaque faceplate of his helmet. "Good. Is everyone here?"

"Two injured in San Francisco, and two more dropped out. We're down to a tight seventeen. It's about typical for the Devil's Run," the Major said. He mounted back up on his bike and kicked it to life.

Manuel called Snowflake immediately, not surprised to get his voice mail. He figured the panda was busily racing back up to the room to move Manuel's few belongings across the hall while he knew Anita was otherwise occupied. "It's me. The tour is starting up, and the race starts at 3, so we'll have to do a quick pre-race check-up once I roll in. Put on a pot of coffee and I'll see you soon. And if you get a chance, try to find me something I can nail El Diablo Blanco on. I don't want him to leave Portland."

Minutes later they were led to a cul-de-sac west of Portland State University on SW College Street. The Major turned them around, and then paused at the intersection. He turned around, and stood tall on his bike, pointing to the crosswalk line. It was clear. This was the starting line. After he had paused long enough for dramatic effect, he led them east on quiet, tree lined SW College until they hit SW 12th several blocks later.

Everything was subdued, the streets silent and all but abandoned about them. Gato Loco fell into an easy rhythm, feeling the asphalt beneath his wheels, letting it lull him into race mindset. He followed automatically, turning north on 12th and crossing over I-405, and then right on SW Market Street, also labeled as Highway 26. They followed this broad road toward the river, hanging a left on the even wider SW Naito Parkway to the nearby Hawthorne Bridge, which is where things became dicey.

The bridge was a lift deck bridge, meaning that instead of having the bridge split and raise up into ramps like most other draw bridges, large metal towers lifted the entire bridge deck straight up. If that were to happen in the middle of a race, it would quickly eliminate anyone caught behind it. Secondly, the bridge deck itself was a metal grid, which was slippery even for cars. On a bike, on a wet night, at a high speed, and changing lanes, it was a guaranteed widow maker. Anyone trying something fancy crossing that bridge, like, oh, trying to pass another vehicle at any speed faster than an aggressive crawl, was in for a life-altering event, like an unexpected dip in the Willamette River or worse.

On the far side of the bridge, they encountered what could be politely called a "poorly thought out" intersection with a busy north-south thoroughfare named Water, all the while merging with traffic coming up from down below as the bridge traffic entered East Portland. They kept heading east on Hawthorne, crossing busy intersections at MLK and Grand that had the potential to still be ferrying some decent cross traffic when the race ran later. Without warning, at 12th, the road turned into two-way traffic, forcing a sudden merge to the right at the risk of hopping the curb-like barrier and being trapped, running head-on into oncoming vehicles. At least the side streets were quiet—almost private in appearance, interspersed with typical suburban décor like convenience stores and bars, with real cross streets every four blocks, at 16th and 20th.

At 33rd, the character of the shops changed, cluttering up with cars parked on the street and more hippie type stores. Gato Loco counted the occult shops, organic bread bakeries, art stores, book stores, coffee shops, and bistros. He doubted there would be much traffic through here when the race ran, and suspected that most of the cars there now would be long gone, but he had no way of knowing.

A huge grocery store loomed on the left, foreshadowing a busy intersection. At the light there on 39th, they turned left, and Gato Loco found himself wondering if the rules of the race permitted him to cut through the parking lot of the supermarket. With the exception of the parked cars, it was a lot less chancy proposition than the intersection. He would have to check with Major Tom before the race.

Another supermarket loomed on the right six blocks up 39th, and then they went through a long stretch that Gato Loco figured would be nicer in the day when the sun was out, as a large park rolled by on the left side. Just past the park was a hill that appeared without warning, but not so quickly that it would be dangerous later in the night when they were racing. The neighborhood was heavily residential and quiet at this time of night. The street was tree lined, with nice upper-middle class homes on either side.

The road appeared to T-bar up ahead, and it was only as Gato Loco got close that he realized that there was a circular park in the middle of a large roundabout, which they circled to the right. Once past the circle, they continued north through streets that were, for all intents and purposes, even quieter and sleepier than the ones they had just left. They were climbing a hill through suburbia that would make Ward Cleaver weep it was so perfect. But then they crested the hill and it was like being slingshot out of the fifties and into the now.

Out of nowhere, the riders found themselves in the middle of a tangle of freeway onramps and overpasses. The neighborhood was instantly different, and the riders crossed the onramp street and over I-84, with 39th getting very cramped as they passed over the two different streets both marked as Halsey, one heading east-west, the other west-east. A bit farther and they hung a hard hairpin left at a busy intersection onto NE Sandy Boulevard, which Gato Loco noticed was also labeled as Highway 30.

They crossed I-84 again, this time going at a diagonal to the regular grid of most other streets. At least Sandy Boulevard was wide open, and the traffic was light, especially at this time of night, although the diagonal bias of the street meant that any cars turning onto the street would be coming in at strange angles. It was a lower class neighborhood they rode through now, filled with car dealerships, burger joints, mechanics and repair shops, and low, windowless buildings advertising "Amateur Night" or "Waitress Contest", which Manuel recognized instantly as strip joints.

He also realized that if anyone was going to make a move, this would likely be the place to do it. The traffic would be light enough for some aggressive riding, and it was a straight enough stretch to get up some high speed. And being at an angle, he suspected there would be a gradual right turn when the course finally did turn off Sandy Boulevard. That would make it possible to extend the break-away even farther, if traffic permitted.

That hope was dashed when, several miles farther on, the racers closed on what Gato Loco felt had to be the ugliest intersection in Portland. Sandy Boulevard cut into a busy intersection of north-south and east-west streets right in the junction, and even at this hour, there were more cars around than he would have liked. The bikes took the gradual right onto E Burnside, but it looked like it would be easy to be forced by busy traffic into going straight through the intersection, missing the turn altogether. He could see a big evangelical church across Burnside with a message board reading "Jesus is calling. Pick up the phone!" Across the intersection from there was a big warehouse style hardware store with female anthropomorphic hippos painted on the support columns, and next to that was what looked to be another strip club, this one called Union Jacks.

Once past the junction, the road was clear, despite the now tame intersections with the busy Grand and MLK. On the downside, the real estate value was going downhill fast. Everywhere

Gato Loco turned were convenience stores, vacant lots, bars, and people sleeping on the street. It was nothing compared to the squalor of the tent city he had recently experienced in the *maquiladora* of Buena Rosa, but by Portland standards, it was a blight.

He glad to leave it behind and hit the bridge crossing back across the Willamette River, even though there was construction taking place on the bridge, necessitating some quick lane changes. But the bridge deck was like regular road, and the asphalt had grip beneath his tires, unlike the other death-trap bridge earlier in the race. As they crossed the Burnside Bridge, his gaze was drawn to a large, white neon deer on the side of a building on the right-hand side of the bridge. He wondered what company it was for, but they passed by too quickly for him to determine.

The race headed into a neighborhood of older buildings that were in some stage of remodel, though old, derelict buildings still stood here and there, like rotten teeth in an old man's mouth. Major Tom had to swerve out of the way of a homeless man who stumbled out into the street in the path of the bike, and Gato Loco and two other riders were forced to follow suit. He hoped the foot traffic was less random when the race rolled through, but there were a lot of homeless on the street here, and unlike earlier where they were already curled up under blankets and sleeping bags for the night, here they were shambling around with paper bags full of liquor. There was going to be an accident here tonight, he knew. It was all but unavoidable.

Shortly, they took a casual left onto SW Broadway. There was another large parking lot on the left, and pending a rules clarification from Major Tom, it was one more way to cut a corner and shave precious seconds off final time. Broadway had the appearance of a major street, but at 3 in the morning, traffic should be light enough to take some ballsy chances.

Next was a relatively quick right onto SW Clay and back through the Portland State University campus.

They took a left onto SW 13th heading south and across I-405. They kept to the right, curving across the interstate, and then took a lazy left just through the first intersection onto southbound SW 14th. Two blocks later, they turned onto the quiet, tree-lined street of SW Hall Street, which changed names to SW Upper Hall for no reason that Gato Loco could see. A sudden hair-pin turn to the left appeared before them, and he looked forward to taking it at a high rate of speed in only a few hours. The street took them south, and within seconds he recognized the street as they crossed the same intersection where they had started.

Major Tom slowed to a stop on the far side of the intersection and pointed to the crosswalk again, marking it as the finish line. Once he was assured that everyone had seen and were still looking in his direction, he held up his gloved hand to show three fingers. The seventeen racers nodded, and then began to pull away from the pack to do whatever race preparation they could in the next few hours.

Rand rolled over in Gato Loco's direction, but a slow turn of the fearsome yowling cat helmet in his direction convinced him silently to just keep on moving. Anita, however, did not look to be so easily discouraged. "Well, this should be exciting," he said to himself.

"You missed dinner." Her face was blank, as if she were having trouble deciding whether to be angry or sad and the two emotions somehow canceled each other out.

Gato Loco waited to see if there was more, but that she said nothing else, her gaze fixed on him for some kind of answer. "I ate."

Her nostrils flared, and anger began to take the lead in her emotional struggle. "I meant you missed dinner with me ... Chinese food with Rand, remember?"

"I remember," Gato Loco said evenly. "I remember saying that I didn't know what my schedule would be like, so I didn't commit to dinner ... to him or to you. You said you would be there and that was fine at the time."

Anita's gaze darted across his faceplate, visibly frustrated that he wouldn't take off the helmet and allow her eye to eye contact. The subtle intimidation had worked countless times on criminals, but Manuel realized that this was the first time it had ever come in handy in a social setting. "No, you didn't commit, but I just ... I assumed—"

Gato Loco fired Shadow to silent life. "Well, then I'll try to be clear to avoid any future misunderstandings. When you get back to the room, you will find that my belongings have been removed. Don't assume that it was theft. You have the room to yourself intentionally. I need to take a step back and focus on my work. I can't do that when I'm having social dinner dates." Out of the corner of his eye, Manuel saw El Diablo Blanco pull away from the pack and out into the Portland streets. "I'm sorry. Now if you'll excuse me, I have some matters to take care of. See you at the race."

He didn't give her a chance to respond, and he realized that was more than a touch unfair. But Gato Loco had bigger problems than jilted girlfriends. He kept El Diablo Blanco within his sight, closing slightly on him as he pulled up Snowflake on the communicator. When the panda answered, Gato Loco didn't waste time with cordial greetings. "I have Blanco in my sights now. Tell me you have something on him other than speeding."

The sound of Snowflake clicking on the computer preceded the report. "Bench warrant for failure to appear for a domestic abuse hearing in Louisiana seven months ago, and an outstanding warrant for the stabbing of three people in Humboldt. Turns out one of the people he cut died in the hospital day after the incident, and another died a few days later. How does that work for you?"

"That's good enough." Gato Loco revved up the engine and began rapidly closing on the figure of El Diablo Blanco. It was high time to catch a killer.

CHAPTER FIFTEEN – TO CATCH A KILLER

Block after dark block, Gato Loco inexorably closed the gap between hunter and prey. His gaze fixed on the back of the white leather jacket like a beacon. This one, easy arrest, he kept telling himself, and he could call Xander and deliver the good news. He couldn't remember a time when he didn't have the vision of his friend's death hanging over his head like the sword of Damocles. Maybe, he found himself wondering distantly, that was why he had received no further visions, that one mental image forming a blockage, like a blood clot before the stroke.

The thought was a disturbing one. Without knowing how the visions worked, maybe it was possible that there was some kind of blockage—some sign that things were not right in the state of Manuel de la Vega. And brave though he was, being felled by a blood clot, psychic or otherwise, was not anything he wanted. Give him a foe he could see, that he could fight, even if he had no chance of winning. The idea that his own body would betray him like that was ... unsettling.

Without warning, El Diablo Blanco slammed on his brakes, going into a hard slide as he clipped close around a corner and into a narrow alley. He's rabbiting, Gato Loco realized. The other rider must have checked his mirrors and realized he was being followed. And the sudden evasive tactics suggested that Blanco very badly didn't want to be followed. At the speed Gato Loco was going, he almost missed the turn. Instead, he dropped his own speed almost to a stop, having to pop out his right leg to brace the bike and keep it from tipping as he cranked hard right to make the turn.

Ahead of him, Blanco shot down the narrow alley, kicking dumpsters to send them rolling partly out into Gato Loco's path. The leather clad vigilante gunned Shadow, using all of the bike's precision engineered acceleration, and lunged forward, slicing between the brick walls of the building to his left and the lazily spinning dumpsters on this right. While his quarry ducked left around the corner and onto the next street, Gato Loco narrowly avoided being pinned by the dumpster, the metal handle clipping his stage field projection just closely enough that it registered on his B.P. meter.

Determined not to lose Blanco, Gato Loco dodged tight around the corner after the killer racer. *Too anxious, perhaps*, he thought, as he rounded the corner just in time to see that El Blanco Diablo had stopped and dismounted his bike. Manuel didn't even see the knife plunging toward his chest. At the speed Gato Loco was riding, there wasn't anything he could do to completely avoid it. The thousands of molecular force fields collapsed one after the other, each one sapping a tiny portion of the kinetic energy until all force from the blow was leached away. However, Gato Loco was still moving forward, applying his own kinetic energy to the equation.

He felt the knife, held defiantly in place through sheer force of will, slide through the leather of the jacket and of the leather mesh below. The cold metal tip of the knife bit through skin and into muscle above Manuel's left breast. Time seemed to slow down as though the moment was being frozen in the unforgiving amber of anticipated agony. The B.P. meter rose up into the yellow in Manuel's field of vision. And then the stage field generator repelled the offending blade, pushing against it suddenly like an invisible trampoline. The knife shot out of Diablo Blanco's hand to skitter away beneath a parked hatchback across the street.

A look of disappointment burned across El Diablo Blanco's angry face. Gato Loco didn't want to give him the chance to formulate another plan and enact it while still raging. The cat-helmeted detective pointed his right fist at the broad-shouldered Satanist, looking for all the world like a karate punch that fell a foot short. "Boom," Manuel whispered into his helmet microphone, activating one of the commands on his vocal menu. The kinetic energy his suit's batteries had been storing—"Boom Points," as the designer Tamika Tesla called them—was released through a tiny condenser ring around his right wrist. It was enough stored energy that it knocked El Diablo Blanco over his parked bike and through the window of a chain coffee store.

The low light filters on his visor kicked in with a sub-vocal command to show Blanco rolling to his feet on the glass-covered tile inside. A second command turned on the miniature hard drive, which began recording an audio and video track of the confrontation. "You want me, you son of a bitch," Blanco growled, "you come on in and try to take me."

"Otis Lee Merriwhite," Gato Loco said, the electronic voice mask adding a darker, more inhuman tone to his voice, "You are wanted for the murder of two men in Humboldt, California. I suggest you come along quietly with me."

Blanco straightened slightly, confusion apparent even if the low-light filter hadn't been active. "What? I didn't kill anyone in Humboldt or anywhere. Those fellas who were messing with my private property were alive when I left. All I did was knock them around some."

Something wasn't right. Manuel could feel it crawl around under his skin for a second. Either Blanco was a world class liar, or he really had no idea about the deaths in Humboldt last year. But it was all he had, false accusation or not. And the fact that the biker had tried to ram a knife through Gato Loco's heart mere seconds ago suggested that he had something to feel guilty about. "That's not what I hear, and that's not what the police seem to think. Steven Sontag, age nineteen and William Reign, age twenty—both died from knife wounds to the stomach received in a park in Humboldt, during an altercation with a motorcyclist from out of town. Does that sound familiar?"

El Diablo Blanco kept his arms out to his sides, balancing on the broken glass on the floor. He wasn't making any move to run or fight, and that suited Gato Loco just fine. "I was there. These three punks started messing with my bike, like they were going to try and steal it. I had some valuables on the bike, stuff that didn't ... valuables I couldn't risk them taking."

Gato Loco had taken a reasonably close look at the bike before. While he hadn't seen Blanco's bike when it wasn't involved in or directly after a race, he couldn't see saddlebags on the low slung racer. And bikes like that were built for speed, not storage. Then again, it was a custom job, reputedly given to him by the Devil himself.

If Blanco didn't know about the murders, he wouldn't be running from Gato Loco over it. And Manuel suspected that he wouldn't be so worried about the bench warrant for the domestic abuse case in Louisiana, either. So what was he running from? What was worth protecting so desperately that stabbing an established vigilante, however retired he might or might not be, seemed like a good option? Blanco didn't strike Manuel as a particularly stupid person, and he had stepped up to defend Lo Ping down in Oakland, so he appeared to have at least a modicum of honor.

Gato Loco couldn't fight the sensation that he was missing something. He saw no avenue but to play it out a bit longer and hope more pieces dropped. "Your guilt or innocence is not for me to decide," Gato Loco growled, "That remains with the state of California."

Blanco licked his lips, his gaze darting around the inside of the store. Gato Loco figured the other rider's eyes had adjusted to the darkness of the store interior by now, but with the low-light vision at his disposal, Gato Loco could see easily that there was no easy exit from the coffee shop. "Let me finish the race, and I swear that I'll turn myself in as soon as I'm finished."

The last time Manuel checked the standings, El Diablo Blanco was sixth overall in the rankings. It would take an act of God, or in his case, Satan, to take the overall win. And somehow, Gato Loco didn't feel that Blanco, for all his trappings, was the kind of guy to kill the four racers ahead of him to secure a cash purse. So why was finishing the race so important? Then something Major Tom had said came to mind. Otis spent a lot of time in Mexico, riding all the way into Central and South America. And then he rode the length of the Pacific coast on a bike belonging, likely, to someone else, not caring about placement, just caring about the destination. "Who are you a courier for, Otis?"

The broad-shouldered Satanist blanched visibly. "I can't tell you that or he'll kill me. You have to believe me. If I could tell you, I would."

One of the broken commandments Xander was focusing on might have involved drugs, but this guy wasn't an assassin. It was less than unlikely that Otis would even come into contact with Xander in a social setting, one where Xander would let his guard down and be in civilian clothes. It was well-nigh impossible. In the

144

distance, he could hear the sound of approaching sirens. He figured it would be only a few minutes until they arrived. "You know what, Otis?"

"What?" El Diablo Blanco looked suspicious.

"I believe you."

Gato Loco triggered the stage-field generator cascade, slipping the courier into an uneasy sleep within half a second. Once he knew what to look for, finding the hidden compartment on the bike took only ten seconds, and opening it revealed close to twenty pounds of pure cocaine. Before he left, Gato Loco fished the knife Blanco had used against him out from beneath the car, tucking it into the straps along his leg. He was well out of sight on Shadow before the police came to arrest Otis.

Several blocks away, Gato Loco retrieved the knife and looked at it beneath the glare of a hissing sodium-vapor parking lot light. Long and slender, like an Arkansas toothpick, it was a functional and not at all decorative blade. This wasn't the weapon he had seen in the vision, not even remotely.

Otis wasn't the killer. He never had been.

And Xander was still in danger.

Snowflake's voice piped through the headset in the helmet. "Hey, I'm picking up an arrest at the place you left Blanco on the police scanner. Sounds like mission accomplished, boss. Head on back to the trailer and I'll give Shadow some tender lovin' before the next race. And while I'm tuning her up, you can call the Tesla kids and give them the good news."

His own voice sounded hollow in his head. "He wasn't the killer."

"What?"

"Otis Lee 'El Diablo Blanco' Merriweather wasn't the right guy. He was just a courier for a drug cartel." Manuel's jaw was tight. He pocketed the knife again and rode off in the direction of the trailer. Just a few days ago, he had narrowed the list of possible suspects down to three, and Blanco had been by far the best candidate. But he was now off the list. And Kemp, or Achilles, or whatever he was going to call himself, was eliminated by virtue of being broken and stuck in a bed in San Francisco recovering.

That left only one person.

It had to be Rand Arthur. All of the variables fit. In the right size category, male, light colored jacket, and associated with the race, at least enough to have touched the trophy. But despite the pieces fitting, Manuel couldn't bring himself to believe it. Why? He couldn't put his finger on it. Gut instinct, maybe. Or maybe it was that he just liked the would-be King. He was personable and trustworthy.

Or was he? Rand had been quick to point out that El Diablo Blanco was bad news, but how accurate was that? Yeah, Blanco was running drugs, but he stood up for Lo Ping in Oakland, and took care of finding an off-the-books doctor for Kemp. There was the Humboldt thing, but he had looked shocked to find out someone had been killed. Maybe that wasn't an act. And the bench warrant in Louisiana was for domestic abuse, but that was all he knew. There was a lot of room for interpretation on that. Was Otis Lee a saint? Not a chance in hell. But bad news? No, he wasn't really that kind of bad news either.

Major Tom had said that Blanco had stabbed the kids in Humboldt, but the only person who Manuel had spoken to who had claimed to actually see anything was Rand. He tried to picture Rand stabbing three college-age kids in a park in Humboldt, and couldn't do it. Rand was too nice, too ... right.

And then he thought back to the night in Oakland, drinking with Rand and Anita. They had been giddy, on some kind of loopy emotional high that had nothing to do with what they were drinking or the adrenalin leaving their bloodstream post-race.

Rand.

Damn.

Snowflake had been right to dislike him. "Ok, I'll be at the trailer in a few minutes, but before I get there, see what you can find on Rand Arthur. He rides under the moniker King Arthur. I'm interested in anything you can pull off the servers. Route it through one of Katherine's data mining services, if you need to."

Through the phone connection, Manuel could hear the squeak of the stool being spun around, followed by swift typing on the other end of the line. "You know that I don't much care for him, but what did this guy do to piss you off?"

"It's not what he did," Manuel clenched his jaw, squeezing another 10 mph out of his speedometer as he rounded a corner so quickly that a newspaper box on the corner was pulled over in the back draft. "It's what he's going to do that I'm worried about." He closed the connection and focused on the road ahead. The internal chronograph in his visor showed the time at 12:50. Less than two hours to research while Snowflake did the tune-up, and then the race. That wasn't much time at all.

Unless Rand had some kind of glaring criminal record with outstanding warrants, it was going to take more time. And that was assuming that there was anything on the record to hold him for. Despite his vision, he couldn't just knock someone out and hold them captive. Preventing future crimes was a slippery slope, he knew. He had seen the movie.

It was clearly time for Plan B.

CHAPTER SIXTEEN – WELCOME TO THE EMERALD CITY

Portland had cost them four racers—two to the Hawthorne Bridge when their bikes had lost control at high speed, one to a collision in the intersection of Burnside and SE 12th, and one due to his arrest for narcotics trafficking. Of the four, it was only El Blanco Diablo's elimination that Manuel had any immediate knowledge of. The other three racers, all injured, two of them badly, had happened far behind him on the course. He had been too focused on the race to notice much else.

The race and only the race, he thought. No scorned lover trying to distract him, no manipulative killer fated to murder a friend, no professional assassin out for revenge, no panda sidekick waiting in the wings, no Manuel. There was only the race—the race and Gato Loco, one man against the organic complexity of a living city. The elegant mathematics of applied physics plus his confidence in his skills divided by a progression of calculated risks.

The witching hour streets of Portland blurred past him, a water-color painting of night and neon; metal and motion. When he crossed the finish line, Gato Loco didn't know if he was first or last. He didn't care. All he knew was that he had run the best race he could, and he had lived. For a divine handful of seconds, he was weightless. Rarified. He had run his best and lived, and right then, that was everything.

Gato Loco sat astride Shadow in the middle of the tree-lined street, sixty feet past the finish line. The hum of approaching bikes built on the air like a coming swarm, and he looped his bike back around to face them. The seconds stretched on forever before the first of the remaining bikers rounded the corner, gunning for the finish. It wasn't until he saw the concentrated fury on Anita's face as she crossed the line and then jetted past him that Manuel fully processed that he had not only won this circuit—he had dominated.

All the racers who would finish crossed the line in the next two minutes, and as soon as the last bike shot through the intersection, Major Tom folded closed the RFID reader he was using to calculate times and monitor the race. He tucked it back into his jacket before starting up his bike and riding over to Gato Loco. He whistled low. "Damnation, boy! What crawled up into you tonight? In all the years I organized the Devil's Run, I've never seen a margin like that before."

"How big of a margin?"

"Fifty-one seconds," the old man said with a lunatic smile. "You're the one to beat now, kiddo. I'd suggest watching your back."

Manuel smiled within the anonymity of his helmet. "You think so?"

"Heh!" Major Tom's gaze trailed off toward the other racers, and Gato Loco could tell he was tracking Anita in particular. "A finish like that pretty much declares that if you get on your bike, you're going to win. Your woman might just smother you in your sleep to make sure that doesn't happen."

Gato Loco turned to look at Anita as she rode back toward them, storm clouds in her eyes. "I see what you mean."

Anita lifted her chin in acknowledgement of the Major, and he gave her his full attention. She avoided looking at Gato Loco entirely—a point not missed by either of the men. "Am I still a strong second in overall time?"

Major Tom nodded. He reached into one of the zipper pockets of his jacket and handed her the second place prize purse for the night. "You have a commanding lead over third, and are within striking distance of first."

She raised one corner of her mouth in a snarl and took the money, jamming it down into her jeans pocket where it lay like a tumor against her hip. "Seattle," she said darkly. "Where and when?"

"I was going to announce—" A hard glare from Anita choked off his explanation mid-sentence, and when the Major found his voice again, it was subdued. "Ten in the morning in two days at the parking lot of the Owl and Thistle, downtown. It's on—"

"I'll find it." Anita pulled away on her bike without another look.

The race organizer was quiet for a few seconds, watching her pull away, as if waiting for her to be out of earshot. He took the night's first place bankroll out of his pocket and handed it across to Gato Loco. "Do you need to stay on my sofa tonight or something?"

Gato Loco shook his head.

"Good luck." Neither of them pretended Major Tom was talking about the race.

Gato Loco tucked the winnings away and rode off after Anita, catching up with her in a cluster of other riders, Rand Arthur among them. As many eyes turned on him with awe as with hatred, and before anyone could congratulate him on the win, the intensity in Anita's expression bludgeoned them into silence. He passed his cat-helmeted gaze over the assembled riders. "Can I have a moment here?" The other riders pulled away to what they figured would be right at the edge of earshot. Rand was the last to go, his expression unreadable as he looked from Gato Loco to Anita and back.

Anita waited until they were gone before acknowledging Manuel. "What do you want? Are you here to apologize for winning or to gloat? Because either way, you're just going to piss me off."

He kept his voice low and neutral as best as he was able. "I wasn't going to mention the race at all. I just wanted to let you know that Snowflake and I are heading up to Seattle at ten tomorrow if you'd like to ride up with us."

"I'm not some kind of trophy," Anita growled. "So don't pretend that you've won me. I know your stuff is out of the hotel room, so where does that leave us? Am I your accessory now? Your entourage?"

Manuel weighed a variety of answers, just as he had weighed the importance of having this discussion. He didn't know who Anita would socialize with once she was no longer with him, but Rand Arthur was a prime contender. Loaded with money, charming, and a good enough racer to be competitive but not as good as she was. And Manuel was reasonably sure that Rand was a killer. What was worse, she wasn't just putting herself in danger. It was entirely likely that her knowledge of the Tesla twins and her conversations with Rand was what would lead to Xander's death. He couldn't allow himself to think that slip would be intentional on Anita's part. But if Rand did have some kind of Svengali hoodoo, either pheromones or psychic persuasion, it would be open season on any secrets that Manuel or Snowflake had confided in Anita.

It was probably too late, he realized, to preserve some secrets. She had eaten dinner with the ubiquitous King just that evening, and had likely been in a rare fit of pique at the time as well. No, it was likely that Rand already knew Gato Loco's real name, all about Snowflake, and probably more than he should about the Tesla twins at the very least. But he couldn't be sure, and minimizing the risk of further damage was preferable to giving her cause to spill all of his secrets willingly.

Manuel had lied before to protect his secret identity. It was simply impossible to maintain one otherwise. For a few years, he had flagrantly deceived his friend and partner in the Cobalt City Police Department, and if Donegal hadn't figured out the secret himself, it might still be secret. But never, in all his time in the leathers of Gato Loco, had he been forced to feign involvement in a relationship. And it wasn't necessarily because he had never been given the opportunity, although he accepted that was part of it at least. But he recognized a clear division between deceiving someone intellectually, and deceiving them emotionally. And the later had always been a line he wouldn't cross.

Manuel took off his sculpted helmet and put on his perfectly sincere face. He felt his heart shrink a few sizes inside his chest and tried to ignore it as best as he could. "Hon, I hope you know it isn't like that. Snowflake and I have been so busy on side projects that I've been keeping odd hours lately. I didn't want to wake you up with all of my fumbling around in the dark with my crutches, so I figured it would be better for you if I let you get your rest and stay focused."

He could see her softening around the corner of her eyes, though her mouth was still frozen in a cold scowl. "You lying son of a bitch."

"Anita, I wouldn't lie to you about something like that," he lied.

Manuel found it devastating how easy it was. "Most of my things are packed and loaded into the truck for tomorrow, but I was hoping to share our room tonight."

One of her thin eyebrows shot up. "Our room?"

"Or call it your room. That's okay. You want your space." He put on Hurt Look Number Three. "I understand if you're angry at me."

One side of her scowl flickered, threatening to crumble. Manuel thought he could see the hint of tears, and seconds later they made a sudden appearance while the scowl gave way. "Yeah, I'm furious. You must have beaten me by close to a minute, you bastard." Despite her words, a crushed smile of relief sprouted on her pretty face, and it bruised Manuel's soul to look at it, to know that the smile was planted in the shallow dirt of comfort lies.

"Fifty-one seconds," he said, using the shame over his manipulation to stand in for his shame of having won by so much time. "Sorry."

He saw her calculating the time difference, applying it to the overall time totals given at the end of the last race. Manuel knew it wasn't pretty. It wasn't impossible, but it wasn't pretty. "If you've been going soft on me all this time, I'm so going to kick your ass, Manuel de la Vega."

"I've been riding to win, baby," he said with a smile. "I just synched up with this course for some reason, and caught some lucky breaks with traffic. Luck like that doesn't come along every race."

But already in his head he was calculating—if he could stop Rand prior to the race, then he would be riding to win. But if he couldn't find anything to pin on the impending killer until after the race, then he might just have to pull his punches and let Anita win the Seattle circuit by a decent margin—anything to keep her happy without her growing suspicious or, even worse, vengeful.

Anita stepped closer, taking Manuel's head in her hands and pulled his mouth to hers in a deep kiss that threatened to take his breath away. When she finally let him go enough to pull his head back, he could see her pupils were dilated, her nostrils flared. "Race you to the room?"

"You really think you can beat me?" He let her see his smile before putting his helmet back on.

For an answer, she hopped onto her bike and kicked it to life.

Anita pulled away so fast that her bike kicked up into a wheelie as she shot down the street. Gato Loco had little choice but to follow her. As he pulled away from the others, he was almost certain that he could feel Rand Arthur's calm gaze watching his every move. *Your time is coming,* Manuel thought, *perhaps sooner than you realize.*

He had Snowflake on the phone within the first block. "You still have my room key?"

The panda sounded tired, the hectic pace of the past few days taking their toll. "I think it's on the table. Why?"

"Toss one of my shirts and a change of shorts and socks into the room for me." He calculated the time based on his earlier sprint to the start line for the preview tour. "I'd say you have about five minutes before Anita gets there."

"Feeling the need for a little sexual healing already? It's been, what, a day?" But despite the petulant tone in his sidekick's voice, Manuel could hear the panda moving around the hotel on the other end of the phone, rooting through the duffle bag for a clean shirt.

"If Rand is our guy, then I need to minimize his access to Anita. *Comprende?*"

"The things you have to do to do in the interest of fighting crime," Snowflake sighed. "Oh, what a hellish life you lead, you Hispanic man-candy, you. Ok, shirt, shorts and socks are in hand. I'm going to run them over now. We still on for a ten o'clock departure?"

Six hours of sleep, Manuel thought. Less for him and Anita, but they wouldn't be driving. It didn't seem like enough, but it would have to do. They could always sleep in Seattle. "You think you'll be rested enough for the drive?"

"Eh, I napped today and there's coffee in the morning. It's not too far to the Emerald City. Five hours tops. I'll be fine."

Manuel pumped up the speed to keep Anita in view on the night-heavy streets ahead of him. "Thanks, buddy. I owe you one."

Snowflake grumbled, "You keep paying the bills and I'll keep the magic happening. Sleep well, you sex-craved deviant. I'll rouse you from your den of sin and iniquity at nine-forty, so for God's sake, have some pants on."

He needn't have worried. Once they got back to the room, Anita attacked him like she was on a day-pass from a women's correctional facility, and then afterward they both let exhaustion overtake them. Manuel woke naturally shortly after nine and decided to grab some pastries and juice from the hotel's free continental breakfast downstairs. He woke Anita so she wouldn't wake up and find him gone again.

After getting dressed and packed quickly, she joined him for what could only be called a breakfast. The coffee had a thin, church meeting quality, little more than lightly brown-tinted water, and the juice was warmer than Manuel would have liked. The bagels were of the previously-frozen variety, and the small pastries were dry and too sweet. Still, it was better than gas station donuts and the powdered coffee-flavored beverages that they would have been stuck with instead, so they had little room to complain.

Now that the passion from the previous night had been sated, and with both of them still tired, they found conversation stilted at best. She avoided talking about the previous night's race and he kept well clear of the relationship topic. Similarly, neither of them talked about the other racers, Rand Arthur in particular. With a leaden silence growing between them, they found themselves back in their room for less than a minute before Snowflake came looking for them.

The sky was overcast, as though reflective of their moods. When Snowflake tuned on a painfully cheery eighties station on the satellite radio, neither Anita nor Manuel complained, though the last thing they really wanted to listen to for the next several hours was whiny Brits and synthesizers. When "Walking on Sunshine" by Katrina and the Waves came on, it only took halfway through the second verse before the cab of the truck was filled with a riot of uncontrolled giggling from all three occupants. The tension dissipated, they sang along with every song they recognized from there all the way into Seattle.

The truck and trailer rolled up I-5, through the southern suburbs of warehouses and industrial buildings between the Boeing airfield and the giant, orange cranes of the waterfront, the cluster of downtown skyscrapers clawing through a misty, gray cloud cover. Manuel judged Seattle to be close to Cobalt City in size, but it was more affluent and with fewer capes—at least if Xander's stories were true. He looked across the cab at Snowflake, who was intently focused on the famous Seattle traffic pressing in on them on all sides. "You know where we're going, right?"

Snowflake nodded and began rapidly rolling down his window. "Yeah, been there twice ... hold on a second." The panda leaned out his window and gestured wildly at a Toyota hybrid with a Dave Matthews Band sticker in the window that had been ahead on his left, signaling to get in front of their truck for the last half mile. "Fucking merge already, lady!" He rolled his window back up. "They have a condo on the other end of town. We're going north and past the University to the Greenwood area. I should be able to find street parking within a block of their place."

Ahead of them, the timid driver still hovered, non-committal about merging, so Snowflake nosed up, only to have her swerve into the space, narrowly missing his bumper. The panda's training eased the foot off the gas, widening the gap between the truck and the offending vehicle, but his innate surliness leaned on the horn. Manuel noticed that his friend had developed a facial tic ever since passing the two big sports arenas off to the side of the interstate, just south of the downtown corridor. What had once been a four-lane interstate had narrowed to two through lanes with several exits to downtown and I-90 peeling into "Exit Only" lanes. It seemed to Manuel that most drivers wanted to travel through the downtown core, or at least to later exits, but so many of them were passive-aggressive about lane changing that Snowflake looked about ready to spit blood. "Isn't there another way through downtown?"

Snowflake ground his teeth, gaze darting to both of his side mirrors as he changed lanes suddenly, eliciting a few angry horns of his own. "Yeah, 99. It's the Pacific Coast Highway, and it's an elevated stretch through downtown, but enough of it has stop lights on either end of Seattle proper that its more hassle than its worth. That and the lanes seem narrow both on the viaduct and on the bridge over Lake Washington or whatever the hell it is we cross over. I think it's called the Ship Canal Bridge when we cross on I-5, which I only know because there was a jumper on it last time I was in town. Jesus, you've never seen a worse traffic mess."

"Worse than this?" Anita said, motioning to the cars around them.

"Hell," Snowflake smiled with the air of a veteran training a rookie. "At least this is moving a little bit at a time. That morning it was a parking lot. If I had been stuck in it instead of watching it on television, I might have been on the bridge thinking about jumping too."

"What happened to the jumper?" Manuel asked.

"Oh, I think she jumped. Broke tons of bones and went into

the hospital, but she lived." He paused and looked pensive. "Or maybe that was another jumper. Lots of suicides here. Welcome to the Emerald City."

As mysteriously as it had started, the traffic suddenly opened up, and the vehicles started flowing again past the skyscrapers of the financial district. Within seconds, they were passing beneath the concrete walls of the Washington State Convention Center, which sat atop the interstate with vines and other greenery cascading down the walls. Underneath the convention center, they passed the cause of the traffic delay—a BMW that had collided with an old hatchback in the center lane was being loaded onto a flatbed while emergency vehicles controlled the scene. Manuel found it vaguely satisfying to see vehicles other than bikes involved in a collision for a change, and also that there was a cause for the delay and that it wasn't just an organic occurrence at this time of day. He found himself wondering when the race might be run and what the prevailing traffic conditions might be at the time.

Almost as an afterthought, Manuel pulled out his cell phone. "About how long now that traffic has cleared up?"

"About ten minutes," the driver shrugged. "Fifteen at the most. Gonna give the punk a heads up that we're almost there?"

Manuel smiled. "Seems only fair. It's just now a little after one. Maybe he hasn't had lunch yet."

Snowflake laughed at the suggestion. "I'd be surprised if he's even awake yet."

Much to his surprise, Xander was not only awake but chipper when he answered the phone on the second ring. "Hey, perfect timing! I just finished up at the dojo. You two almost in town?"

"We're passing the Space Needle now. The estimate is ten or so minutes," Manuel informed his young friend casually. "And there are three of us. Are you sure you have enough crash space?"

"Right. This mysterious girlfriend Snow has been telling me about. No worries. Tam has been crashing at her boyfriend's most nights up on Beacon. She already said one of you could use her room."

The idea that Tamika had a boyfriend, let alone that she was spending the night with him regularly was strangely disconcerting to Manuel. He had to remind himself that the Tesla twins were adults now. They were still young—at least compared to him—but adults nonetheless. "Who is this boyfriend? Does he check out?"

"Guitarist in her band, name of Jake. He's a nice enough guy who doesn't know she used to do the hero gig in her wild youth, so we're keeping that on the down-low."

Another thought came to Manuel suddenly. "Wait, does Katherine know about Jake?" The silence on the other side of the phone spoke volumes. He wasn't sure how Katherine would feel about Tam co-habitating with a civilian. She had always been much more of a den mother than she would have readily admitted, and had been closer to the twins than he had. She had been more like a foster mother figure next to his fun uncle. "She's going to have to tell Kat, you know. Tamika knows stuff that is confidential and even though she can be trusted to guard those secrets, Kat at least deserves to know that there is a risk. And, you know, Kat needs to give her the talk."

"What talk?"

"The talk. You're a bio specialist Xander," he chided. "You figure it out." He could picture the young genius rolling his eyes on the other end of the phone. "Anyway, we'll be there soon. If you haven't had lunch, we could meet you somewhere, or we could pop out after we've unloaded the truck and get something to eat. The continental breakfast in Portland gave out on me ninety minutes ago."

"I'm famished. Sensei gave me a solid work-out today. How do you feel about barbeque?"

Manuel mouthed the word "barbeque" to Anita and Snowflake, to be met by an indifferent shrug by Anita and an enthusiastic nod from the panda. "If I say no, Snowflake will likely never forgive me."

Xander laughed. "Like he won't ever have another chance to eat ribs! I'm about a block away now. I'll grab us a table and you can park in the drugstore parking lot next door. See you in a few minutes."

Manuel hung up and tucked the phone back into his breast pocket. Would it be tonight, he wondered? Would this be the night when Rand tried to kill Xander, or would it be tomorrow on race night? Snowflake seemed to sense what Manuel was thinking and fell grimly quiet himself.

By the time they pulled off the interstate onto 85th, Anita realized that something wasn't right. "You caught the guy who was going to attack your friend, right? Wasn't it El Blanco Diablo?"

Snowflake kept his gaze locked dead ahead, his jaw set as Anita looked from him to Manuel and back again. "Yeah," Manuel finally said, realizing that something needed to be said. There wasn't any way Anita was going to let this one go, and in the interest of everyone's safety, it was time for some things to come out. "About that. It wasn't him. He was loaded down with drugs and stabbed me when I started looking at him too closely as a suspect. But he wasn't a killer."

She snorted. "That's not what Rand was saying at dinner the other night!"

Outside the window, houses with big trees in the yard scrolled by, and Manuel tried to focus on them instead of Anita, for fear that he would betray his suspicions. "Really? That's interesting. Did Rand have any other insights?"

She opened her mouth to say something, and it was only her reflection in the window that gave away her eventual lie. "No. Not that I remember anyway. Why?"

"How much do you know about him?" Manuel asked. "Rand Arthur, that is. What can you tell me about him? Have you raced with him before or heard any stories?"

"I've raced him a few times." Her voice held a trace of suspicion, but it couldn't be helped. "He has money, so he doesn't race as hard as some of us who don't. He wrote a book, a fantasy ... no, horror novel a few years ago. He mentioned the name at dinner, but I don't remember it. I guess it never sold well, but he said that he runs into it in used book stores from time to time."

"But it was published under his name and not a pseudonym?" Snowflake asked as he rounded the corner onto Greenwood Avenue, revealing a thriving little neighborhood of shops and restaurants on the tree-lined streets.

"He didn't say. Why?"

Snowflake pointed out the passenger side window, indicating a used bookstore with several racks of cheap paperbacks out front on the sidewalk. "I'm going to pop in and see if I can find some reading material after lunch."

Manuel nodded, thinking the same thing. "I'll join you."

The mood in the cab of the truck was somber, and they rode the next block in silence, broken by Anita only when they pulled into the parking lot of the Walgreen's Drug Store on the left. "Why all the interest in Rand? Do you think he has something to do with the imagined attack on your friend?"

A ramshackle building that looked more like a condemned barn than a restaurant greeted them on the other side of the parking lot, a clapboard sign and awning with fading paint advertised it as the "O.K. Corral BBQ." Xander Tesla was waiting for them as well, his compact, athletic frame clad casually in skater shorts, checkerboard slip on shoes, and a red hoodie with a tribal flame design on the sleeve. The hood was down to reveal the inventor's shoulder-length brown hair, which he brushed casually out of his eyes with the back of his hand. He looked Anita over with a grin as she stepped out of the truck. "Hey there, baby doll. How you livin', girl?"

"Down boy," Snowflake barked. "She would likely ruin you for other women, and then you'd have to join a monastery or something."

Manuel could hear a mixture of joy in the panda's voice as the thrill of reunion was tainted by the sorrow of what could be a final few days. Manuel felt the same tightness of the chest, and chose to say nothing, instead hobbling over to give the young genius a clumsy, one armed hug, his weight balanced on the one forearm crutch.

Anita sauntered past toward the front door of the dive barbeque restaurant, an extra bit of sway in her hips. The curl of her lip suggested that she was flattered by Xander's attention, but had no intention of encouraging it. She held her hand up to her shoulder level. "Must be at least this high to ride, junior. Nice try, though."

The three men watched her go, lingering enough for proper reunion. "A swing and a miss," Xander smiled sheepishly at Manuel. "Anyway, your post-Wild Kat rebound girlfriend would hardly be in my division ... she'd probably kill me."

"Keep eating your spinach and hitting the gym, and you too can hook up with unbalanced biker women," Snowflake muttered. "Anyway, good to see you in the flesh, kiddo."

"And that goes double for me," Manuel said as he got his crutches back beneath him. He started stumping off after Anita with Xander securely between himself and the panda. "We need to puzzle out how to keep you safe until this thing blows over."

"You know, I've been thinking about that," Xander said quietly. "And I think the best solution is to let him kill me."

Xander walked alone into the heavenly scented interior of the establishment. Manuel and Snowflake had stopped moving, jaws open on the sidewalk out front.

☐

CHAPTER SEVENTEEN – SUICIDE CAPITAL
OF THE NORTHWEST

The pared down group of racers met in the parking lot near the Owl and Thistle, in the crossing shadows of the pedestrian bridge from the ferry and the looming concrete of the Alaskan Way Viaduct, which looked both dangerously old and eternally patient. The street that ran beneath the viaduct was narrow, particularly at this time of day, when cars were parked at a diagonal down both sides between massive, crumbling support pillars, and it reminded Manuel briefly of the movie *The French Connection*. He sat astride Shadow and gazed down the stretch of street and anticipated that at least a little of that street would be used in the race.

It was a much better thing to focus on than the insanity of the plan he had worked out with Xander the day before. Too many days, too many stressful hours, had been spent trying to figure out a way to avert Xander's apparent fate that wrapping his brain around embracing the vision was enough to give him a headache. Not that he felt the idea was without merit. Quite the opposite, despite the madness of the central conceit—that you couldn't change fate, but if you knew what fate was, you could use it to your advantage. It was better than any plan that he had come up with on his own. *It just goes to show*, Manuel thought, *that a creative and brilliant mind with enough time to plan and a lick of self-preservation can think himself out of most problems.*

"Is Rand there yet?" Snowflake's voice buzzed through on the helmet ear piece.

"He got here a few minutes ago and has been talking with Anita," Gato Loco responded, glancing over at the other racers out of the corner of his visor.

"You trust her to stick to her story?" the panda grumbled.

Manuel had been wrestling with a variation on the same thought for the better part of the day. While he didn't have an answer that completely satisfied him, he had at least figured out a way to articulate his thoughts better. "I'm pretty sure we didn't tell her anything damaging, and she's not really deviating from the truth as she knows it: we're staying with old friends who I feel are in some kind of danger, and while we're worried, our friend appears cocky and full of himself. The master plan was never discussed with her anywhere around, so she couldn't spill the beans on that if she wanted to."

Snowflake sighed on the other end of the line. He didn't sound convinced, but also didn't have any reason other than his inborn stubbornness to belabor how little he liked and trusted Anita Cruz. "Whatever. If you get a chance to chat with the King there, tell him his book sucks, will you?"

"The first half wasn't bad." Manuel said with a grimace, wishing he had made time to read more of the battered paperback they had picked up for three dollars at the bookstore after lunch yesterday. But between keeping Anita sufficiently distracted, plotting with Xander and his twin sister Tamika, and a minimal amount of sleep, halfway through the horror paperback was pretty commendable. So far, the small group of occultists had found themselves locked into an old tobacco warehouse in Raleigh, which had been converted into expensive loft condos. Some cultist was in there with a book that they had let slip into his hands, and one by one he was killing the heroes and the other building residents off for his dark god. It wasn't Dickens, but Manuel had read worse. "Have you finished it already?"

"Page one-seventy-three," the mechanic confided. As Manuel recalled, that wasn't much further than he had gotten himself. "If I were Archon, I would have been able to read it, write an analysis of it, and turn out a better sequel by now, but lack of sleep and furry panda-fingers make this hard. And the actual book, what's the word I'm looking for ... oh yeah. Poop. The book is poop, Manuel. You shouldn't read books like this. You should put them in a flaming bag on someone's porch."

"I never saw you for a book burner."

Oblivious to the jab, Snowflake kept going, his complaining winding down to his typically disgruntled mumble. "How this yahoo got a book deal is beyond me. There hasn't been a single frickin' decapitation. Anyway, just my two cents."

Up ahead of him, Major Tom signaled the riders to start their bikes. "We're about to roll. What's the status on Xander and Tam?"

"They stepped out—" There was a pause as the panda checked his watch. "—oh, about ten minutes ago, to grab a coffee from the Wayward Coffeehouse down the street, and then they were headed to the condo for a final fine tuning. Unless there was a line, they're probably there now."

Gato Loco started his bike and joined the other riders on Post Avenue headed south. "Good. I'll keep our target in sight, and let you know if there are any changes. I still wish you could have found something we could actually charge him with. I don't like this wait-and-see tactic."

"Other than literary crimes, he's either clean or he's covered his tracks real damn well. I'm guessing its number two. Have a good ride, and I'll see you afterward up at base camp."

Major Tom waved his finger in a circle above his head, then started off. The remaining racers followed at a respectable distance and speed. Manuel watched as Rand jogged up toward the front of the pack with him and nodded a greeting before falling back into the middle of the group of racers. With as few racers as remained at this stage, it was virtually right behind him, and while it made Manuel just a shade nervous, he found he could easily keep an eye on this King Arthur with his mirrors.

The procession headed south past the Owl and Thistle Irish Pub in a generally southerly direction until they hit Yesler and turned right. At this time of mid-day, the traffic on Yesler was only moderate, and Manuel noticed most of the license plates were not local. Tourists, he figured, or visitors of some other stripe. They wouldn't be here when the race ran, but with all the bars and clubs in the area, the likelihood of busy evening traffic was still a good bet.

Less than a block away, they turned underneath the viaduct, and Gato Loco realized this stretch was little more than a series of long parking lots. Only cars pulling out of spaces or circling to find the infrequent open parking spots took this route, and their progress was stop and go for blocks. Again, Manuel thought, at bar-closure time, this would be a tricky path to navigate at high speed. He was relieved when they turned left onto Union for a slight jog heading toward the large pier buildings less than a block away. And then almost immediately, they turned right onto the ground level Alaskan Way, running along the waterfront. Traffic was a little heavier here but faster. They curved left with the city on their right hand, piers and the Puget Sound beyond on the other.

Farther up, when Alaskan looked to be terminating in a park, the riders took a right turn across some railroad tracks and up steep Broad Street. Two intersections followed where they were forced to sit at the light on a steep incline. Of course, when the race was going, they wouldn't be stopping for lights. Crossing Western and 1st Avenue would be exciting considering that both looked to have decent traffic at all times and were essentially "blind" cross streets. Entering into either of those intersections at high speed, a rider would have to be prepared to make sudden adjustments based on traffic volume that might as well have just materialized. If there wasn't an accident there during the race, then the gods of motorsports were watching out for them.

Broad leveled out more or less past 1st Avenue, and approached the signature skyline element of the Space Needle on the left. The bikes passed the tourist hot-spot in heavy traffic and then passed a brightly colored metallic blob of a building that was pierced at midpoint by the monorail tracks overhead. It took him a few horrified seconds to remember Tamika telling him that this was some kind of hands-on music museum, built to look like music sounded. She loved it, and had gone on and on about how looking at it in the morning sunrise was one of her favorite things in Seattle. Try as he might, Manuel couldn't share her enthusiasm.

Not long after the blobby red, gold, and purple music building, they hung a gradual right onto Republican, a side street that was not as well maintained as Gato Loco would have liked. They buildings transitioned from commercial to light industrial. Loading docks off the side streets and alleys became commonplace. They crossed through a couple of relatively busy intersections, but nothing as bad as the ones on Broad before turning left onto the busy thoroughfare of Westlake.

Westlake had the advantage of being one way, but it was exceptionally busy with commuters and busses. They merged and changed lanes aggressively to the far right to make a quick right turn onto Mercer one block later. This intersection was the worst yet, as it comprised not only the north-south arterial of Westlake, but it was also where Mercer fed the major onramp to Interstate 5. They took a hard right, being careful to stay on Mercer and not get into either of the two on-ramps.

Just shy of I-5, Mercer hit a "T" intersection, and Major Tom took them left onto Eastlake Avenue. They kept right, moving quickly onto Lakeview Boulevard E, taking that across the packed interstate and up the hill. The road forked on the other side of I-5, and they took the right fork onto Belmont Avenue and headed in a southerly direction up Capitol Hill. The road was getting steeper and narrower, as houses gave way to apartment buildings. They took a gradual right onto E Roy Street, which was just as steep as Belmont had been before it. The traffic was light, which was a blessing on the narrow streets, but what cars were driving through were moving quickly.

A crooked right turn onto Broadway met them just past the top of their ascent, and here they hit a relatively active neighborhood. Most of the traffic was on foot, the sidewalks packed with shoppers and people with cardboard signs begging for money. The crowd was largely young, college students and cultural vanguard types. Manuel had thought that the trendy hipsters had died out, but apparently they had instead moved to Capitol Hill in Seattle. A casual glance also showed him a disheveled and bearded man in his fifties walking down the street shirtless, with something held in front of him just below waist level. Upon further inspection, it appeared that the man was exposing himself, walking down the street with his cock in his hand while no one on the street paid him any attention. "That's what I get for paying attention," he said to himself, almost disbelieving that he had seen it at all.

As they followed Broadway, the foot traffic lightened up as they passed Seattle Central Community College on the right and, he figured, possibly on the left as well. The street took a dip, and then began climbing gradually back up, and a large hospital could be seen off to the side of the street. The neighborhood had changed entirely by this point, the trendy hipsters, restaurants, glitter-goth clothing boutiques, and neon-garnished facades replaced by discount groceries and old brick buildings in need of repair. This, he realized, was not the "fun" part of the hill, and the prospects looked a bit bleaker. This was much the same as they took a gradual left onto Boren Avenue across Yesler into a kind of messy intersection with 12th Avenue South. They turned right onto 12th, and followed that south onto S Jackson Street, where they turned right again.

They were headed downhill again, back toward the water, and while the city's two big sports arenas came into view on the left, Gato Loco gauged the traffic and their eventual destination. They passed the International District, and then the rail station on the left, and the big green-glass wave of an office building beyond that, dropping ever lower in elevation. The foot traffic took on an unmistakable air of desperation. Seattle's government buildings, the county administration and courthouse and such were on the right, as were residence hotels and apartment buildings packed with what, if the pedestrians of the neighborhood were any indication, an overwhelming tide of junkies and people stuck in low-level government housing.

It astounded him. A pristine white building with construction scaffolds up around it, advertising a new boutique hotel opening next year, while across the street an ambulance was parked with its flashing lights on in front of a shabby building where someone was being treated for an overdose. The juxtaposition was surreal. A check cashing place next door to a gleaming bank—a greasy convenience store with metal accordion gating over the windows across the street from a gourmet coffee shop. He couldn't even begin to imagine what this neighborhood would be like at night when the race was on. He could barely accept what he saw now.

Jackson passed through Pioneer Square Park, which, at a glance, he took to be little more than a cobblestone stretch with a few statues, trees, and benches occupied by sleeping homeless. Once past the park, they turned right onto 1st Avenue. This took them through Pioneer Square proper, with high stone buildings fronted by classic, hundred-year-old façades. A small, triangular courtyard-style park rolled by on their right, decorated by a Victorian iron and glass pergola on the corner with a tall, wooden totem pole just beyond. This area was also packed with foot traffic, but of a much different kind than elsewhere. While a few homeless could be seen panhandling for change, the sidewalks were awash with office workers on coffee and cigarette breaks and thick clusters of tourists with their shopping bags and cameras.

The street bent to the left and they followed, in the home stretch now. A few blocks later, they took a left onto the downhill slope of Madison, the Owl and Thistle in sight. Another left again, this time on Western, and then a block farther, a final left onto Marion to the same point in which they had started.

It was a respectable course, Gato Loco figured. Plenty opportunity to make mistakes taking chances, enough straight stretches, such as on Alaskan, Broad, and Broadway for a chance to break away, and some unknowns, such as the behavior of foot traffic. Heading through Pioneer Square, he had noticed a lot of bars and clubs. With the 2 am start time, that was a chaos storm waiting to happen.

Major Tom removed his helmet and stepped off his bike. It was clear to Manuel that the Devil's Run was taking a toll on its creator. While the elderly organizer had never looked exceptionally spry, he was looking more and more worn down since end of the San Francisco circuit. Maybe it was the deaths or the injuries. Maybe, Manuel thought, it was the knowledge that Cross was out there, shadowing the event, waiting for the chance to move in and avenge his son's death. There was no telling. And Manuel wasn't even sure if he should ask. He couldn't help shake the thought that Gato Loco's presence amid the illegal race wasn't helping the old man sleep peacefully. "Two am," he said loudly enough for all the racers to hear, "Don't be late. Any questions?"

The only remaining female racer other than Anita hesitantly raised her hand. The razor-thin woman was dressed in black denim, and she looked awkward, as if the raising of the hand was an automatic response, trained from years of school. Manuel seemed to remember her name being Susan or something, and while she hadn't placed well throughout the entirety of the series, she was still there, and that wasn't to be discounted. Racing smart and finishing in the middle of the pack was better than racing fast and not finishing at all. "Um, what happens if we're here late? I mean, I don't plan on being late, but what if?"

Major Tom's eyes narrowed suspiciously, as if he was missing an obvious angle, and if he squinted at it long enough it would present itself. "Then you miss the start of the race," he said slowly, as if explaining to a child.

Gato Loco suddenly saw what Susan might have been dancing around the edges of. He cleared his throat, the voice mask in his helmet turning the sound into more of a growl. "But are we disqualified for being late?"

"Like I told you back in Tijuana, if you're late, you're disqualified and forfeit the entrance fee." Manuel thought he saw a certain caginess in the Major's eyes that showed he saw the angle. "Anyway, you'd be behind the rest of the racers, and with your cumulative time, you can't afford it."

"Not exactly," Susan said. "We aren't really racing the other racers, right? We're racing the clock. We're each individually timed, and that's based on when we cross the start and the finish lines."

The realization spread to the other racers, and Manuel suspected that they might be considering how to exploit this new information. Delaying start times until the bar rush had died down, perhaps. Major Tom saw it as well, and his face turned to flint. "I told you the rules at the start. Anyway, I'm not waiting around in the rain all damn night for you punks to lollygag in and race on your own schedule." He looked around the assembled riders. Either his exhaustion got the better of him, or the time he'd spent with the few racers still in the chase had softened him somewhat. "But here's what I'll do. I'm going to be here just before 2 for the start time, but I pack up at 2:30. Anyone who hasn't crossed the line by then, I don't care how fast they finish the course, I'm going to go get some goddamned French toast and that's final."

Half-an-hour, Gato Loco thought. It wasn't much, and it wouldn't help those trying to scheme a better start time. But it was an interesting wrinkle, he had to admit.

"Oh, and after race party will be at the Hurricane Café," Major Tom said before putting his helmet back on. "I'll announce the final meeting point there for anyone who is still riding." The august biker pulled his helmet down snug and rode off, several of the other riders in his wake.

Rand flipped up his visor and smiled casually over in Manuel's direction. "Are you spending the day hanging out with your friend who lives here?"

Despite his anticipation of a conversation with Rand, Manuel still felt his chest tighten up a bit. "That was the plan. Is there anything on your schedule?"

Rand's smile was dazzling—flashing white and perfect. The reflection of sun on his teeth filled Manuel with a just the slightest hint of nausea. "I have a special project I'm planning for, and I figured I'd get in some shopping too." He paused, looking around as if realizing for the first time that it was only he and Manuel there in the street, Anita long having started back to base camp up in Greenwood. "I understand your friends are twins. Is that right?"

The mysterious unease was gone, but a vague discomfort at the memory of the experience lingered, and Manuel had to pause to keep his voice from shaking just a bit. "Not identical twins, but yeah. Same mom within a few minutes of each other."

Rand slid his visor back down, and though Manuel couldn't see the smile anymore, he could hear it in King Arthur's voice. "Ah, fraternal twins. My favorite. See you tonight."

Manuel didn't know someone could have a favorite kind of twins, but he would have believed just about anything about Rand at this point, save that he was harmless. He watched the canary yellow jacket of King Arthur disappear around the corner before he started his own bike again. *The twin angle*, he thought. Maybe that was it. There had to be some reason for Rand to target Xander. Without a previous connection, the attack would either have to be a completely random coincidence or motivated by something he couldn't fathom. Maybe he was too much of a detective, always looking for connections, but Manuel was never happy with the explanation of "random coincidence." It reeked of bad detective work.

But twins.

It might be crazy, but outright murder was rarely a sane act.

He voice activated the helmet phone and Snowflake picked up immediately. "Time to fetch the kids. Our target is on the move, and I don't want them anywhere near their condo as long as he's mobile."

From the background noise on the line, Manuel took it that his partner was outside, walking along the relatively busy Greenwood Avenue. "I have it covered. Are you on your way back now?"

Manuel checked the visor chronograph. More than enough time to squeeze in a nap and then dinner, maybe even some reading at the coffeehouse. "I think I can hop on 99 from here. I'll be up in about fifteen to twenty. Where can I meet you?"

Snowflake snorted derisively. "Don't bother with the 99. Head north on Western. You should be right there anyway, right? Just take that all the way across the bridge, it turns into 15th and you can just ride that all the way to 85th. It's a hell of a lot better than dealing with finding the highway onramp and then crawling up Aurora this time of day once you get across the water. As for meeting us, there's a theatre not far from here. You want to catch a movie?"

The idea of sitting in a dark theatre for two hours wasn't the worst idea he had heard in a while. It had been days since he had seen anything, and didn't even know what was showing when he thought about it. "Did you have something specific in mind?"

The speed with which Snowflake responded indicated that this had been the plan all along. "There's this zombie western showing. It starts at 3:10. Is Anita going to be joining us?"

"She had mentioned something about wanting to see some of the tourist things, like the Market and the place where Bruce Lee is buried. And then she was going to get her bike serviced. I think she's going to take advantage of the fact I'm distracted to win this leg of the race. I can't really blame her. She'll probably join us for dinner around eight or so."

This answer also had the net effect of cheering the panda up. He gave Manuel directions to the theatre, and promised to be there with the truck and trailer so that he could change in time for the movie. True to his word, the by now familiar pickup and mobile base were parked in a dirt side lot across a side street from the Oak Tree Cinema. Manuel had plenty of time to slip into jeans and a heather gray Cultivate Peace ringer t-shirt, relishing the sunny warmth of the Seattle summer weather. Rather than have to explain the scars on his forearms, courtesy of early bike accidents and a fight with a possessed Wild Kat a few year ago, he slipped on a long-sleeved red silk shirt, buttoning the cuffs carefully. Snowflake was waiting for him at the ticket counter, a pair of tickets in hand.

"Where are the twins?" Manuel asked as he stumped up to his partner on his forearm crutches.

"Tam is getting popcorn and Red Vines, and Xander is holding down seats for us. Don't worry, buddy. This is supposed to be a relaxing afternoon."

Snowflake wasn't wrong. Despite the camaraderie of his friends and the high-octane violence on the movie screen in front of him, the seats were too comfortable, the room too dark, and save for the periodic bursts of gunfire as the serape wrapped zombie Texas Ranger cleared out the town of Queira Junction, Manuel found he was hard pressed to stay awake. It was Tamika who roused him when the credits had started rolling. Her wryly beaming face hovered over him in the near darkness of the theatre where she was standing and stretching. "Hey, old man. The silly movie is finished."

Manuel looked around in a moment of brief confusion. "It wasn't a silly movie," Xander protested on the other side of Manuel, like a competing angel of conscience on his other shoulder. "That was the best zombie western ever made."

"It was the only zombie western ever made, and it was silly," she countered.

Snowflake joined the fray from down on the end of the aisle. "Of course it was silly. It was a zombie western. It wasn't like they were doing Shakespeare. But as zombie westerns go, it wasn't the first, it won't be the last, but it might be the best."

Tam smiled dismissively. "Whatever. I'm going to walk back over to Greenwood. We're doing dinner late tonight, right? In another few hours?"

"After eight," Manuel said, looking at his watch. "So, we have over two hours to kill. I'm voting for the coffeehouse near you guys. Snowflake or I can use the time to finish reading *Souls in Carcosa*. I heard something about a vegetarian Chinese place downtown you wanted to go to?" He worked his way to the end of the aisle with one crutch and the back of the seats in front of him, joining Tamika on the worn red aisle carpet.

Something had been bugging Manuel about that book almost from the beginning, and he had chalked it up to being the work of a murderous mind. But the more he thought about it, the more it kept picking away at him. While he waited for Xander to join him at the end of the aisle, Manuel looked up and realized he was being watched by a slender white man with dark hair, seated a few rows back. Once this stranger realized that he had been noticed, he half-waved at Manuel and company. "I'm sorry," the stranger said over the lamentable closing credit music, "but did you say something about Carcosa?"

"*Souls in Carcosa*—it's this bad horror novel we're reading. Do you know it?" Manuel said casually. The stranger who was addressing them was probably somewhere in his late thirties, maybe early forties, wearing a dark t-shirt and jeans, with shoulder length hair and an affable smile. There was no indication one way or another that he might be anything other than just another curious movie patron, but Manuel had been deceived before—recently in Rand's case.

At the mention of the book title, the stranger seemed to think it over then shook his head. "There's a lot of Carcosa stuff out there, but most of it's in short stories. Or it just shows up other places. I can't think of any novels that have it in the title. Pretty bad though?"

"Not a single decapitation," Snowflake piped in.

The stranger laughed. "Who wrote it?

Manuel watched their new friend carefully, trying to gauge a reaction. "Randal Arthur," got only a blank stare. He was just another random fiction aficionado, from the looks of it.

"Yeah, I've never heard of him. You want good Carcosa stories, stick to the big names. Chambers or Lovecraft or Derleth, or even go all the way back to Bierce. Since the city is public domain, any hack with a pen can use it, and that means there's a lot of crap out there."

"I've never," Manuel started then looked to Snowflake for confirmation, getting a slow shake of the head for his efforts, "I mean, we've never heard of Carcosa. Where is it? The novel we're reading doesn't say. In fact, until now, we thought it was a fictional place."

"Oh, Carcosa is fictional," the stranger agreed quickly, "Ambrose Bierce created it in a short story right about 1890. Then Robert W. Chambers used it in a series of short stories he published a few years later and expanded it quite a bit. Good 'ol H.P. loved the book and added it to his mythology in the 1920's. So did his friend August Derleth. It's been associated with the Cthulhu myths and cycle of stories for eighty years, and even straight up science fiction and fantasy authors have worked the city into their stories. Carcosa is the whore of the literary community— the mystical lost city home to the King in Yellow."

The name sent chills down Manuel and Snowflake's spine. They had yet to encounter it in the novel, but they both had friends and acquaintances who had encountered an entity calling himself the King in Yellow only a few years ago. Just a few years ago, around

Halloween, Manuel had been introduced to the King in Yellow's anchor, a cut-rate occultist named Malenfant, when there was a demon problem in Cobalt City. There was no doubt in either of their minds that the King was very real indeed, and not a fiction dreamed up by a loose affiliation of speculative fiction writers almost a century ago. They mumbled a collective "Thanks," to the helpful stranger, and then staggered out into the light through the back door exit.

Tam and Xander Tesla watched their friends with concern for a few minutes as four sets of eyes blinked to adjust to the light of the sunny afternoon. "The King in Yellow? We know that name, right? There's no way this racer Rand Arthur is the King in Yellow," Snowflake finally said.

Manuel had no answer for that. Years ago, before he was actively dating Katherine Wilde and the Protectorate were still relatively newly formed, she and her team-mates had been involved in a cross-dimensional crisis involving an attempted invasion by a hostile alien force of decay. During the completion of this endeavor, they witnessed the transformation of a Louis Malenfant into a figure calling himself the King in Yellow. Claiming dominion over a lost and dead city on the eternally dark shores of a vast alien lake, this King in Yellow was not a person so much as force of nature. The ubiquitous Dr. Shadow said that the King was an avatar of something much bigger, a concept that could not be encompassed by a single person. Other members of the team wouldn't mention the King in Yellow until they had a few drinks in them, and even then they did so in hushed tones. Manuel had only met the human host, not the real deal, but as far as he knew, Malenfant was still the closest thing to the actual King in Yellow.

The Protectorate were among the most powerful heroes on the planet at one point, able to topple armies. Every one of them feared the King in Yellow. Manuel remembered something Rand had told him, about how he didn't buy into the Arthurian mythologies. They weren't his myths. Yet he was a king, or at least painted himself as one. And not a king of the road, as he had joked. No. His ambitions were much grander than that.

There was no way Rand Arthur was this King in Yellow. But Manuel could easily believe that he wanted to be. And there was already evidence to suggest that Rand had some para-human abilities. "Snowflake, do we still have that blood sample you took off me back in San Francisco?"

"In the cooler in the trailer," Snowflake said with little hesitation.

Manuel looked at Xander, proud to see the young man standing straight, his shoulders back, ready to get to work. The look in his eyes showed he knew what was expected of him, the thought of this pretender to the throne of the King in Yellow trying to kill him pushed far from his mind. "You want a full work up. Any idea what I'm looking for?"

"Anything that doesn't fit," Manuel said. "Beyond that, I have no idea. You're a bright kid. You'll figure it out."

"Where can I help out?" Tam volunteered.

"Who do we know with a background in the occult?" Manuel asked Snowflake.

Snowflake pulled a PDA out of his pocket and flipped to one of the most useful rolodexes in the superhuman community. "Dr. Shadow skipped the dimension with Huntsman and the Libertine a few weeks back way I hear it, so he's a no go," he said, tapping the screen with the stylus. "There's always Archon, but he's been in and out of deep cover for months, so there's no promise I can get a speedy reply. It was hard enough to tap him to get us across the border. And the occult really isn't his thing. Mr. Gray—" He started, and an awkward silence filled the small group. "I really should take that him off my phone list."

"Who do we know that's available?" Manuel corrected.

"I might be able to go through channels and get a contact for Louis Malenfant. I don't know how forthcoming he'll be. And, well, he's crazy, so that's also a strike against him. Oh, and there's a tarot reader in Cobalt City who used to be a member of Mr. Gray's Perdido Street Irregulars. I can give her a call, but she's not an expert, just the closest we have available."

Tamika and Xander shared a brief look before she spoke up. "We know someone here," she said. "Well, not here, but over on Bainbridge Island. I can be there in an hour or less."

Xander nodded in rare agreement with his sister. "He used to be a government spook, loosely tied to the Black Cabinet before he found out what they were up to and retired. He knows his stuff."

"You can't just call him?" Snowflake asked.

Tamika shook her head. "He doesn't use phones. Won't tell us why, but his wife says he has his reasons. I think his retirement didn't go over well with his employers. Or maybe he pissed off a ghost. I don't know. I have to visit in person or not at all. And I'll have to hurry to catch the ferry over."

Snowflake and Manuel shared a long look. It seemed like just the other day, Tam and Xander were merely the junior league. Now here they were with their own lab space and their own secret contacts. Kids—they grow up so fast. "Ok. Be fast, make a recording if you can," Manuel said, provoking a "well, duh" look from Tamika. Being a sound engineer and musician, she was never anywhere without her DAT recorder. "And call when you're on your way back so we can coordinate."

"Come on." Xander tapped his sister on the arm. "I'll drop you downtown since I have to hit the lab anyway."

The twins hustled off to Xander's Honda that he had proudly customized himself over a long weekend, including neon running lights, green jewel-tone paint, and twisting black vine work along the running boards and hood. Xander, always thinking ahead, had gone the extra step to convert the engine to hydrogen cells, making it the fastest "green" car in the city. Halfway to the car, the Tesla twins were already arguing about what music to play on the stereo. They were good kids. He really hoped they pulled this off so he would have more opportunities to see the adults they would grow into.

"You know, I think I finally figured that book out," Snowflake said suddenly, shaking Manuel from his reverie.

"How do you mean?"

"All this time, I figured the author meant for us to identify with the main characters, the ones who were trying to survive the novel. But they were all flat and, I don't know, cardboard. The only good points are when you're in the head of the killer, dreaming of these sacrifices buying his way into Carcosa where he can join with his dark god."

"Rand identifies with the killer," Manuel said quietly. "He can't write the main characters because he can't empathize with them. They're just meat—just tools to be used and discarded."

They stood there silently, watching Xander's car until it disappeared around the corner. "You don't think he's the real King in Yellow yet, do you?" Snowflake asked, his voice wavering just on the edge of being afraid.

"I think Louis Malenfant is the only one who can answer that, and we don't have any good way to get ahold of him to ask. But I met Malenfant a few years ago and this guy is no Malenfant," Manuel said. "He wants to be, though. That makes him even more dangerous. We need to stop him, amigo. Because he isn't the King in Yellow yet, and I don't think he'll stop killing until he is."

CHAPTER EIGHTEEN – HAIL TO THE KING

True to their word, the Bamboo Garden had a menu chock loaded with meat dishes, but the distinction was that all of the meat was fake, made with wheat gluten. It had confused the hell out of Anita, and Manuel himself was a little taken back by it as well. To enter a restaurant proudly proclaiming itself to be vegetarian, only to be greeted with pages of chicken, beef, and pork dishes. And while it was all tasty, it was nothing like the real thing, not even with their eyes closed.

"What I don't get," Anita finally confessed at the end of the meal, "is why it has to pretend to be other food? I can understand not wanting to eat meat. Fine then, don't eat meat. But then why eat something that's pretending to be meat? Isn't that hypocritical?"

"I'm that way about soy," Xander agreed. "I like tofu as much as the next guy. In fact, there's this place up the street that makes a red pepper tofu that I'm just in love with. But it's like soy has this self-esteem issue and it keeps trying to be other stuff, like tofu-dogs or tofu burgers, or tofu chorizo."

Manuel's ears perked up at the mention of tofu chorizo. He would have never in a million years have expected such a thing to exist. "You're making that up."

"He isn't," Tamika confirmed. "I can't eat meat anymore, and I won't even touch the tofu chorizo. It's an abomination. It tastes like an ashtray."

"Why would someone do that to chorizo?"

"Because some people can't eat meat," Snowflake offered.

"But most vegetarians don't eat meat by choice. It's not because they can't," Xander said. "At least at first. They go long enough without and they lose the enzymes to digest meat, and then they feel sick if they try to eat it again."

Anita smirked at the thought. "So they decide not to eat meat for philosophical or religious reasons, but they still want to pretend to eat meat—they still want the flavor, they just don't want to feel bad about it? And then, after a while, they can't eat it even if they want to? America is a messed up country," Anita said with a laugh. "You have the money to eat meat, but you'd rather spend more money on stuff that tastes like meat, but doesn't hurt poor, defenseless cows or chickens. You won't see crap like that in Mexico."

"You aren't in Mexico anymore," Tamika said with a condescending smile. "We do things differently up here."

The two women stared each other down—the scrappy Mexican bike racer and the young blonde acoustical engineer musician with dreadlocks. Neither one looked ready to budge anytime soon. It took Manuel inserting himself physically between them to break the tension. "Anita, we have over four hours before the race. Do you have anything going on?"

She finally broke eye contact with Tamika and fixed Manuel with a distracted smile. "I have my bike ready to go and I don't want to intrude on baby-sitting time." Her gaze flickered back over his shoulder to Tam and then back to Manuel. "There's a band I like playing at this place called El Corazon. I thought I'd go and catch that before the race started."

Manuel ignored her jab and gave her a quick kiss. "Have fun. I'll see you at the starting line."

They parted ways without further words, Anita mounting up on her bike parked in the lot beside the restaurant and riding away in the direction of the Space Needle. "Damn," Tam finally said. "I wanted to go to that show too, back before some whack-job got the idea to kill my brother."

"Sorry for being alive, sis," Xander said with a smile.

"Apology accepted."

They piled into Xander's car, with Snowflake and Tamika crammed into the back seat, and Manuel riding shotgun. Since the ferry had delayed Tamika getting to dinner, it was the first time all four of them had been alone together since the movie theatre. Manuel reached out and turned the stereo off before pivoting sideways as much as possible. "Ok, Tam. Why don't you start with what you learned from your contact?"

"Ok, so this King in Yellow is a real entity, which I guess we already knew," she began. "The background I was provided tells me he's the avatar of some inter-dimensional god-type figure called Hastur. It's like a mantle or role, a kind of persona or template worn by whoever has the attention of Hastur. And there's a connotation of madness associated with him, though I don't know if that's from Hastur or the King in Yellow. This Malenfant character was kind of born into it. The mantle was his to claim by genetic predisposition or some vagaries of fate. No one knows. But apparently he doesn't want to be the King in Yellow, so it's possible for someone to take the mantle from him if they want it bad enough and know what they're doing."

"And it's clear that Rand Arthur wants to," Manuel said, having finished the book earlier in the afternoon. It still gave him chills, not because of the quality of writing so much as the sadistic and sociopathic tendencies betrayed by the narrative.

"Right. Well, since my contact has never entertained the idea of making a play for the crown himself, he didn't really know what steps someone would have to go through to get there. That said, tonight is an auspicious night astrologically speaking, and as the King and his human host are kind of each other's reflection— different but linked—there is significance in Xander and I being fraternal twins."

"So if he pulls this off," Manuel interjected, "what are the odds that he'll actually be able to become the actual King in Yellow?"

"No way of knowing," Tamika paused, and Manuel craned his head enough to see that she was looking at the back of her brother's head. Her jaw was clenched tight with concern, a trace of emotion beading her eyes that her voice did not betray. "If this is his first sacrifice, his odds are not good at all. But apparently magic is all exponential. If he's done this a few times before, his chances go from bad to pretty damn good in relatively short order."

Snowflake joined the discussion from the back seat next to Tam. "So, worst case scenario, he manages to—" He paused, his voice a bit choked up. "—he becomes the actual King in Yellow, what then?"

No one said anything for several somber seconds, all of them knowing without having to say it what would have to happen for

Rand to take the crown. Finally Tam broke the silence. "Then he isn't really human any more. He's more the conduit of an alien god's powers in our dimension. He can step between worlds, and focus this sort of crushing presence on anyone he surveys. He rules over a giant dead city, which, while not having any practical applications, is still creepy, and he can go back and forth freely from there to anywhere, and can take other people with him when he does. He might be able to do a lot of other things, but no one knows what. The fact that he hasn't done something like that in Cobalt City is testament to Louis Malenfant not really being that committed to his role. No one has really seen the King in Yellow off the chain, so there's no good way to know how that would manifest. But I don't really want to be around to find out."

"But he can't do any of this now?" Manuel asked carefully.

There was a trace of fear in Tam's eyes. "I don't know. If he's pulled off some rituals already, he might have a degree of Hastur's blessing. What that means, I have no idea. From what you said before, you think he might have killed some people in Northern California?"

"Two people that he pinned on El Blanco Diablo," Manuel said. "Yeah, I'm pretty sure that was him, but I don't know if it was ritual or spree killing. And I can't prove he did it either way. It might just be a coincidence."

"I'd rather not assume anything is a coincidence, if you don't mind," Xander added. "You got anything else, sis?"

"Calliope had a lead on a weapons shipment, small arms mostly, coming in via cargo container next week. Give her a call."

Xander looked over at Manuel, a half smile on his face. "She's the wife of the guy Tam went to talk to. He did the occult stuff, and she was his handler. She walked when he did, but still has all kinds of contacts with various underground informants."

"It's good to have friends," Manuel said, meaning it on a level that he hoped everyone in the car would agree to. From the brief silence that followed, he took it that they were all on the same page. "Ok, Xander, fill us in on what you found out? I know you told Snowflake some of it already when I was on the phone with Anita, but I didn't catch all of it, and your sister is completely out of the loop."

"Right. So your blood was awash with endorphins—um, natural biochemical compounds produced by the pituitary gland and hypothalamus," Xander started. "It's like an opiate. They fill you with a sense of well-being, and are what causes the so-called 'runner's high' that you read about. No one knows 100% what activity causes the release of endorphins, since science uses animal models rather than human ones. If I were to venture a guess, I'd say that Rand might have some way of stimulating the parts of the brain that produce the endorphins. In addition, there were other biological agents that I couldn't identify. For all intents and purposes, they looked like viruses, but they were sluggish, like they were dying already. I've never seen anything like it, but I'm sure it will mean a paper for someone. Virology isn't my bag, but it's still strange."

"Is there any way to counter that?" Manuel said, turning the idea around in his head. He was distantly glad that he had noticed a change in his behavior that night. He couldn't risk Rand getting the upper hand on him by using some kind of mind control, whether it was psionic, chemically, or biologically induced. And at least this way, there was a chance they could do something about it.

"I have something cooking in an incubator in the trunk," Xander admitted reluctantly. Tamika shot him an angry look from the back seat, hinting that this was an ongoing argument between them. "The seals are solid, so we won't have any contamination risk, and there's a chance I might be able to concoct an aerosol that will counter the endorphins if nothing else."

"Only a chance?" Snowflake said forlornly.

"It's a work in progress. If you have a little table space in the trailer, I can bring the incubator in and run some tests."

Very conscious of the space limitations in the trailer, Manuel raised an eyebrow. "How big is the incubator?"

"About the size of a rock tumbler," Xander said, meeting the blank stares of the other people in the car. "Like a blender lying on its side."

"I have some space," Snowflake said after a moment's thought. "It's not particularly level, but I can jury rig that with a shim and clamp in a few seconds. You don't need an outlet or anything, do you?"

"No, it has a self-contained power source. I usually use it to synthesize the paralytic agent on my darts when I know I'll be away from the lab for a while," Xander said, avoiding eye contact with his sister in the mirror as he pulled off the highway toward their temporary base camp in Greenwood.

Tamika took the opportunity to sneak in just one more playful jab at her brother. "Except it looks enough like a bomb that he shut down the Edmonds-Kingston ferry for two hours while a bomb squad evaluated him as a terrorist threat."

Snowflake and Manuel suppressed a laugh. "That made the national news feed," the panda said with a hint of respect in his voice. "I had no idea it was you."

Xander's ears had turned red with embarrassment. "And I'd prefer if you don't mention it to Wild Kat."

"Your secret is safe with me," Manuel said, patting his young friend on the arm.

Minutes later, Xander parked on the street behind the truck and trailer. Manuel hobbled over to the back door while Snowflake helped Xander gather the incubator from the trunk. Tamika watched from the sidewalk until things looked well in hand. "The trailer is too small for all of us, so I'm going to get my gear and run a last minute wiring check on the audio and video rig in the condo. I'm still pretty good on time, aren't I?"

Manuel checked his watch, noting that it was still well before ten. By his count, that left more than five hours before his vision was due to come to pass. "You're still well in the clear. Nothing's tripped the alarms yet and we have hours. Just be fast, be alert, and expect Snowflake up there in a few minutes to be your back-up."

"Shiny! You hear that, Snowflake? You're my sidekick now," she said. She beamed at him then turned on her heel to get her meter kit from the lockbox in her vintage VW Bug. Snowflake looked indignantly wide-eyed at Manuel, as he tried to form some kind of protest. He settled down quickly, realizing that it didn't matter if she thought he was a sidekick or not. Having either of the twins alone in the condo for any period of time was looking like a worse and worse idea the closer they got to 3 am.

Manuel was the first one into the trailer, and rather than wait to suit up, he decided to start putting on his leathers early. He was pulling on his boots when Snowflake entered the trailer grumbling. The panda mechanic looked at both of them for a few seconds accusingly with a pair of c-clamps one hand and a short length of 2x4 in the other. "Have either of you been in my tool chest that I keep in the pickup?"

They both shook their heads. "Wait," Manuel said. "Didn't Anita borrow a socket wrench from you to tighten her side mirror?"

Snowflake shook his head, still angrily unsettled. He began clamping the board to the underside of a compartment lid, creating a level surface for the incubator. "Yeah, but that was over a week ago. And it was in the top drawer, not down in the bottom where I have my clamps."

Concern began to nag at Manuel. Xander, however, became distracted by the computer at the end of the trailer that had been tasked to use as a monitor for the cameras in the condo. "Was anything missing?"

"No," the panda said. He picked the incubator up and set it on the improvised shelf. He jostled it a bit with one hand, confirming for himself that it was secure. "Everything was there, but it had been moved around, like someone was looking for something and they didn't know where it was. And I don't like that."

"Any idea what they would be looking for?" Manuel slid on his jacket. He thought he could see the reasons for Snowflake's concern, but before he could say anything else about it, Xander interrupted them.

"Hey guys, is this set up on a recorded loop or are the camera feeds live?"

"Live," Snowflake said without hesitation. Manuel quickly zipped up his jacket and snatched the helmet off the chest where he had laid it. "Why? Are you seeing something?"

"Look back in the corner there, at the clock on the side table? Is that a three or an eight?"

Snowflake clicked the cursor over the clock and blew up the image. The microphones in the condo picked up the sound of Tamika as she was singing "Quando, Quando, Quando" in the other room, and over that was the sound of the porch door being slid open. Once highlighted, the clock in the corner could be read clearly. "3:11? How can it say 3:11?"

"The building gets odd power surges," Xander said flatly, his voice hollow and haunted. "That clock restarts at midnight automatically if the power flickers but doesn't actually go off. I never count on it for reliable time anymore ... I have to reset it every few weeks."

On the screen, the clock ticked over to 3:12, and a shadow moved silently through the camera's frame. Xander and Snowflake turned, shouting, "He's in there! Go!"

But Gato Loco was already gone, the trailer door swinging shut as the grim vigilante ran to protect Tamika Tesla from a death he had never seen coming.

CHAPTER NINETEEN – CHECKMATE!

———

The synthetic muscles and hard-wired reflexes of the body suit propelled Gato Loco in bounds up the balconies of the Tesla twin's condo to the top floor. The gauzy, white curtains billowed in the wind, the door already wide open. The inside was dim but not dark. The low light filters in Gato Loco's visor provided as much illumination as daylight, but Rand Arthur was nowhere to be seen.

The clock along the wall read 3:14, and the body of Xander Tesla lay on the floor. But it wasn't Xander Tesla. Not really. "That's a clever trick," Rand said from around the corner in the kitchen. "Robotic or something?"

Manuel scanned for some sign of Tamika, but wasn't seeing anything except her canvas kit-bag on the sofa. "Something. It's a floating globe about the size of a grapefruit that projects an automated hologram. A friend of friend designed it for other purposes. Xander thought it would be useful here."

"Smart. Very smart," came Rand's voice. Still very calm and still around the corner, out of sight in the kitchen. "And the blood?"

"A bladder bag hung from the globe and filled with a synthetic blood. It burns off with exposure to air. Another few minutes, and all sign of it will be gone. It had to be convincing, but they didn't want to lose their damage deposit." Manuel activated the internal microphone to the trailer with a sub-audio command. He toggled the sound for internal mic only, keeping his conversation private. "Any sign of Tamika, team?"

"Nothing," Snowflake said, his voice taut.

A throaty chuckle from the kitchen sent a shiver down Manuel's spine. "You knew I was coming, didn't you." It wasn't a question. Manuel wondered how much Anita had told Rand. He also wondered, not for the first time, how much Anita had known herself in order to tell Rand anything. "Did you see this?"

Without warning, two figures stepped around the corner from the kitchen. Tamika was in the front, face slack, her eyes rolled back in her head, while Rand stood behind with a wicked, bloody knife to her throat. As Gato Loco watched, blood seemed to steam off the blade ... an effect of the synthetic blood, he knew, but eerie nonetheless, and at least proof that the blood currently on the knife wasn't Tamika's.

"I might not need the hostage," Rand said. "I'm pretty sure you can't touch me. Hastur provides, you see. But I need this sacrifice, and as long as I have her, you aren't going to do anything stupid, are you?"

Gato Loco was very temped to prove him wrong, but he couldn't take the chance. Sure, Rand might be bluffing, but Manuel had no way of knowing for sure. If a directed burst from the stage field generator failed to drop him quickly, there was nothing to be lost by simply slitting Tamika's throat where she stood. As long as she was a hostage, she was alive. As long as she was alive, there was a chance she could be rescued. He toggled on the outside mic again. "I can't let you kill her."

"And yet you can't stop me from killing her either," Rand said, his voice soothing and calm. Manuel was alarmed to realize that his resistance was fading. He found his arms getting slack, relaxing against his will. Even Rand seemed more relaxed and removed the knife from Tamika's neck. She made no attempt to run, slumping to her knees beside the bookcase along the wall to her right.

"I need help here," Gato Loco said, and after a second he realized that he hadn't toggled the microphone, and his voice had been projected to trailer as well as to the room.

Rand smiled. He put his arms out to his side, the deadly looking knife balanced in his hand. "Who can help you, Manuel? There isn't anyone here who can help you."

"Dart Frog is on his way," Snowflake said with steel in his voice, referring to the costumed identity of Xander Tesla. *Great*, Manuel thought, *one more hostage twin for the King in Yellow*.

Gato Loco realized after several seconds had passed that he had a wide open shot. He had no kinetic energy built up for a concussive blast, but if ever he were to try to use the stage field generator against Rand, this was the time to do it. He triggered a focused blast directly at the knife-wielding cultist, but to no effect. "I almost felt that," Rand said with a bored expression. "Like the beating wings of a thousand million ghost fly wings. Yet we both have auras around us, do we not? You have layers of resistance that protect you in miniscule increments that ensure that no one can ever get close to you. I have layers of corruption that break down and destroy anything that gets too close. It would be a stand-off were it not for the fact that I have sacrifices, and you have nothing."

Out of the corner of his eye, Manuel noticed that Tamika had pulled something off the bookshelf that looked at a glance to be a square CD boombox. Xander's voice broke through onto the radio channel he was using with Snowflake. "Tam has been talking to me for the last minute on our own channel," he said. "When she makes her move, drop your protective field. Don't ask why, but trust us."

"I love you kids," Gato Loco said, earning a momentary confused look from Rand Arthur.

Tamika jammed her hand into the back of the boom box and pointed it languidly in the direction of Rand's knife. A dull "THRUM" sound burst through the room, and the knife dissolved like smoke in the killer's hand, destroyed on a molecular level by a vibrational frequency Tamika had developed as Steel Pan. Against organic targets, it barely tickled, but against inorganic compounds, it was amazingly effective. She smiled, relaxed, and dropped her hand.

Before Rand could react, Manuel took Xander's advice and dropped his stage field generator, only to find himself shot in the ass a second later with drugged dart. "That's going to sting," Xander said from outside the window, "but you'll thank me later."

Rand roared, his jaw unhinging like a snake as he charged Gato Loco, knocking him into Xander/Dart Frog on the balcony. His strength, fueled by rage and possibly the might of Hastur, forced all three of them off the balcony and into the night. Manuel had the good sense to reactivate his stage field generator, while Xander merely clung to the other side of the balcony, held tight with his adhesive gloves.

And Rand, much to everyone's disappointment, flew.

Well, Gato Loco thought as he fell to the sidewalk four stores below, charging his Boom Point meter with the impact, *that explains how he got up to the balcony so easily.*

"Oh come on!" Xander shouted with exasperation. "The bastard can fly? No one told me he could fly!"

Gato Loco looked around and spotted Rand's bike parked twenty feet away. "Look after your sister. I'm going to put an end to this."

"How?" Snowflake chimed in over the headset. "It's not like you can fly."

Hopping onto Rand's bike, he stripped off the casing and had it hotwired within seconds. "I'm still working out the details."

"I feel good about this plan," Xander shouted encouragingly. "Go get him!"

The rear tire of the stolen Pegasus bike screamed and kicked up smoke as Gato Loco revved the engine. He spun out toward Greenwood and shot south in the direction he had last seen Rand headed. "Snowflake, can you track Rand's RFID tag from there?"

The click of fingers on keys filled the confines of the helmet for second. "Yeah, pulling that up now ... Ok. I have him heading mostly south."

"Mostly south? Is he following the road grid?"

"No, it doesn't look like it."

"Then he's probably heading somewhere specific. Either to get another weapon to try again, or after a back-up target he had picked out just in case he needed another sacrifice. If he's not on the road grid and we don't know where he's going specifically, catching him is going to be difficult at best. Patch the map feed through to my HUD," he said, watching as seconds later a mini-map appeared on the heads-up display inside his visor down in the right corner. He saw a green arrow representing himself, while a deep yellow dot marked Rand's location. He was relieved to see that while Rand could fly, he couldn't fly particularly fast, nor did his earlier charge paint him as particularly agile in the air. There was hope yet.

He gunned the bike hard down Greenwood southbound, screaming around the corner on 80th. *Elevation,* he thought. *I need elevation.* His gaze plotted a course, calculations working lightning quick in his mind as he tried to remember the terrain. "Snowflake, give me a zoom for about five seconds on where 70th hits I-5, and give me satellite view, not map. Then pull back to give me the overall map."

"On it chief," the panda said, complying with lightning speed. *It might work*, Gato Loco thought. *Maybe, just maybe.*

"Can you get me the elevation on our target?" Gato Loco asked, "And more importantly, is that staying fairly constant?"

"That's a bit harder. Give me about ten seconds," Snowflake said as he typed quickly away with his big, furry fingers.

"You have five seconds, and then it won't matter quite so much," Gato Loco warned as he dodged between a pair of oncoming SUV's in the other lane, trying to make the perceived checkpoint in time.

"Thirty feet above ground, and that only seems to vary by a few feet. He's skirting taller buildings, so I think he has a maximum distance he can get above the ground, and he seems to be dropping slightly. Yeah, twenty-five feet now."

The curving bridge of 70th as it crossed the interstate presented itself to Gato Loco, and as he neared the apex of the curve, he sighted the yellow-jacketed figure of Rand Arthur, the man who would kill to be king. With a quick prayer to the Father, Son, and Holy Ghost, Manuel gunned the engine for one final push and popped the bike at high speed over the median and straight at the imposter King in Yellow.

Rand either heard the impossible sound of a bike engine approaching through the air or felt the mass of something big heading for him, for he turned in his flight. Gato Loco kicked himself free from the bike into a lazy backward jackknife. He looked up in time to see the bike buckle as it hit the aura of corruption around the King in Yellow. Manuel pointed his forearm at the collapsing bike, careful to point toward the nearly full gas tank. "Boom," he whispered into the microphone. A bolt of kinetic energy lanced from his glove, discharging the inertia winder that was his Boom Point meter.

A fireball engulfed Rand Arthur, and he fell, hitting the railing on one side of I-5 along with the wreckage of his bike, before falling between the north and southbound sections to the quiet dirt and gravel below.

Gato Loco landed on the railing on the far side of the southbound lane. Comforted that no accidents had been caused by his improvised pyrotechnics, he dropped to the ground below. He was at Rand's side within seconds, removing the King in Yellow's smoldering jacket and beating out the flames on his legs with it. No aura of corruption sprang up to prevent the assault, just as it had failed to protect Rand from the impact of the fall. It was obvious at a glance that the King was broken, barely clinging to consciousness.

Manuel set the audio/video rig on his helmet to record. "There were other sacrifices. Were, when and who?"

In flat, broken monotone, Rand listed off six other murders, dating back three years and across four states. When it was over, Manuel cuffed him with plastic zip-cuffs and stopped the recording. A reduced burst of his stage field generator slid Rand the rest of the way into unconsciousness. In the distance, he could hear police and fire sirens. He popped a mini-disk with the confessions out of the recorder in his helmet, blazoned with the Gato Loco icon, and placed it on his captive's chest.

"You have my location, Snowflake?"

"Got you, boss."

"The road that runs around the lake is four blocks west. I'll meet you there for a pick up. And Xander and Tamika, if you're listening in, it's over. You're safe."

Xander's voice piped in, "Tam isn't on this channel. Her sub-dermal communicator is only keyed to one frequency that we use to keep tabs on each other. But I'll let her know."

"Thanks, kid," Gato Loco said, relief heavy in his voice. He picked up his pace, moving shadow to shadow in bounds as people started to look out their window in the direction of the fireball that had recently appeared over the interstate. "And for the record, you guys did great. It was a thrill working with you again."

"We learned from the best. I'm going to shut down for the night. Busy day tomorrow and all that," Xander said, a playful tone creeping into his voice. "And don't you have a race or something to win?"

Manuel laughed. He was momentarily relieved to think that the race was his biggest concern. But the cold hard fist of reality grabbed a hold of him again. No, there was still the Marco Cross problem. But that wasn't a problem for the twins. "Good night. We'll try not to wake you when we show up around 3 to crash on your sofas."

Minutes later, Gato Loco stepped from the shadows of some

bushes alongside Green Lake Park and into the back of an anonymous travel trailer. He had a race to win, and one more mystery left to solve.

CHAPTER TWENTY – A MATTER FOR CATS AND COYOTES

The field of racers had narrowed throughout the course of the Devil's Run. Starting at thirty, it stood at only five when Gato Loco pulled up to the line outside the Owl and Thistle at two in the morning. Major Tom was pacing nervously, very aware of the gazes of the racers on him, as well as the suspicious stares the small group was getting from the patrons leaving the Irish pub. "I guess King Arthur is running late?" the race organizer said quietly to Gato Loco.

"He's retired," Gato Loco said softly but with a weight that didn't invite questions. Major Tom blinked, taken aback and wondering if he should feel threatened. It wasn't fair to him, Manuel realized. "The murders in Humboldt that you thought El Diablo Blanco was responsible for? It was Rand. Those and more, it turns out. He's going away for a while. Don't expect him at any further races."

"Ah," the old man said. He looked at the assembled racers, paying particular attention to Anita. "So it's between you and the Coyote now, is it?"

Gato Loco looked over at Anita, but she was focused, her race face set. It was between the two of them. Maybe it always had been. Before he could answer, Major Tom walked out in front of the racers and raised his kerchief above his head.

The five bikes started.

The kerchief dropped with a snap and the five remaining racers shot south on Post Avenue for the Seattle circuit of the Devil's Run.

The first couple of turns kept everyone tightly clustered, and even at the first break-away point under the viaduct, no one pushed for too much of a lead. Anita took point, but Gato Loco jumped ahead to run vanguard for a block at a time before falling back. A car backing out of a space almost clipped him in the side, and he had to adjust quickly, dropping enough speed to fall into an easy third, behind Anita and, if he was right, Susan.

One of the racers who Gato Loco didn't remember the name of made a challenge for first, pulling ahead on the long straight shot of Alaskan Way. He kept pushing it, pulling ahead by thirty feet when he shot up Broad Street through the first intersection. The small, finely tuned café-racer cleared two lanes before its tires touched down, and encouraged, he cranked the throttle up even higher, widening the gap by another fifteen feet before he hit the intersection with 1st.

Even over the roar of engines, Manuel and Anita, now fighting for second place, heard the collision. As they topped the hill onto 1st, they saw what was left of the bike hit the ground, the rider a broken mess still astride it. A bus had been crossing through the intersection in the far lane, thankfully out of service at this time of night. Being in the air as he was, the rider could do nothing to prevent the impact. *He might live*, Manuel thought. But it would be a long time before he did anything like that again. It was a cautionary message that encouraged the other riders to drop off the throttle and not risk blind corners at every other busy intersection they came across.

Riding conservatively, they were still the fastest things on the road, and the four remaining riders zipped through the nocturnal shadow of the Space Needle and past the ugly metallic blob building before sliding around the corner onto Republican. These streets were dead quiet at this time of night, and it was only the poor road conditions and the two busy intersections that caused anyone to be cautious at all. They took the left on Westlake, jogging between the surprising number of late-night drivers to make the quick right onto Mercer, busy even at this time of night.

Gato Loco slid back a bit, herding the third and fourth place bikes for fear of losing another rider to an accident. Anita took full advantage of his apparent timidity, and widened her lead to seventy feet by the time the curved right onto Lakeview Boulevard E and across I-5.

The other racers started pushing the pace, and Gato Loco stayed just in front of them, slowly inching up on the Coyote as they took the uphill right onto Belmont, and then again as the turned onto East Roy. By the time all four bikes were on Broadway heading south, there was only a sixty foot difference between first and last place. It made Manuel smile within his helmet. *This*, he thought, *is what racing is all about.*

Traffic on Broadway was only mildly active, and the bikes were able to weave in and out of cars with impunity, and with the exception of the intersections near the huge QFC grocery, the cross streets were relatively quiet. Gato Loco let the other racers push up into second place while he fell all the way back into fourth. He didn't think of it as toying with them. Far from it. These two racers had been there since Tijuana. Without the aid of high-tech bikes or enhanced body suits, they had stuck in there, surviving where others had failed.

It wasn't a question anymore of if he could win. He knew he could win. And they knew it too. But for a few, glorious seconds, they rode ahead of Gato Loco. And somehow, for him, that was enough.

The group made the series of turns onto S Jackson, and Gato Loco pushed back up into second place so quickly that it looked effortless. Up ahead, he saw Anita loose precious seconds navigating around a cluster of people crossing the street from some kind of industrial club. He had closed the distance with her by the time they hit 1st, and he slid around the corner a mere second ahead of her.

He saw the fury on her face as he passed. This race was everything to her. It might have been the only thing that had mattered to her all along. "Snowflake, can you hear me, amigo?"

"I have my ears on. What do you need?"

"Your tool chest. Can you give me an inventory for everything that was in that lower drawer, particularly anything that looks like it might have been moved?"

"I've already built my list, but I don't think I really need to read it to you, do I?" Snowflake said.

"That was it, wasn't it?"

Snowflake managed to keep the sound of smug satisfaction out of his voice. "Running tests now to confirm, but it's the last piece for me. I've been leaning that way for days."

Manuel's heart felt heavy in his chest. Without thinking, he slid around the corner onto the slight downhill slope of Madison, and then again on Western. "A few days, and you didn't say anything? And it was still there?"

"It had been returned. Not the same as still being there. And I thought of it a few days ago. It was the tire print that made me think of it, but I couldn't say anything without proof, and with Xander still out there in the wind."

Gato Loco popped a foot down to make a final left turn onto Marion and then across the finish line two seconds before Anita. "Call me as soon as you know anything." He coasted around the corner to a stop and took off his helmet.

Anita was grinding her teeth when she stopped, her eyes hot coals despite a forced smile. "That was close. I guess it will be Vancouver that decides this."

Manuel looked at her carefully, aware that Major Tom and the other two racers were well within earshot. "About that. I'm not going on to Vancouver."

Four pairs of eyes widened, and Major Tom practically gave himself a whiplash looking back at Gato Loco. It was Anita who gathered her wits first. "What? Why?"

Gato Loco shrugged. "I was worried about a friend, and it's been a big distraction for me. Now that I know he's okay, I'd really rather stay here for a few more days and visit than push on to Canada. Sorry to disappoint you."

The other two racer's eyes lit up. With only three racers left in the Devil's Run, one of them was certain to get the second prize purse, and that would be more than justification for them having stuck it out this far. Major Tom watched the whirlwind of emotions move through the assembled crowd and a wistful smile snuck onto his face. "Are you sure I can't change your mind?" he said.

It was a formality, Manuel knew, and he didn't rise to it. "So you said something about an all-night diner? I could go for something with meat in it after that vegetarian stuff I had six hours ago."

Major Tom smiled and started off in the direction of his bike, parked in the next lot. "Follow me to the biggest omelet in Seattle."

Anita looked conflicted. "You're sure you want to do this?"

"I'm sure. And I'll be here for about a week, so you can come down after you win and meet up with me again," he said, knowing deep down inside that that just wasn't going to happen. "In the meantime, how would you like to get a real meal?"

She leaned in close and kissed him hard. For a second, he thought he felt her tears on his cheeks, but when she pulled back they were gone. "I'll follow you."

CHAPTER TWENTY-ONE – END OF THE AFFAIR

―――――――――

Inside, Susan and Lo Ping listened to Major Tom regale them with tales of Devil's Runs past, one of the juicer nuggets being how high stakes gambling on the race, run by the Major's backers, was what enabled him to put on the Devil's Run every year. Snowflake, despite his enjoyment of a full vegetarian dinner earlier, was deep into a plate of nachos that would have happily fed three. Tom Waits was on the jukebox, singing about tragic lovers and highways. Overhead, the stars fought to be seen through the light pollution of downtown Seattle, while the smells of exhaust and summer filled the air. Manuel looked up at the sky, wondering what it was that he was looking for.

He became aware of Anita's presence beside him beneath the parking lot sign for the Hurricane Café. "Snowflake said you would be out here," she said, cozying up and taking his right arm in hers. "Thinking about finishing or not finishing the race?"

Manuel sighed, his gaze fixed on invisible stars. "Not really. I was wondering why you did it, and I figured asking you would be the easiest solution."

"Why I did what?" Genuine confusion laced her voice, but he could sense the scales dropping from her eyes by the second.

"Why you sabotaged the bike back in Los Angeles. Why did you do that?" he said. "Was winning that important? And would you have gone that far to beat me?"

"I don't know what you're talking about."

Manuel lowered his gaze from the sky the color of a television turned to a dead channel. He met her gaze calmly and without emotion or pre-conceived ideas. She was lying, and he didn't know whether to be more upset over the fact that she had killed someone to win a race, or that could be so cavalier lying to him about it for so long. "When you came into the deli in Los Angeles before the race, you had grime on your hand. There was a distinctive pattern on your palm from where you had leaned on Victor Cross's front tire to sabotage the fork. Snowflake remembered the pattern, and he didn't think it resembled the tread of your tires. But it matched Victor's. You used a tool from Snowflake's tool chest, getting access by asking to use some ratchets. You didn't bother to wear gloves, so even though you put it back, your prints are all over it. And there is particulate matter in the tool that matches the custom fork composition."

Anita bit her lip. She looked around for a police car or a witness or anything. She was on foot, her bike twenty feet away, while Manuel was out of his Gato Loco leathers and limited to forearm crutches. There wasn't anything he could do to stop her if she chose to run, but survivor that she was, she was suspicious of anything that looked this easy. "What are you going to do about it? Are you going to turn me in?"

"Nope," he shook his head. "But I'm giving you a chance to turn yourself in. It's the only chance you're going to get."

"Turn myself in? You're crazy."

Manuel's gaze burned into her. "There is a police car parked a few blocks north of here on Denny. You walk up there and turn yourself in. You'll probably get a few years, maybe less if you throw yourself on the mercy of the court."

"Or what? Are you going to arrest me?"

"Or I let Marco Cross have you," he pushed himself away from the concrete and steel sign support. "I strongly recommend that you take option one. But either way, we're done. Sorry, Anita. I'll put up with a lot, but not murder."

Manuel began hobbling his way back toward the front door. He heard footsteps on the sidewalk and paused, eyes closed. Seconds later, he heard the distinctive sound of her bike starting. She was a block away when he reached the door. He was unable to get inside before he heard her bike explode as the assassin's tracer bullet pierced her gas tank.

Patrons spilled past him out onto the street as he fought his way inside. Snowflake had remained seated, as had several of the more inebriated clientele. Manuel slid into the seat across from his friend and sidekick.

"Sorry," Snowflake said. Though he didn't look up from his nachos, Manuel believed that the panda actually meant it.

"She had a choice."

Snowflake nodded. "Still. Sorry your girlfriend got blown up. That's never good." They sat in silence for a few minutes, Manuel picking at the cold remains of his chicken strips and fries while Snowflake continued to dismantle the nachos with a layer by layer strategy that looked like it would pay off in the end provided he had the endurance of finish. "So," the panda finally said, "what's next?"

Manuel shrugged. "I'd like to spend a week up here with the twins, maybe take in some sights. Eat something that wasn't prepared in a restaurant for a change. Maybe read a book that wasn't written by a serial killer. And all this time on the road and not enough time in the gym is going to make it hard to fit into the leathers after another week of this so-called high life. After that, who knows?"

"You know, with the twins up here, we could put down roots, maybe set up as protectors of Seattle."

The idea had some merit, but Manuel ended up shrugging it off. "I'm not really ready to settle down anywhere yet."

"Good call. This city seems nice now, but it's all a vicious lie. Winters up here suck. So, where to?"

Manuel shrugged again, feeling the weight of the past few weeks slide off him. Maybe he should find a massage therapist while he was up here. And a hot tub, come to think of it. The next week was looking better by the minute. "I picked last time, and you saw how well that turned out for us. It's your turn now."

"Vegas," Snowflake said without hesitation.

"Take your time, think it over," Manuel smiled.

"Vegas," the panda repeated with no loss of sincerity.

"Well, let me know when you've made up your mind," Manuel de la Vega laughed. On the jukebox, Tom Waits finished his complaining, to be replaced by a much more up-beat Louie Armstrong. The duo made a conscious effort to ignore the irony of "A Wonderful World."

After a few comparatively quiet moments, the familiar strains of the Magnificent Seven theme sounded from Manuel's pocket. He made no move to answer it, and Snowflake, while saying nothing, stared pointedly at Manuel's jacket pocket, nacho poised halfway between plate and mouth. When the phone stopped ringing, the panda sidekick reached into his own pocket and retrieved his own cell phone. When it started ringing a second later, he flipped it open immediately, a patient look in his eyes.

"Yeah, he's here," Snowflake said quietly into the phone. Manuel sighed deeply, and held out his hand for Snowflake's phone, only to have his friend hold up a finger, asking him to wait. "No, really, thank you. Be gentle."

Without another word into the phone, Snowflake folded his cell closed and tucked it into his pocket.

"That was Kat?" Manuel said, already knowing the answer.

Snowflake fished a fist-full of quarters out of his pocket and stood next to the table. "Well, since you weren't taking her calls, she decided to call me. I suggested the two of you talk, which is made tricky because you won't answer your phone, so she came up with another solution." Snowflake's gaze was drawn up, past Manuel's shoulders to the door of the Hurricane. "Now if you'll excuse me, I have to study the jukebox at some length."

Manuel had been dreading this, and had almost convinced himself that he could put off a discussion by ignoring Katherine's phone calls indefinitely. He still wasn't sure, entirely, what he had to say to her, just that there was still a lot left unsaid when they parted the last time. When she touched his shoulder on the way past to take Snowflake's now-vacant seat, it sent a mild electrical charge through him.

She looked flawless as always, if a bit tired, her porcelain face framed in waves of flowing auburn. He guessed the suede jacket she wore probably set her back about $800, and the high-heeled boots as much if not more. She slid in behind the deconstructed plate of nachos, careful not to get any on her clothes.

"Is this about the loan of the equipment?" Manuel asked as casually as possible, hoping against hope that her answer was yes.

She offered him a warmly fragile smile. "Is that what you think this is about?"

"No, but hope springs eternal." He cleared his throat. "Then what exactly is this about?"

"Us."

"Ah." He nodded, comforting himself that at least his instincts had been correct. "Right. Us and ghost fish."

Katherine's smile revealed a bit of nervousness, which he found disarming. He hadn't realized how much he had missed that. "So, I understand they have good coffee in Seattle. How is it at this dive?"

He shrugged. "I haven't dared to find out."

"Well then, let's get a few cups. We have a lot to talk about." She waved her empty coffee cup at the waiter. "Now, why don't you start?"

Manuel flipped his coffee cup to right side up. He waited until it was full while he put his head in order. And then, with a sigh, he began.

ABOUT THE AUTHOR

Nathan Crowder is the author of several fine novels and a small battalion of short fiction. He lives in the untamed wild of north Seattle, and is occasionally spotted in his natural habitat taking in a movie, drinking way too much coffee, belting out Bowie at karaoke, or enjoying the vast panoply of exotic foods and micro-brews which make Seattle not unlike heaven on Earth.

He is the proud father of two wonderful and dangerously smart and creative adults who inspired the Tesla Twins. His career is managed by his cat Shiva in exchange for board and kibble.

Soundtrack for *Ride like the Devil* courtesy of Calexico, Chuck Mangione, and Neko Case among others. A corresponding reading playlist titled Ride Like the Devil can be found on Spotify.

Find Manuel's earlier adventures in the Protectorate novel *Cobalt City Blues*, *Cobalt City: Los Muertos*, or the first de la Vega Mystery, *Greetings from Buena Rosa*. He and Snowflake also appear in *Cobalt City: Resistance*, and will return in further adventures.